Unmask Me If You Can

The Survivors: Book IV

Shana Galen

UNMASK ME IF YOU CAN

Cover Design by The Killion Group, Inc.

One

Jasper could remember when his face had been whole. He could remember feeling the breeze on his skin instead of the sticky silk of the mask plastered to his raw, irritated flesh. He could remember when ladies' heads had turned as he walked by. Now the ladies, and even the females who couldn't rightly be called ladies, turned away.

The sun was hot as Jasper made his way through the village of Penbury on the southern coast of England. The breeze off the English Channel would have cooled him if he'd removed his mask, but it was bad enough being out in daylight. He'd send the people already staring at him running and screaming if he revealed his burn scars. As it was, the black silk covering his hair, forehead, and the upper half of his face attracted enough unwanted attention. He tried to ignore the whispers and furtive looks and followed the directions he'd secured from the local he'd treated to ale the night before in exchange for information.

Fewer and fewer people were about as he left the village behind and neared the rocky shoreline. Only then did Jasper realize he should have set out earlier. The trek would involve more climbing than he expected, which was his own fault. The Duke of Withernsea had warned him the woman was elusive. She'd managed to evade the other investigators Withernsea had hired.

But she wouldn't escape Jasper. He hadn't come on behalf of Withernsea. Even if the duke hadn't been a miser too cheap to pay Jasper's rates, Jasper wouldn't have worked for the man. Jasper had no desire to drag women into matrimony with men they didn't fancy, especially not to a man with Withernsea's vices. Jasper would never understand why the girls' parents had promised her to such a monster, but now that the mother, Viscountess Carlisle, was ill, and her dying wish was to see her daughter again, he didn't think it appropriate to ask. The pleas of the viscount and his wife had moved Jasper. And surely Miss Carlisle would want to know that her mother was on her deathbed.

If not, well, Jasper didn't exactly need the money. He could have used it, but as a retired member of The Survivors and the son of the Marquess of Strathern, Jasper had other means available to him.

Sweat streaked down his face, burning the sensitive tissue around his scar, and making Jasper wish, for the thousandth time, he could remove the mask. He'd gone far enough that the beach was mostly empty. Squinting into the distance, he spotted the large rock the informant had described. Jasper just had to climb up the narrow path marked by the boulder, and the cottage would be at the top. It was a clever arrangement. The cottage could not be seen from below, and there was enough soil on the outcropping that a dozen or more trees had grown there, giving the cottage additional shade and cover.

If the cottage was indeed up there. Only one way to find out.

Jasper started up, but halfway he paused to shake out his boots. The rocks stabbed the bottom of his feet, and he needed a drink. He sat on a small patch of leaves and dirt, pulled out his flask and drank deeply. The water was warm now, but it eased his thirst, wetting what felt like a desert in the back of his throat.

He took hold of one boot and struggled to yank it off. The effort almost caused him to fall back, but the boot came loose unexpectedly and shot out and into the path. "Damn it," Jasper cursed under his breath. He moved to rise and retrieve the boot, then froze.

The stab in his ribs was all too familiar. He knew the feel of a knife pressed to his side, and he knew whoever held it was serious. The trickle of blood running down his skin was serious as hell.

"What do you want?" Jasper muttered, barely moving his lips. His instinct was to leap away, but he'd fallen on his arse when the boot came free and jumping up was out of the question.

"Your blunt," came the hoarse reply. "And anything else of value."

The accent was indistinguishable from any other, not lower class but not of the higher ranks either. Jasper couldn't even determine whether it was from the north or south of England. He rather doubted this was purely by chance. His assailant did not want to be identified. A professional then? Surely not simply someone who happened upon him. Someone who'd known he'd come this way and who lay in wait.

"I have a wallet in my coat pocket," Jasper answered.

"Get it out." The man's voice hitched slightly, indicating excitement.

"I have to reach for it."

"No sudden moves," the knife-holder cautioned.

Jasper blew out his breath. Sudden moves or not, the man with the knife at his flank would use it. Jasper didn't care much about the money he'd lose. But he sure as hell didn't intend to bleed to death on the side of a sea cliff with one boot on and one boot off. "I'm reaching for my pocket," he said, moving his right arm slowly. The wallet was in his left inside pocket and the knife rested against his left side. Jasper's hand slid inside his greatcoat then inside his tailcoat. But instead of reaching for the wallet, he lunged for the knife, gripping it with the fabric as his shield.

It was a risky move, but it took the assailant by surprise. He sprang back. Unfortunately, the knife went with him, and Jasper couldn't keep hold of it through the fabric. Jasper lunged to his feet, but his awkward position hampered him, and the attacker came at him with the knife. Jasper raised a hand to deflect the blow, but he was off-balance and aimed too high. Instead of the weapon grazing his arm, he gave his foe an opening. The sharp prick of the knife took Jasper's breath away as it slid through the fabric of his coat and into his skin.

The dull pain ratcheted up to a shrill scream of agony as the assailant yanked the knife back out. Ignoring the pain, Jasper threw a punch at the man with the knife, hitting him on the side of the jaw. The man went down, but so did Jasper. He fell hard, and when he tried to rise again, he saw black spots dancing in front of his eyes. His entire left side felt as though he had fallen into a pond. Blood was gushing from the wound. He struggled, but the attacker rose first. Jasper knew this because the man used his booted feet to land a hard kick to Jasper's uninjured side. Jasper huffed out a curse and reached for the man, who landed another kick, this one to Jasper's jaw.

That was when the spots grew too big for Jasper to blink away. That was when the light faded, and the last thing he knew was the feel of the man's rough hands rummaging through his coat pockets.

***

"Mama! Mama!"

Thunder sounded in the distance and Olivia was relieved to hear Richard's voice approaching. She wanted him inside before the rains started.

"Come inside now, Richard. I don't like the look of those clouds."

"But Mama, I found something." He held up what looked like a man's boot.

Olivia had no idea where he would have found something like that, but anything related to men made her uneasy. "Leave it outside for now," she said. Later she would go to the cliff and hurl it over the side. She wanted nothing of men near her cottage.

"But Mama! That's not all. I found a man. He was lying beside the boot!"

Olivia was tempted to chastise her son for telling a wolf story—their term for a make-believe tale that demanded she save him—but though Richard had told many fanciful stories in his five years, he had never told one about a man or had a boot as evidence. Almost as though he could read her thoughts, Richard held the boot higher. "It's true, Mama! Come and see!"

Olivia did not want to see. She wanted to go inside her cozy cottage, close the windows and bar the doors, and hold her son tightly. But she couldn't ignore a man, not one who had come close enough that Richard discovered him.

"Wait here." She might have to face a man, but she wouldn't do so unarmed. She went to the high shelf where she kept her cooking knives and pulled down the largest, sharpest she had. Sliding it into her apron, she smoothed back her hair and took a deep breath. She'd known this day would come. She'd known she couldn't hide forever. Now she just had to muster the courage she'd been praying for all these years and do what had to be done.

For her son and herself.

She strode out of the cottage, feeling the light mist of rain on her face. At least it hadn't begun to rain in earnest or the path would be slippery and dangerous. Though she wore boots with her serviceable gray dress, even boots were no match against mud on slick, narrow pathways. When she reached Richard, she grasped his hand. He stood shifting impatiently from foot to foot, and as soon as she took his hand, he yanked her toward the path that descended toward the seashore below.

This was the path Olivia hated. She had to travel it once a month to go into town and buy what she could not make or grow. She always dreaded those days and did her best to appear unattractive. It wasn't difficult. Almost five years on the sea cliff meant her looks were not what they had once been. Olivia didn't care. Once, when she'd been seventeen and innocent, she'd cared very much about dresses and ribbons and all sorts of lace. She had not thought she could possibly exist without a lady's maid, a modiste, and a copy of *La Belle Assemblée*. Olivia didn't know that girl anymore. She's been murdered, snuffed out, one careless night.

She gave a wistful look over her shoulder toward the path that wound behind the cottage and led to the garden she herself planted and cultivated. She would much rather be pulling weeds and harvesting the last of the ripe vegetables than taking this path towards the shore.

"Hurry, Mama," Richard said, tugging her hand impatiently. His red hair lifted from his forehead as he ran, like a robin taking flight. "He might be dead by now."

"Why would you think he is dead? And why are we past the boulder? You know you aren't supposed to wander this far."

Richard looked back at her, his big blue eyes apologetic. "Sorry, Mama."

She'd have to have a word with him later, but it almost seemed like an exercise in futility. She wouldn't be able to keep him hidden for much longer. At five he was still—mostly—obedient, but what about when he grew to nine or ten or even thirteen? He wouldn't be content to stay in their little world forever. And though it was for his own safety, it was hardly fair to keep him from having any friends or even any company other than herself.

The path curved, and when they came around the other side, Olivia gasped and grasped at a small tree growing on the rocky slope. Richard grinned at her triumphantly. "Told you there was a man."

There was definitely a man. And he was definitely missing a boot. One stocking-clad foot stuck out of the brush where he lay while the other boot-clad foot rested beside it. Neither foot moved, and from the position of the feet, she could tell the man lay on his belly.

"Is he asleep?" she whispered.

"He didn't move when I crept close," Richard said. He was looking at the man or he would have seen the way Olivia's face went rigid with anger and terror and wouldn't have continued. "I saw blood. A lot of blood, Mama." He looked up at her now, his blue eyes full of concern.

Olivia felt relief. If he was injured, he wouldn't be a threat. They could leave him his boot and after the rains fell and their footprints were destroyed, he'd never know they'd been there. "Run back to the cottage," she told Richard.

"Why?" he protested. "I want to see the man again. I want to see if he's alive."

"Richard, go back to the cottage. It's not safe."

"Yes, it is. He's not even awake."

"Richard!"

His shoulders drooped. "Yes, Mama. But how will you carry him back to the cottage on your own?"

This was precisely the reason she wanted him out of sight. Olivia had no intention of carrying the man back to the cottage and every intention of leaving him right where he lay and to whatever Fate had in store for him. But Richard wouldn't accept that, and it would be better if she could return to the cottage and tell him the man had woken and went his own way.

Lies.

She'd told more than her share. She'd never realized how many lies a mother had to tell a child. Too late she'd realized all the lies her own mother had told her.

"If I need your help, I'll come for you," she told him. "Now go."

"But Mama…"

"*Go.*"

He sighed and trudged slowly, very slowly, up the path and back toward the cottage. When she was certain her son was gone, Olivia crept closer to the man. Her breath caught in her throat, making her lungs burn when she forgot to breathe. He was a large man, much larger than she, and quite powerful looking. He did indeed lay on his stomach, his face down, legs spread, and one hand tucked against his side. There was the blood Richard had spoken of. It stained the ground and the man's great coat. The coat was finely made. She looked down at the boot she still held before dropping it. The boot was expertly made as well, the materials expensive and fashionable. Whoever this man was, he was not from Penbury.

Had he come looking for her?

She didn't think she'd ever seen him on her trips to the village. She had to go into Penbury every few months to replenish her supplies. There she could sell needlework she'd done or even take commissions from those who wanted embroidery for something special. Mostly, she was self-sufficient, but she couldn't make fabric or metal pots and utensils. She also had the money she had taken with her when she'd run away. It would not have been much if she had lived like she did in London, but it was quite sufficient if she was careful and lived modestly. Since she didn't want anyone looking at her too closely, wondering where her coin had come from, she spent it sparingly and she tried to do business with women whenever possible. It wasn't always possible, since women rarely owned shops or tended them. That was why Olivia dressed shabbily and kept her face ducked and her hats low. She even wore a half veil, though that tended to attract more attention.

Now she peered down at this man intently, but he wore some sort of black silk mask over the top of his face. She could not see anything above his lips and jaw. She knew his hair was golden-brown because the mask ended in the middle of his head, leaving the wavy hair at his nape exposed. A hat lay not far from his body, obviously knocked off when the man had…

What *had* happened? Had he fallen? Had he lost consciousness from whatever injury he'd incurred? She did not need to know that. She realized one hand had been curved about the hilt of her knife, and she released it now. She'd returned the boot. It was time to depart.

She took a step back and her gaze fell to the crimson splash blood again. The mist of rain had turned into a drizzle and little rivulets of blood had begun to run down the hill, away from the body. She should leave him.

But how could she leave him to die?

And how could she not? Perhaps he'd come to kill her.

She swore under her breath, torn between what she wanted to do and what she should do. Finally, she bent down and put a finger against the man's neck. *Please let him be dead.* If he were dead, all her problems would be solved.

But there was no denying the weak pulse beating against her fingers. He was alive, barely, and if she walked away, she condemned him to the hereafter. She couldn't do it. Not only because Richard would ask about the man and even a consummate liar like herself couldn't look him in the eye and say the man had been fine and walked away. But also because she hoped she hadn't lost all of her humanity. She was still a decent person. She still had compassion. This man needed all the decency and compassion she could muster.

She nudged the man's shoulder with her hand. "Sir?"

He didn't move.

She shook his shoulder, this time with more force. "Sir? Are you awake?"

Nothing.

Perhaps she should try to turn him and see his wound. She tried for almost five minutes to do so, but he was too heavy. Instead, she managed to move his hand, which was bright red with blood. She couldn't see the wound under the layers of clothing. She prodded at it, though, and the man let out a low groan.

Olivia jumped back like a frightened cat. The man's eye opened, the one on the side he wasn't resting on, and he stared at her with an unfocused gaze. He had hazel eyes—not quite green and not quite brown—and he blinked at her once then closed his eye again.

Olivia's heart pounded in her chest so hard she thought it might explode. Why did it have to be a man, a big man at that, lying on her path? And why had Richard chosen today of all days to disobey her? Would that she'd never discovered this beast of a man.

But she had, and somehow he'd become her responsibility. She had to find a way to move him up the hill. There was only one way she could think to do that, and she would need Richard and Clover's help.

Two

Jasper woke in pain. Pain so great he couldn't even open his eyes. He couldn't do anything but breathe through it, and even that hurt. Gradually, the wave of pain that precipitated his waking subsided to the level of mere agony, and he had time to process the fact that he was no longer lying face down in the mud. In fact, he wasn't outside at all. There was no mistaking the yeasty smell of baked bread or the mouth-watering aroma of thyme and rosemary. He couldn't yet manage to crack his eyes open, but what he'd thought was the thudding of blood rushing in his ears he slowly realized was the sound of rain pelting a roof and windows.

At least he wouldn't die out in the open. Not that he intended to die, but it was hard to argue with the stabbing sensation in his side. Unlike most of the wounds he'd suffered during the war, this was no mere scratch. The knife had plunged deep. But the pain was nothing compared to that of being burned. If he'd had to think of it in colors, this pain was red, while the burns he'd suffered had been a blinding white for weeks. He'd wanted to die then. Now he wanted to live. He tried to open his eyes again, and they wouldn't obey. A bad sign.

He tried to rise. Something held him down, pressing on his chest and binding his arms. He fought the restraints until another scent teased his nose. Jasper froze.

The scent was that of a woman. He had no doubt of that. It might have been some time since he'd been close enough to a woman to inhale her fragrance, but it was a heady combination no man ever truly forgot. The scent was a mixture of the herbs cooking, the sea air, and a light note of femininity.

A warm hand touched his cheek. *Her* hand, judging by the size and weight of it, and it was so cool that Jasper realized he was burning with fever. Something cool pressed against his lips followed by wetness, and he opened his mouth to take in the water. It quenched his thirst, but it must not have been the first liquid he'd been given for his throat wasn't parched. Still, it was an effort to force words past what felt like a swollen throat.

"Where am I?" he croaked. His eyelids fluttered, and he was able to see a gray haze before him and firelight behind it.

"Just rest," said a low female voice. It was a young voice. The woman whose hand had touched his cheek?

His cheek…Panic reared inside him as he remembered his mask. Had she removed it? Was his scarred face exposed for all to see? His hand flew up to touch his face, relief coursing through him like a great avalanche when he felt the silk mask still in place.

"I tried to remove it earlier," said the woman, "but you fought so hard I left it."

Jasper reached out to touch her. She sounded nearby, but he couldn't locate her. All he saw was that gray haze.

She caught his hand and held it lightly. "May I remove it now? You have a fever, and I'd like to bathe your face."

"Where am I?" he asked. His voice sounded less hoarse now and more like it usually did.

"With friends. You're injured."

"The bastard stabbed me." He heard the soft intake of breath. He was no longer used to speaking in front of ladies. "Forgive me."

She spoke softly, and someone responded. So they weren't alone. There were others here. The gray was beginning to take shape. It was cloth, material for a dress. She was standing before him, and he was staring at her dress. He tried to look up, but the effort of lifting his head was rather more than he could manage.

And then she surprised him by obliging him. She knelt beside the cot or pallet where he lay, and he could see her quite clearly. Her brow was furrowed in concern. It was a delicate brow on a delicate heart-shaped face. He didn't think it was pain or delirium that made him see her as somewhat more than merely pretty. Dark hair framed the pale face, little pieces of it—what were those called?—falling down around her ears. Her eyes were the blue of the sky at dusk and framed by thick black lashes and dark brows. Her lips were like a bow, small and pink, pursed in a look of concern. Concern for him, of course.

"Do you know who stabbed you?" she asked, and from her tone he did not think it the first time she'd asked the question. He'd been so caught up in looking at her, he hadn't been able to concentrate on anything else. And not simply because she was extraordinarily pretty. Because he knew her, and she would have known him as well if his face hadn't been ravaged in that fire.

"No," Jasper finally said. "He came out of nowhere."

"I found you on the trail. Had he forced you off the sea shore so he might accost you? I've seen a few smuggling ships and heard stories of pirates, but we've never had any trouble."

He understood what she wanted to know.

"No. He was hiding on the trail. I was looking for you."

She shrank back, her eyes widening. "You know me."

He tried to nod and found it hurt too much. "I do. And you know me, though I don't expect you to recognize me with the mask."

"May I—?" She reached out one hand.

"Touch it at the risk of losing your hand," he said in a much more menacing tone than he'd intended.

She snatched her hand back.

"You're Miss Carlisle. We danced together years ago. Before I wore this mask. Before you disappeared from Society."

"You have me at a disadvantage."

"Jasper Grantham."

She stared at him as though willing her brain to place him. "That's the surname of the Marquess of Strathern."

"His third son, at your service." He'd foolishly tried to make a flourish with his arm, and it brought on a coughing fit, which made his side hurt as though someone was digging the knife in all over again. He tasted blood in his mouth and knew that to be a bad sign.

"And why have you come looking for me?" she asked when he'd stopped hacking enough that he could hear her. Through tears brought on by the pain, he saw her pretty blue eyes were wary and shadowed by those long lashes.

"No need to worry about that now." She was going all gray again. Had she stood? Was he staring into the folds on her dress again?

"Why is that?"

"Because I'm dying. Won't live long…enough…to…"

Blackness, blessed for its lack of sensation, descended and Jasper went willingly into its embrace.

When he woke again, he knew she was near. He could detect her fragrance, just barely, but it was there. It still rained, so the storm hadn't yet passed. It was either a remarkably strong storm or he hadn't slept very long. Jasper did a mental accounting of his body. He still wore the mask, which surprised him because most people he knew were far too curious to leave something like that in place. He still lay on the bed, but his chest was bare beneath the sheet that covered him. He wore his trousers but wiggling his toes a bit told him he didn't possess his boots. The one boot might be lost forever.

His blasted side hurt like the devil, but now the pain was only a raw pink as opposed to searing red. His throat felt dry and his skin hot and itchy, which meant the fever hadn't left him, but it had lessened. There must have been something in the water she'd given him, some sort of medicine to ease the pain and fever. He had the first fleeting hope that he would not die.

Of course, he wasn't about to stand up and walk out of here. And he certainly wouldn't be able to take Miss Carlisle with him. For all the strength he had, she could push him over with one finger.

He opened his eyes and stared at the wide oak beams that supported the roof. They were not painted, though they had discolored slightly from the fires that kept the cottage warm. Jasper allowed his gaze to travel across the ceiling and then down the wall across from where he lay. There was the hearth and in it a small fire burned. It had been banked for the night, and expertly so. It would burn cheerily for hours to come. Beside the hearth a large pot hung on an iron arm that could be swung into the fire so its contents might heat. On the other side, a small wooden rack held a pair of stockings and a small shirt. These were drying with the aid of the fire's heat.

Jasper stared at the shirt for quite a long time. It looked like a man's shirt, though it was too small for any man.

In the center of the room a good size oak table took up most of the rest of the space in the cottage. On it lay two plates and two bowls, stacked on top of each other. A basket filled with what looked to be herbs and vegetables was in the center, and several books were at the end farthest from the fire. Benches ran the length of both sides of the table, and Jasper could just make out several small objects on the bench farther from him and thus in too much darkness for him to identify. A ladder lay against the wall across from the table, and it led to a loft, where Jasper assumed Miss Carlisle slept. As to where he now lay…he tried to move his head enough to determine where he was. It was a bed, not a cot as he'd earlier assumed. A small bed with soft sheets and a warm blanket over his legs. It must have belonged to the person he'd heard her speaking to earlier. A maid? A friend? The voice had not been low enough to belong to a man.

He heard a sound and turned to look on his other side, and there she was, asleep. Her hands were folded in her lap, a piece of fabric still held loosely, the thread dangling. Jasper remembered seeing his nanny thus many times. He'd always taken advantage of those moments to sneak out of the nursery and play tricks on his young sisters. This woman sat in a rustic-looking rocking chair, her head fallen to one side and her eyes closed. Her dark lashes cast a shadow on her cheek, which looked pinker and warmer than it had earlier.

She still looked far too pretty, with all that dark hair and translucent skin, like a painting one might see in a museum. Again, he questioned why her parents, who seemed to love her enough to pay him an exorbitant amount to have her returned to them, had ever engaged her to a man like the Duke of Withernsea? The man was a brute, a great bull of a man with little grace and well-known proclivities. As a man who made his way in the world slinking through the shadows of London's rookeries, looking for people who did not want to be found and whom Bow Street could not find, Jasper knew a thing or two about the seedier side of the city. He knew the brothels and the gaming hells and the streets where the beggars were as thick as flies on a dead dog.

Though Jasper himself had no interest in the business of prostitutes, he found himself in their company more often than most. For a farthing or two, the women would give him the odd bit of information. When he needed information on someone of the upper classes, he would spend an evening in the brothels the men of the *ton* frequented. The whores still had most of their teeth and enough rouge to cover the pox marks on their skin, but the price was a thruppence or even a tanner.

In some of those brothels, he'd seen more than one ladybird sporting a bloody lip or a bruised cheek. And those were only the wounds that showed. Several men had reputations for such violence. The whores knew who they were, and the abbesses charged them extra. Jasper doubted the broken girl was paid extra for the nightmare she endured, but it compensated the abbess for the expense of doctors who would be called to sew the chit back together.

And one of the men who always paid extra was the Duke of Withernsea.

Had the Carlisles not known of Withernsea's reputation? Jasper couldn't remember if he'd known of it all those years ago, before the war and before Napoleon. Regardless, he knew of it now. He knew the duke had searched for his betrothed for years. By now he might have married any young lady with parents destitute enough to offer their daughter up as a sacrifice. But Withernsea wanted Viscount Carlisle's daughter. He wanted what he'd been promised.

The fact that the woman sleeping just a few feet away had defied the duke for so long impressed Jasper. She had to be resourceful and independent to run away and stay hidden all these years. She can't have had much money or any way to earn more. Jasper looked about the cottage. And yet she seemed to be making do—more than making do. The cottage was cozy and inviting. If the rain and winds hadn't been rattling the shutters and battering the walls, it might have even been peaceful. But she couldn't want to live away from her family, in seclusion. Why had she stayed away for so long?

What had the duke done to her?

The effort of looking about had tired him and Jasper allowed his eyes to drift closed again only to snap them back open. His skin prickled painfully, and he tensed. He had the same feeling he'd had when in France, right before an ambush. His gaze returned to Miss Carlisle, but she slept on. Then he darted his attention across the room and up to the darkness of the loft above the ladder.

There was a figure crouched there who hadn't been there before.

Jasper wished he had some sort of weapon. He would have preferred a pistol, but even a knife would have sufficed. As it was, he lay helpless, his chest exposed. And then, as he watched, the figure took shape, and Jasper felt his body relax. This was not a man or a beast, crouched in anticipation of attack. This was a child, peering down at him and attempting not to be seen. Jasper lifted a hand, silently indicating he had noticed the child. He expected the youth to shrink back, but instead the boy moved forward until he knelt beside the ladder.

Even in the dim light, there was no mistaking the boy's resemblance to his mother, who slept on unawares. But Jasper also knew the boy's father, and Withernsea's red hair was the exact same color as the lad's.

Jasper swallowed, his dry throat protesting the movement. He had his answers now. What Withernsea had done, why Miss Carlisle had remained hidden. And as usual, now that he had the answers he sought, he wished he'd had the wisdom to remain ignorant.

***

Olivia woke to blackness. She hadn't meant to fall asleep. She'd intended to stay awake and vigilant, keeping an eye on the injured form of Lord Jasper.

The man seemed to think he was on the verge of death, but in Olivia's view, he still had plenty of strength remaining. He'd barely responded when she'd led Clover down the trail and dragged the unconscious man to the travois she constructed from a harness, some old wood, and a study old horse blanket. She had huffed and puffed in order to move the man uphill to the travois. For a few minutes she'd been glad of the rain because it cooled her heated face and washed some of the man's blood from her hands.

She'd half wondered if her efforts were even worth it. He'd seemed to have lost so much blood. Having Clover pull him up the steep cliff might kill him even faster. But she couldn't leave him. He terrified her, but she refused to act any more the coward than she already had. What example would that set for Richard? Of course, if the man ended up murdering Richard and her in their sleep, that wouldn't be the best example either.

Clover had easily hauled the man, who must have been eleven or twelve stone, up the cliff and right to the door of the cottage. Richard had stood there, eyes wide with shock, as she unfastened the horse blanket and pulled the man inside. The rain had been coming down in earnest, and if she'd looked out at the ocean, she would have seen the white caps pitching and rolling with a vengeance. As she struggled to maneuver the man into the cottage, she'd used her eyes to dare Richard to say something. When her son, who was no fool, kept his mouth shut, she ordered him to ready her bed.

"Your bed, Mama?"

"I can't drag him up to yours, darling," she'd wheezed. Together they'd wrestled the man inside and onto her bed, which Richard stripped first so all the linens wouldn't be soiled with blood. And then she'd gone to work.

She had a rudimentary knowledge of the sick room. Her mother's health had always been poor, and Olivia had watched surgeons do their work from the time she was Richard's age. She knew the wound had to be cleaned and that spirits would work well for that. She had a bottle she kept in case she or Richard were ever injured, and though she hated to waste it now, she did so anyway. She'd removed the man's shirt—and wasn't that a new experience—and cleaned the wound by dousing it with a quarter of the bottle of gin.

If she'd thought he was half dead, he had disproved it by sitting up and roaring. She'd jumped back just in time to avoid being backhanded by his flying fists. One look at his face told her he wasn't aware of what he was doing. His eyes had been blank and wild. He was probably barely conscious. When he lay back down, she'd spooned some of the gin into him. It probably wasn't the best cure, but she figured he would need it when she sewed his wound closed. Surprisingly, he'd only moaned when she'd completed that task. And then he seemed to settle into a deep sleep. She hoped it was a healing sleep, though he might just as easily slip into death. She had no way of knowing if the knife had punctured something vital, and no way to repair the organ if it had. But at least he was no longer bleeding all over everything.

She'd made soup for Richard and baked the bread she'd spent the morning kneading, then when Richard had eaten and was playing quietly with his wooden animals, she returned to the wounded man and cleaned the blood from his body.

She'd tried not to look too closely at his chest. It was probably very much like any other man's chest—muscled and hard with a smattering of hair. The skin was darker than her own as though it had been exposed to the sun on occasion, and while he was not prone to any fat, he was also not slim or slight. He was strong and big and even the ugly knife gash she covered with a clean strip of linen looked insignificant compared to the heft of him.

She'd noticed other smaller details she should not have. His nipples were a pale pink. She didn't know why this should intrigue her so. But it had made him seem less formidable to have nipples of such a tender color. She'd wiped the cloth over them, and they stiffened, much like her own when she was cold. That too had been interesting. Interesting enough that she'd glanced guiltily at Richard to make certain he hadn't seen.

Not that she'd done anything wrong. She hadn't. But what she felt inside when she looked at those nipples was not exactly innocent.

And then there was his belly. That part of him had not been covered with much blood. His back and side had taken the worst of it. But she had found his hard, flat belly infinitely mesmerizing. The hair on his chest seemed to flow into a line on his belly that thickened below his navel and disappeared under his trousers. Since he lay on his back, his belly was flat, but she could make out the definition of muscles there too. How did one achieve muscles in such an area? Fencing? Riding? Some other manly pursuit?

"Mama?"

She'd jumped up and tried not to look guilty when she faced Richard. "Yes, darling."

"Why does the man wear a mask?"

That was a good question, and one she might have considered if she hadn't been so absorbed in staring at the hair dipping below the waist on his trousers. In fact, the mask was quite concerning. Only people who did not want their identities known would wear a mask. What was this man hiding or whom was he hiding from? What if he was some sort of bandit? Perhaps it would be better if she didn't see his face.

On the other hand, she'd come this far. If he lived and then he intended to kill her, she doubted he would spare her because she'd had the forethought to leave his mask in place.

"I don't know," she told Richard. "But I expect with a wound like this he will soon develop a fever. I can brew some of the tea with the herbs I keep for fever, but we should probably bathe his face as well."

She started the water to steep the herbs for the tea then lifted the man's head and attempted to remove the mask. She would have sworn he was unconscious, but as soon as she'd tugged at the mask's ties, he had grasped her wrist and yanked it away. His grip was tight but not painful. Still she was frightened when he pulled her close to his lips and hissed, "Do not touch my face."

"I am trying to help," she'd replied in her most pleasant voice. She didn't want to scare Richard. She'd been scared enough for the both of them. "You have a fever, and it will be worse before it becomes better." *If* it got better. "I need to keep you cool—"

"Do not touch my face. I'll kill you."

Well, that was that then. Bathing his face wasn't worth dying over. Let him keep his secrets. "I won't touch your mask," she'd promised. He released her hand and collapsed back into unconsciousness. When she was certain he'd been sleeping, she'd tied his ankles to the foot of the bed. She didn't expect that would hold him long, but it might stall him long enough for her and Richard to escape.

And now as she sat staring at the darkness outside the window nearby, darkness that should have been daylight if not for the storm that still raged, she remembered the exchange they'd had in the middle of the night.

He was burning with fever, but he'd been strangely lucid. He'd introduced himself, and though she couldn't remember him very well, she knew who he was. Lord Jasper. She had danced and flirted with him at balls before the war.

Perhaps that was why he wore the mask. He'd been injured in the war.

Or perhaps he wasn't Lord Jasper at all, and the mask concealed his true identity.

But the even bigger question was why a son of the Marquess of Strathern was here, on a cliff near the unremarkable town of Penbury. She knew it was no coincidence that he'd been on her cliff. He'd admitted he'd been looking for her.

Olivia turned her head now and studied the man sleeping in her bed. The sheet had been pulled to his chest, concealing much of it from her. His hazel eyes were closed, making it seem as though the entire upper half of his face was covered. The lower half had begun to sport a bit of stubble. It caught the light from the low burning fire, and looked somewhat lighter than his hair, more of a golden brown. His breathing was shallow, and his face pale. The sheet clung to his body in a way that indicated he was damp. Perhaps the fever was breaking.

She should bathe him with the cool cloth again. She had taken him in, and she now had a duty to see him survive. But if he did survive, she knew she was in danger. She'd bathe him and then begin her preparations. Much as she hated to leave, this place was no longer safe for Richard or for her. They would have to run. Again.

It was the only way to stay alive.

Three

Her scent woke him. Jasper was smart enough not to open his eyes. He never opened his eyes before he knew the situation around him. There had been many times when it was better to pretend sleep than let anyone know he was awake.

This turned out to be one of those times. She was bathing him with blissfully cool water. His skin felt hot and tight, and the cool water eased the scorching pain of the heat momentarily. Jasper knew he was burning with fever. Men often died of fever. And if he were to die, he wanted to enjoy the scent of her and the feel of her hand on his chest as her other hand ran from his shoulder to his waist. If he hadn't been so weak, he might have wished she'd dip lower.

Hell, who was he kidding. He did wish it. He was just too weak to do anything about it if she did. How long had it been since a woman had touched him like this? With tenderness and care? Years? Decades? Never? Before his face had been ravaged, he'd had his share of lovers. Those women had touched him with greedy fingers and scoring nails, not soft caresses. He hadn't touched them any differently. And though Miss Carlisle's touch was not sexual in the least, he couldn't help but imagine how she would have touched him if the two of them had been in this bed together. If he hadn't been burning with fever and she playing nursemaid.

Ridiculous thoughts that would never come to fruition. But lying here, teetering somewhere between life and death, sleep and wakefulness, Jasper had time to entertain the ridiculous.

He woke again when she lifted his head and poured some foul-tasting brew into it. He identified it as willow bark tea, which had pain-relieving properties. But that didn't mean he had to like the taste of it. "You might warn a man before you pour something like that down his throat," he said when she lay his head back down. He opened his eyes when he spoke and saw the look of panic on her face when she realized he was awake.

It was the same sort of frozen, desperate expression a rabbit adopts when it realizes the fox is poised to pounce.

"It's an herbal tea," she stammered. "To help with—"

"The fever. I know. It could do with some honey."

Now her dark brows lowered. "I don't have any honey, and even if I did, I wouldn't waste it on you. Bad enough I'm wasting my herbs and gin on you."

"Gin?" Jasper tried to sit up and immediately regretted it when his side throbbed in protest. "Why didn't I know there was gin?"

"Because you've been half unconscious for the last eighteen hours and waiting on you hand and foot hasn't left me with much inclination for conversation."

She was right. He hadn't exactly been acting grateful for her efforts. "And if I didn't feel like my head or my flank might split in two, I would be…" He almost said *more of a gentleman,* but after spending so much time in the rookeries, he hardly remembered his gentlemanly manners, much less had call to use them. "I would be more vocal with my thanks. You saved my life."

"Not yet," she said, arching a brow. He couldn't help but grin at her meaning. He didn't think she'd kill him in his sleep, but he admired her for thinking about it.

"Where's your son?" he asked.

She'd been about to turn away, probably to place the mug on the table, but she stiffened at his words. "Who?"

"The little boy." Jasper gestured to the dark loft. "I saw him peering down at me last night. He must be yours. The resemblance is notable."

"He's sleeping."

"Is it still night?" Jasper looked at the dark window, streaked with raindrops from the continuing rain. "I've lost track."

"It's early morning. You should rest again."

"I don't seem to have much choice. My eyes close without my permission." In fact, they were heavy now, so heavy he could barely keep them open. "Miss Carlisle," he muttered as he forced the lids back up.

She looked down at him, her expression tense.

"I haven't come to hurt you or your son. I haven't come from him."

"Who?" she asked.

"We both know who. I've come at the request of..." But sleep was taking him, and it didn't matter why he'd come at the moment, only that she not fear him. "I came to help. Protect..." He didn't know why he said the last. Ewan was The Protector in Draven's troop, not he. Jasper had always been the man who found what they needed. They'd all joked that Jasper would make a good bounty hunter. And so when he'd come back after the war, that's exactly what he'd become. And while Viscount Carlisle had promised him a rum ribband for finding his daughter, Jasper wasn't hunting her for the bounty. Not any longer. If he lived, he'd do everything to protect her and her son, and that he would do because he'd already been paid—in tender caresses and sweet scents and rank herbal tea.

He owed her what no amount of blunt could buy: his loyalty.

***

"Why does he wear that mask, Mama?"

Jasper heard the little boy's voice as though from a great distance. He wasn't certain how long he'd slept. He could still hear the rain outside, and though he hadn't opened his eyes, he could sense the darkness in the cottage. His tongue felt swollen, his head pounded, and his throat ached as though someone had coated it in salt. He wanted water.

"I don't know, darling. Eat your potatoes, please."

"Can we ask him when he wakes up?"

Jasper heard the clink of silver on a plate or bowl.

"I think we had better not. A man is entitled to his privacy."

"What's privacy?"

"It's like…when I go behind my curtain to change clothes. Or when you think something, but you don't say it."

"I always say what I think."

"Yes, you do." Jasper thought he heard a smile in her voice. "Now eat your potatoes."

For a moment there was only the sound of silver scraping plates, but the silence was short-lived. "Mama, when will he ever wake?"

"I think he's awake now," she answered.

Jasper opened his eyes. How had she known? He must have given it away somehow.

"I thought so," she said. She was sitting at the table, facing him. The little red-haired boy had his back to Jasper, but he turned now, fastening his eyes—very much the same dark blue as his mother's—on Jasper. "Are you hungry? I have some broth." She rose, wiping her hands on her apron. It struck him then how strange it was to see this woman who he remembered in silks and jewels wearing a plain gray dress and dingy white apron.

"Water," he croaked. "Please."

She crossed to him, her strides quick and efficient. None of the graceful way of walking she had most likely learned from dance instructors and tutors. She placed the back of her hand against his cheek, and Jasper had the strangest urge to lean into it. It felt so soft and cool.

"Your fever hasn't climbed," she said. "But it's still high."

"I might live yet," he said.

"Mama says after all the effort she's made, you had better live." The little boy stood on his other side and looked down at Jasper with undisguised interest.

"Who am I to defy your mother?"

The little boy's brow furrowed. "What does that mean?"

Miss Carlisle, who had poured water from a pitcher and into a cup, knelt beside Jasper. "Let's not ask too many questions right now, darling. Our guest needs rest." She raised the cup to his lips, and Jasper drank greedily. He felt some of the water slip down his chin, but he didn't care.

"More," he said, and Miss Carlisle obliged him.

"Would you like some broth now or do you want to sleep again?"

"Oh, don't sleep again," the little boy said, his tone pleading. "All you do is sleep."

"How long have I been sleeping?" Jasper asked. With the rain darkening the skies even during the day, he could not track the time.

The boy answered. "I found you the day before yesterday."

"*You* found me?" Jasper asked, then nodded to the lady. "Yes, broth, please."

"Uh-huh." The lad nodded.

"Richard." His mother's voice had a warning in it.

"I mean, yes, sir. No. Yes, *my lord*."

Jasper made a face. "Don't start that nonsense. I only make people I don't like call me *lord*. You can call me Jasper."

"I can?"

Miss Carlisle appeared with a bowl of broth. "No, you cannot. That's far too informal."

Jasper looked down at his bare chest under the sheet where he lay on her bed. They weren't exactly in a formal setting. But considering he was relying on Miss Carlisle to keep him alive, he wasn't about to argue.

She pushed his pillow higher and helped him sit so he could swallow without choking. The movement made him clench his hand into a fist to ward off the pain, but he tried to keep his expression neutral. She was watching him for signs of pain.

"Master Richard," Jasper said, "you were saying you found me. Could you elaborate?"

"Huh?"

"Richard…" His mother warned.

"I mean, pardon? What does *laborate* mean?"

Jasper almost smiled. He'd been careful not to use the cant he knew so well from all the time spent in the rookeries, and his speech had still confused the lad. "Give me the details. No. I can do it." This was in response to Miss Carlisle who attempted to feed him with a spoon of broth. "I'm not an infant who needs to be fed." He held out a hand to take the bowl.

"What are *details*?" Richard asked.

"The particulars." Jasper met Miss Carlisle's gaze. They locked eyes, and he saw the glint of stubbornness that must have kept her alive and hidden all these years. Finally, she gave a short nod and handed him the bowl. He almost dropped it, which would have proven her point entirely, but he caught it at the last moment.

"What are *particulars*?" Richard asked.

Jasper blew out a breath. As a man who often had to ask many questions before gathering the information he needed, he had boundless reserves of patience. He could see how young Richard here might exhaust them, though.

"His lordship is asking you to tell him how you came to find him," Miss Carlisle said finally, saving him.

"Oh! I saw your boot. I was walking down the path"—he glanced at his mother—"just a tiny bit further than I should, and then I saw the boot. There was never a boot there before, so I went to inspectigate. That's when I saw you and ran to get Mama."

Jasper dipped his spoon into more broth. It was delicious broth, thick with carrots, potatoes, and green vegetables he couldn't name. "And how did I move from there to here?" he asked.

"I moved you," Miss Carlisle said, pushing her shoulders back in what was obviously pride. She was a small woman, petite and slim, but when she pushed her shoulders back like that he could just make out the roundness of her breasts. Not that he should be looking at such things with her child at his elbow.

"Clover helped," Richard added.

"Who is Clover?"

"Our horse. Mama said you were heavier than three horses, and she had to drag you onto the blanket."

Jasper glanced at Miss Carlisle again, feeling a new sense of admiration. She'd moved him with only the help of a horse. Even with a horse to pull him up the steep incline, she still had to exert no small amount of strength in order to position him. "I'm in your debt," he said.

"You can pay it by surviving and then returning from whence you came."

"I assume without ever mentioning I saw you."

"Preferably."

"What are you talking about?" Richard asked.

"When I go home," Jasper said, scraping the bottom of the bowl. He'd already finished his broth. How had he eaten it so quickly? Miss Carlisle took the bowl but didn't fill it again, much to Jasper's disappointment.

"You can't go home," Richard whined. "You just got here."

"Darling, we had better allow Lord Jasper to rest now."

But to his surprise, Jasper didn't want to rest. He didn't feel as tired as he had the past eighteen hours. He still felt as though a horse had stomped on him and then kicked him in the flank for good measure, but he was sitting for the first time in days and wanted to stretch his legs, test his wound and his strength.

"Actually, I'd like to—" He'd attempted to swing his legs out and place his feet on the floor, but he found he couldn't move his feet. For a moment he feared something had happened to his legs, but then he threw aside the sheet and saw the ropes. Miss Carlisle's face went red.

"Do you want to see my wooden animals?" Richard asked, oblivious to the tension now vibrating between Jasper and Miss Carlisle.

"That's a good idea. Run up to the loft and fetch them," she told Richard. The boy didn't need to be asked twice. He scampered away as though chased by a swarm of bees.

"You bound me?" Jasper asked, voice low.

"I didn't know who you were, and I didn't trust you," she said in the same muted tone. "In my place, you would probably have done the same. I have a child to think of."

"Why only my ankles?"

"Because I'm not foolish enough to believe these ropes will hold you. I just wanted to ensure I had a few additional minutes if the need to escape arose." Escape. He could understand why that was her strategy. It had clearly been her *modus operandi* for some time.

"And if I remove them now?"

Her gaze slid to the ropes and then back to his face. "I'd rather you didn't. If you need a chamber pot—"

He waved a hand. "I need to stand up and stretch my legs. I want to have a look outside." It must have been raining for days. He wondered what effect that had on the trail.

"Maybe tomorrow," she said, her voice shaking. Jasper had never been very good with horses. That was Nicholas's forte, and he'd always been in charge of the troop's horses when they'd been fighting Napoleon on the Continent. But Jasper knew enough of skittish animals to move slowly around them and speak softly.

"Maybe today." He slid the sheet aside, revealing both of his legs. His feet were bare, his ankles bound to the posts at the bottom of the bed's footboard. "I promise I will just walk around. Nothing more." He reached for the bindings and the pain in his side lanced through him. Damn it. He looked up at Miss Carlisle, whose face had paled.

"Will you loosen the bindings?"

"I really think you should rest another day. The fever has not yet passed and moving too much may open your wound again."

"Will you loosen them or do I have to open the wound by doing it myself?" He met her gaze, knowing he could be as stubborn as anyone when he wanted. She glared right back at him, hands on her hips. Her blue eyes turned darker and her small, sweet mouth turned down. Bloody Christ. She wouldn't do it. He could see the defiance in her small frame from her head to her toes.

"I found them!" Richard announced. He dropped them in a pail beside the ladder and lowered it with the use of a rope attached to a pulley system down to the first floor. Jasper hadn't noticed that contraption before. Rather ingenious. He made another mark in the Impressed column for Miss Carlisle. Then Richard was scampering down the ladder, scooping his toys into his arms, and heading toward them. He stopped mid-step. "What's wrong?"

Jasper looked at Miss Carlisle. It hardly seemed possible, but her glare intensified. Then it vanished, and she turned and smiled at her son. "Not a thing, darling. I need to help his lordship with the bindings on his feet." She moved to the end of the bed and knelt on the floor beside the headboard.

"Why are his feet tied?" Richard asked.

"I didn't want him to fall out of bed and hurt himself." She lied smoothly. He shouldn't have added that to the Impressed column, but as a consummate liar himself, Jasper admired the trait more than he ought.

Miss Carlisle grasped his ankle and loosened the rope, and Jasper found himself riveted to the sight of her hands on his skin. He'd never thought of his ankle as an erogenous area, but her touch was making him reconsider. While Jasper tried to tamp down his lust, Richard held up one animal after another to show to Jasper. There were about seven in all—a horse, a hedgehog, a fox, a baby fox, a chicken, a pig, and a cow. They were carved from smooth wood and then painted. Jasper could fit three in one hand, but each was about the size of Richard's small palm. "These are good craftsmanship," Jasper said, not certain what other remarks to make about wooden animals. "Did your mother carve them?" He rather doubted she had that ability, but from what he knew of her so far, he wouldn't put anything past her.

"No, sir. We bought them at the little shop in Penbury. You must have seen it when you came through the village."

A shop with toy animals. Even if he had seen it, Jasper wouldn't have noted it. "I'm certain I did. What was it called?"

"The Curious Cabinet. It's my favorite shop in all the world."

As he prattled on, one rope binding fell away, and Jasper moved his foot from side to side. His feet felt rather numb and no wonder, as he hadn't moved them for days. He watched as Miss Carlisle moved to his other ankle, her small fingers working the knots on the binding and brushing against his skin in the process.

"And my friend Martin lives there."

Jasper arched a brow, though no one could see it with his mask on. "You have a friend named Martin?" This surprised him. He hadn't thought Miss Carlisle would risk friendships.

"Uh-huh."

"*Richard*."

"I mean, yes, sir. He's six, and sometimes we play with our animals together. Mama said I can go to his house for dinner one day."

"I said I would think about it." She rose, and Jasper almost wished she'd tie him again just so she'd have to keep touching him. "There you are." She took a step backward, her hand on Richard's shoulder so he moved back, and away, from Jasper as well. "Just move slowly so you don't fall." Her voice trembled, and Jasper had the feeling if she hadn't had to hide her fear from her son, she would have run as fast and as far from him as she could. As it was, she continued moving backward, putting the table between herself and her son and Jasper.

"Mama, I can't show him my animals over here," Richard complained.

Jasper set one foot on the floor then the other. Just the act of sitting up made the world tilt. "She just wants you out of the way, Master Richard. It's a good idea as right now the room is spinning and I see three of you."

"Three of me?" This was obviously an entertaining thought for the boy. He held up one of his animals. "How many of Horsey do you see?"

"Six." Jasper heaved himself up from the bed then rested an elbow on the wall behind the headboard. He didn't really see six wooden horses, but he really did feel like he might lose consciousness at any moment. It wasn't the fever, though surely that played a role, as much as the searing pain in his side that made him want to double over and moan.

He gritted his teeth and stood. It was all he could manage at the moment, and he was determined to support himself. When he felt a good deal steadier, he lifted an arm and peered at his side. White linen bound his upper abdomen, covering the stitches. He slid it down and peered at the epicenter of the pain. The skin looked raw and red, but the stitches were neat and even. He didn't see any indication of infection. He'd seen that all too often during the war, and he knew the signs. He wished he had a mirror so he might have a better view.

Slowly—no reason to fall over by moving his head too quickly—he looked over at Miss Carlisle. When he saw her face, all thoughts of a mirror vanished. She had both arms wrapped around her son's shoulders. Her eyes were huge in her face, like twin bruises against her waxy complexion. She was trembling, and even her son must have known she was afraid because his face had fallen and his eyes welled with tears.

Jasper failed to understand how she could fear him. He could barely stand on his own. What did she think he'd do to her in this condition? But he wanted to calm her and the boy, not chastise them. "I said I wouldn't hurt you." He kept his voice low and level. "Even if I thought to hurt you, I couldn't. I'm completely at your mercy, Miss Carlisle."

She blinked and swallowed visibly. "We are not used to visitors, my lord. And with the mask, you look—" She gestured as though unable to find the words.

"Like a monster," her son added helpfully.

"Richard!"

Jasper held his hand up then regretted releasing the wall and grasped it again. He lowered himself onto the bed, resting his elbows on his knees and breathing far more heavily than his minimal effort should require. "It's fine, Miss Carlisle. He's only curious." Like everyone else in the world. "Perfectly natural."

Jasper raised his head to look Miss Carlisle and her son squarely in the face. She had relaxed slightly, but she still had her arms around Richard and kept the table as a protective barrier.

"If you think I look like a monster with the mask, you would be even more terrified if I removed it."

Richard's eyes widened—not in fear but in fascination. "Do you ever take it off?" he whispered.

"Richard!"

Jasper held up a hand again. "Of course. In fact, I'd like to remove it and bathe my face and hair." He'd like to bathe more than that. Miss Carlisle had kept his wound clean, but the rest of him felt grimy.

"We usually bathe in the stable," she said. "But with all the rain, the path is muddy, and I fear you'd return from your bath dirtier than you left."

Not to mention the fact that even if the stable were close by, he couldn't have walked the distance in his present state.

"Then perhaps I might trouble you for a basin of water, a towel, and some privacy?"

"Of course." She nodded. With what seemed practiced efficiency, she shooed her son up the ladder and into his loft, then she gathered the necessary supplies. Jasper did not move. He didn't want to scare her, but he also knew he'd need his strength for the coming task. She set the basin of water, a clean cloth, and a small bar of soap next to a chair in one corner. Then she grasped a long piece of floral fabric that had been secured to the ceiling. Turning to him, she pulled the fabric to the side and tied it with a ribbon on the other corner. "This should give you some measure of privacy. I'll go into the loft with Richard and won't come down until you give the word."

He nodded. "I don't suppose you have any clean clothing that will fit me?"

She shook her head. "Your shirt is a complete loss. It was stuck to your skin with dried blood, and I had to cut it off. I could wash your trousers, but I haven't any way to dry them save hanging them by the fire. The rain has made a clothesline outside impossible."

Clean trousers were something. He could wash his own small clothes and hang them on the rack by the fire as well. Of course, that would mean he'd be naked until his clothing dried, but he would be under the bed sheets and thus unlikely to send Miss Carlisle into hysterics.

"I'd appreciate that. Thank you."

She started for the ladder then paused. She spoke without turning around. "I suppose you should call for me if you need assistance."

"I won't," he said.

"But if you do…"

"I'll call out." But the last thing he wanted was for anyone, especially this woman who was already afraid of him, to see his scarred face.

She climbed nimbly up the ladder, giving him nary a flash of her ankles, and Jasper made the slow, onerous trek to the chair just a few feet away. There he sank onto the chair, stripped down, and proceeded to tackle the difficult task of washing his body.

Four

He was naked. A naked man was in her cottage, and she was sitting in the loft doing nothing. Olivia didn't know if she was terrified or excited. Probably a little of both.

Fortunately, she had Richard to distract her. She helped him prepare for bed. It was a little early for his bedtime, but she didn't know how long they would be up here. By the time Lord Jasper finished his ablutions, it might be past Richard's bedtime. She resisted peeking down to see if he'd made it to the chair and helped Richard don his nightshirt.

"Read me a story, Mama?" Richard asked.

"Very well. You find the book, and I'll light the lamp." She took the tinder box from the shelf and lit the lamp she kept on the other side of the shelf. She did not look down, though she would have had a perfect view of Lord Jasper, a view from above that would have made the curtain useless.

"This one, Mama." Richard pointed to the page in the book that began the story he wanted, and Olivia smiled. It was a story of a mother bear who loses her cub and searches all night to find him. She can't locate the baby bear and returns despondent to her cave, whereupon she finds the cub fast asleep in his usual spot. Richard loved it, no doubt, because he saw himself as the bear cub—bravely exploring the world and then returning safely to a mother who worried for nothing. Olivia liked it because it showed the love and dedication a mother, a mother of any species, has for her child. Like the mother bear, Olivia knew she would have searched all night for her baby. Unlike the mother bear, she would have gone to the ends of the earth before she'd given up. If her little cub returned home, she would probably never find him because she'd still be out searching.

Richard climbed under his covers, and Olivia snuggled beside him, using her finger to follow the words in hopes that Richard might be able to read some of them one day soon. She didn't need to look at the words herself. She knew this story very, very well.

When that story was done, and Lord Jasper still had not called for her, she started another. About halfway through, Richard went limp, and she closed the book, tucked him in and blew out the lamp. The loft was darker now, but the lamp and the fire below still burned and she had plenty of light. She sat beside the bed and watched her son sleep, tracing the line of his brow, the slope of his cheek, and the roundness of his lips with her eyes.

Finally, he rolled over and settled into a deeper sleep, and she pulled her knees to her chest and rested her head on them. She had a thousand things to do before the day dawned tomorrow, and none of them could be done in the loft. She hoped the rain finally passed because she would like to air out the cottage and sweep the floors. Not to mention, her garden was more of a pond at the moment, and poor Clover was restless in the stable. Olivia had gone to feed and groom her, of course, but, like Richard and her, the horse wanted to stretch her legs.

Lord Jasper had wanted to stretch his tonight too. She had known that when he began to feel better he would be more of a threat. She had just thought his recovery would take longer. He still had a fever, and he was obviously still weak. She did not think if she had been in his position she would have been able to stand. But Lord Jasper was obviously a remarkably strong man. When he'd stood beside her bed, she couldn't help but note he was also a large man. She felt like a child standing in his shadow. He could have grabbed her and hurt her or Richard with very little effort indeed.

But he hadn't.

He'd made no move toward her or Richard and again insisted that he meant them no harm. She would believe that when he was gone. Men lied, and as far as she could see, he was no different than other men.

Except for the mask.

But the mask wasn't what had drawn her attention tonight. When she'd sent Richard upstairs to safety and Lord Jasper was once again seated, she couldn't help but steal peeks at his chest. Again. Olivia didn't know why it should fascinate her so. It was just a part of his body. His very *male* body. When she looked at it, she had the urge to touch it the muscled ridges and the smattering of golden brown hair. She had touched his chest because she'd cleaned it and bathed it, but she wanted to touch him far less platonically.

How could it be that she both wanted to run from him and wanted to touch him? She didn't understand herself in moments like this. She knew why she wanted to run. Withernsea had made certain she would never see men as interesting or diverting. For years now, she had shuddered with disgust when she even thought about a man touching her. She avoided all contact when she went into Penbury, keeping her face partially obscured with a veil she wore because she claimed to be a widow.

And Olivia wasn't certain that Lord Jasper touching her wouldn't make her shudder with revulsion. But for the first time she actually wanted to touch a man. She had the urge to run a finger over his strong jaw and his pale pink lips. She might thread her fingers through the straight ends of the dark blond hair that hung below his mask. She could imagine his hazel eyes fixed on her, and her chest tightened at the thought. Yes, she definitely wanted to touch him.

The very thought made her head pop up and off her knees. Olivia couldn't remember the last time she'd been attracted to a man. She supposed it had been when she'd been one of those silly girls during the London Season. So many of the young men then had been handsome and charming and graceful dancers. She'd found any number of them attractive and interesting.

Never Withernsea. Even then he'd been older than she and had a look about him that made her cringe. But she'd enjoyed dancing with the younger men. She'd liked placing her hand on their arms and feeling the warmth of their breath as they whispered to her. She'd liked the light brush of an arm across her back or the quick clasp of a hand on her waist.

Olivia felt her face grow hot. Perhaps Withernsea had seen how much she'd liked all of that and given her just what she'd deserved. That was what he'd said at any rate. She was a slut, and he was just treating her like the little strumpet she was.

But she hadn't been a strumpet. She hadn't done anything inappropriate. And even if she had been a slut, it didn't give him the right to…to…

She bit her lip to stave off tears and heard the chair scrape on the floor. She should call down and see if Lord Jasper needed assistance. Or she could just take a quick peek. That was far quieter, and she didn't want to wake Richard or make Lord Jasper feel as though he should hurry.

She rose to her knees and leaned to the side so she might see around the wall of the loft. She only wanted to be certain Lord Jasper wasn't lying on the floor, injured, but when she caught sight of the curtain, she could not look away.

Dear God in Heaven.

The curtain had parted slightly, or perhaps he'd never fully closed it, and she could see directly inside. She'd thought she would only be able to spot his head from this height, but with the curtain askew she could see far more than that. And what she noted was the man wore nothing at all. He stood facing the chair, his back to the room and her, and the firelight flickered gold over long legs, taut buttocks, and a wide, muscled back.

Her mouth went dry and her face burst into flame. And yet it wasn't embarrassment she felt. If she had, she might have looked away. It was desire. She hadn't felt it in a long, long time—she hadn't thought herself capable of feeling it ever again—but here it was. The longing was palpable, pulsing through her like the blood in her veins. The hair on her arms tingled, her chest tightened, and her belly felt warm and soft.

With reluctance, she pulled back and out of sight. But not before she caught a glimpse of the side of Lord Jasper's face. It must have been the side that was uninjured—either that or he'd lied about the injury—because it was absolutely perfect. He was a handsome man with a strong nose and a square jaw. He was also vaguely familiar. She had most certainly seen him at the theater or a ball all those years ago during the Season. And that meant he wasn't lying about who he was.

Her chest rose and fell as she tried to calm her breathing and push the ache of attraction away.

A moment later Lord Jasper called quietly, "Miss Carlisle, I'm finished."

"I'll be down in a moment," she called back. She was grateful that they were speaking in hushed tones because she wasn't certain her voice would have functioned. She still hadn't composed herself and she still felt a flush heating her face. She shouldn't have spied on him. He deserved privacy, and he wasn't some object put here for her to lust after.

She should have felt ashamed of herself, but that wasn't the sensation overwhelming her at all.

***

Olivia climbed down the ladder a few minutes later, studiously avoiding looking in Lord Jasper's direction. She kept her head down, her eyes on the floor.

"I'm under the sheets," he said. "I may not be decent, but at least I'm not indecent."

She nodded, afraid if she spoke her voice would betray the tumult of emotions she felt. And if she looked him in the eye, would he know she had seen his body bare and uncovered? She went to the chair and lifted his trousers from the back, where he had hung them neatly. How strange to touch something that had so intimately touched him. She would wash them in the soapy water she'd saved from the dishes and then hang them to dry. Happy to have something to occupy her, she knelt beside the tub and began scrubbing.

"Where is your son?" Lord Jasper asked.

Olivia caught her breath. She couldn't nod in answer to that question. She'd have to give a response. She cleared her throat. "Sleeping," she said. "It's his bedtime."

She rinsed the trousers in the clean water in the second tub, rung them out, then moved to hang them on the drying rack near the hearth. What she saw there made her pause. Lord Jasper must have washed his own small clothes and hung them to dry. She didn't know when he'd done it, but there they were. Pretending she didn't see them, she laid the trousers on the rope beneath them.

"I hope you don't mind that I did some of my own washing," he said. She shook her head, not trusting herself to look at him. "I would have washed the trousers, but I didn't want to fall over. I thought you'd rather not have to lift me into bed again."

The image of her lifting his naked body into bed made her flush even warmer. She should move away from the fire. She was becoming overheated.

"I don't mind." She squeaked the words more than spoke them.

"Miss Carlisle." His voice had an edge to it that might have frightened her if she wasn't so completely mortified already.

She began to gather the plates from the table. She would wash them and be thankful for another activity. Never had she been happy to wash dishes before.

"Miss Carlisle." This time it was more an order than a query. She looked up and met his gaze. Her breath hitched at the way his gaze seemed to caress her face. Quickly, she looked down again.

"Do you need something?"

"I trusted you to give me privacy."

She glanced at him again, looking back down just as quickly because she could well imagine her face was the picture of guilt. "I-I did."

"Then why won't you look at me?"

"I-I suppose seeing such personal items…" She gestured vaguely to the rack by the fire.

"We both know that's not it."

Olivia squeezed her eyes shut and clasped her hands together. Would he call her names? Accuse her of behaving wantonly? She didn't think he would attempt to punish her with his fists. He didn't have the strength.

"You couldn't stand not seeing what was underneath, could you?"

She twisted her hands. How had he known? Had he been able to read her thoughts, to know she wondered what he looked like without his clothing?

"And now that you've seen you can't even look me in the eye."

She raised her gaze to his then. She might as well accept responsibility for what she'd done. "I'm sorry. I didn't intend to look. It just…happened."

His hazel eyes, so pretty ordinarily, flashed fire. "And now you can't stand to look at me, is that it?"

She touched her hands to her flaming cheeks. "I…I…"

"You're disgusted by what you saw."

With her hands pressed to her cheeks, she felt her jaw drop. "Why would I be disgusted?"

"You can't have thought it attractive. I've sent men and children screaming at the sight of it."

She stared at him. When had he shown other men and children his bare backside? Unless… "Are you speaking of your face?" she asked.

His eyes, hooded by the mask, narrowed. "What do you think I am speaking of?"

Best not to answer that question. "I did not see your face, my lord. I…" *I was looking much lower*. "You were turned away."

He did not move and since she felt practically frozen in place, the entire room was still for three long heartbeats. Then very slowly his mouth quirked up in something of a smile. Or perhaps it was more aptly termed a smirk.

"Then what was it you saw?" He gestured to her. "What has your face so pink?"

"It was a very quick peek. As I said, it was more of an accident."

"If you weren't looking at my face, what were you looking at?"

"Nothing! Not intentionally, at any rate."

"So you caught an accidental glimpse and then looked away immediately."

She nodded. "Exactly."

"Your gaze didn't linger?"

"No!"

"You didn't stare?"

"No!"

"Miss Carlisle…"

"Oh, very well!" The truth seemed ready to explode out of her. She could turn purple and expire from embarrassment or she could just admit her sin. "I looked. I saw your bare backside. I didn't intend to, but I did."

"I see." He seemed amused, but it was difficult to tell with the mask.

"And, no, I didn't look away immediately. I should have, but I suppose I was interested. I've never seen—" She made a vague gesture toward him.

"You've never seen…?" he asked, and she knew from the tone of his voice he was enjoying this exchange.

"That is all I am saying. I apologize."

"You've never seen a naked man?" he asked, pressing the issue where she did not want it to go.

"Correct. I assure you I will not violate your privacy again."

"I believe you, but indulge me for a moment, Miss Carlisle."

"No." She shook her head. "No indulging."

He went on, ignoring her. "What did you think of what you saw? Did you like it?"

She wasn't certain how to answer. She felt embarrassed, guilty, and decidedly too warm. She needed a few moments alone. "Excuse me. I should tend to Clover."

Immediately, his smirk faded. "You don't plan to go out into the dark alone. It's still raining."

She listened, cocking her head. "It's slackened enough that if I throw my shawl over my head I shan't be soaked to the skin." And she lifted her shawl, tossed it over her head, and then made the mistake of looking back at him.

Olivia balked.

Her patient had swung his legs over the side of the bed and was sitting with only a scrap of cloth covering his…lower regions.

"What are you doing?" Did he plan to deliberately expose himself to her?

"I'll go out with you." He said, his voice sounding rough. She immediately understood why as he gritted his teeth as he spoke the next words. "It's not safe for you to go alone."

"You will do no such thing! The last thing I need is you lying in the mud bleeding." *Naked and bleeding*, she thought, but she would probably implode before she had the courage to say those words.

"You could slip and—" He'd tried to rise but grimaced when the pain was too much for him. She thanked God when he sat back down, remaining covered.

"And you think to assist me?" Anger slowly replaced her mortification. "I don't need your help, my lord. I've been tending my own horse and my own house by myself and in every kind of weather for years now. All you will do is hurt yourself, and then I will have to worry not only about the horse but about an injured fool as well."

His back went rigid and he turned a gaze hot with anger on her. "Did you just call me a fool?"

"If you think you have the strength to walk to the stable and back with me, then yes. You are a fool."

He made a low noise in his throat that sounded very much like a growl. "Madam, no one has ever called me a fool. No one has ever dared."

"Well, they should have." She knew she should be frightened, but she was too annoyed to care. Later she would probably shake with delayed nerves. How dare he assume she couldn't take care of herself and her horse? How did he think she'd managed all these years? And she hadn't just had herself to see to. She'd had a baby and then a toddler to care for as well. The man couldn't even stand and he thought he would save her. In her mind, that was the exact definition of a fool.

She marched over to the bed, hands on her hips, eyes trained above his shoulders. The black half mask he wore did nothing to hide his anger. She could see it in the tenseness of his stubbled jaw and the tightness in his shoulders.

"Unless you want to open those stitches I sewed or drag yourself back up from the floor, I suggest you lie back down and rest. You can prove what a strong man you are another day."

His eyes narrowed, looking like little more than slits with the mask over them. "You will rue the day you gave me that challenge."

"I'm sure."

But he lay down and tugged at the covers. When even those eluded him, she pulled them up to his shoulders for him. Clearly, he was exhausted because he was fighting to keep his eyes open. "If you were a man, I would pummel you bloody. Since you are a female, we will have it out in words. Later."

"Why not just punch me?" She didn't know why she'd said it. Perhaps because she could only exist in a state of fear for so long before she broke and teased the angry tiger into action. "You'll feel better and I won't have to wait for what I know is coming."

His eyes, which had been drooping, opened. Surprisingly clear now, they focused on her face. "I don't hit women." And then his eyes closed and he did not move again.

Olivia waited until she was certain he was asleep before she felt his cheek. It was warm but not overly so. The fever was waning. She wished he would allow her to remove that mask. It couldn't be comfortable, and if he wasn't wearing it, she could bathe his brow with a cool cloth. She'd settle for preparing more herbal tea when she returned. If he stirred in the night, she'd force some down his throat.

Her hand lingered on his cheek and then slid to his slightly parted lips. She licked her own lips in response to the softness of his. Hers tingled, and she swallowed hard trying to ignore the feeling. She had no time for infatuation. She had chores to see to. And now that her anger was fading, she realized how reckless she'd been to call him a fool and challenge him. She'd surely pay for such imprudence on her part.

I don't hit women.

She had heard that before. She was neither young enough nor naïve enough to believe it anymore.

Five

By Jasper's count, he was out for two more days. At least. He'd paid for overtaxing himself by standing up and then arguing with Miss Carlisle. He'd had no strength to do anything but sleep and allow her to spoon tea and broth down his throat. He was completely disgusted with himself. Never had he been so weak, so pitiful. Here he had been sent to find Miss Carlisle and bring her home. Instead, she had found him and was stuck playing nursemaid. He hated himself for needing a nursemaid. And he was helpless to do anything but accept her kindness.

Finally, on what he thought was the third day, he opened his eyes and felt somewhat like his old self. His body didn't ache. His head didn't pound. His flank was still tender, but he could all but feel where the skin was beginning to knit together. He turned his head toward the window and was surprised to see the pale light of early morning filtering through the lace curtains.

Sunlight.

He'd almost forgotten what it looked like. It seemed like he'd been trapped in a nightmare world of pain and darkness for years. But now the sun was out. The rain had stopped, and he was awake. All good signs.

His gaze slid to the chair between the bed and the window. She'd placed it carefully—not close enough that he could reach out and grab her but near enough that she could be of help if he needed it. Jasper vaguely remembered an argument where she called him a fool. He remembered thinking she'd seen his burn scars. He'd been angry about that, so angry he'd said words he didn't mean. But then he'd realized she'd just seen his bare buttocks, and her prudish response amused him. An arse was an arse. Why should seeing his embarrass her?

Unless she had liked what she'd seen?

And then he'd been interested in her blushes. *Had* she liked what she'd seen? He had his suspicions about what had happened between her and Withernsea. He'd assumed she would have an unshakeable antipathy toward men after the abuse she'd no doubt suffered. But perhaps time had healed those wounds.

He shook his head, grateful it didn't throb in protest. It wasn't for him to worry about her body's wants and desires or lack thereof. Even if she hadn't been a job for him, he knew he was little more than a scarred monster. No woman would want him, especially not this one.

It had been so long since he'd spent any time with a woman that being constantly in Miss Carlisle's presence was discomfiting. Jasper had decided long ago that he wouldn't pay for a woman as though a body was a commodity to be purchased. He'd resigned himself to celibacy, and it was generally not too difficult. He didn't see many women who attracted him, not in the rookeries, where he spent most of his time. Both men and women there had been ravaged by poverty. Their bodies proved the outward manifestation of their ruined spirits—pox on their skin, rotting teeth, oily hair, broken bones.

But he wasn't in the rookeries now, and when his gaze lifted to Miss Carlisle's face it was difficult to pretend she didn't stir his blood. In sleep she was pretty in an innocent, almost child-like way. He felt more protective than anything else. But when she was awake and moving about efficiently, ordering him to swallow the tea, or challenging him with her hands on those slim hips, she was spectacularly beautiful. Jasper had wanted to pretend his heart thudded because he was weak, but that wasn't the only reason.

Enough!

She didn't want him, and he should stop torturing himself imagining she would ever overcome her past or see him as anything more than a scarred wreck of a man.

He threw back the covers and sat, making himself move gingerly so his head wouldn't spin. Wrapping the sheet around his middle, he shuffled to the fireplace. His small clothes were dry. He slipped them on and then lifted his trousers. They were dry as well. He pulled them on and wished his shirt or coat had been salvageable. But he'd survived several weeks in the Russian winter. He could tolerate England's crisp fall with a bare chest. Shoving his feet into his boots, Jasper lifted the door's latch. It didn't open. A key hung on a nail high enough so the lad couldn't reach it, but Jasper used it to unlock the door. He wondered if the lock was to keep her son in or others out.

Jasper closed the door quietly behind him so as not to wake Miss Carlisle or the lad and surveyed the yard. Leaves and small tree limbs littered the muddy ground, while a light breeze rustled the branches that remained and made him shiver. To his right was the trail down to the shore. To his left, footprints marked the path to the stable. He went left, pausing after only a few feet to marvel at the view of the ocean. It was calm today, the waves rolling in gently and white wispy clouds on the pinkish horizon. It was too early for the morning tide, and he didn't spot any ships. He imagined he could see halfway to America up here, though from the letters he'd read from his friend Rafe, who'd traveled to the former colonies, the distance was much greater than that.

Turning from the view of the ocean, Jasper trudged through the thick mud until he spotted a small building with a wide window. This must be the stable. As he neared, he heard the horse nicker. The animal was probably hungry and eager for fresh air.

Jasper lifted the bar on the stable doors, wincing a little at the twinge of pain in his side, and swung them open. Inside an old brown mare lifted her head and neighed at him, her ears flicking back and her eyes rolling nervously. Jasper spoke quietly to her. He wasn't quite up to mucking out stalls yet, but he found the feed easily enough, as well as a bucket of clean water. Obviously, this reassured the horse because she only snorted when he entered her stall and opened the window. She lifted her head and blew out a breath then went back to eating. No doubt when Miss Carlisle woke she would take the horse out to stretch her legs.

There was little else to see in the stable, so Jasper left. He would have walked back to the cottage except the footprints he'd followed wound around the back of the stable. He followed them to a clearing where neat rows of vegetables had been planted. At least they had been neat rows at some point. Now the plants had toppled over and what might have been carefully tended soil was little more than a shallow, muddy pond.

Jasper walked on, his side beginning to throb now, past the rear of the cottage, and toward the path leading back down to the ocean. The path he'd taken to the cottage. A fist had closed around his heart, but he tried to ignore the ominous feeling that he would be trapped here by more than his injury. There was no ignoring the truth, however, when he looked down the steep incline of the path. What had been a somewhat challenging but traversable path was now little more than a steep muddy descent. Rocks and tree limbs that had provided purchase had been washed away, and Jasper stared at what amounted to a precipice. A few yards down, the path curved. It had once been a gentle curve but was now a jutting of land where the rest of the cliff ended.

Jasper supposed the lower half of the trail might have fared better, but he didn't think he could make it down in order to assess the terrain.

Not with his injured side and not with the mud still wet and slippery.

He was stuck here. There was no way to return to London.

Worse, he was forced into close quarters with a beautiful woman. He couldn't help being attracted to her, and she'd made it clear she wanted him to go away.

This was supposed to be an easy job: find Miss Carlisle, tell her about her mother dying, and escort her to London to say her farewells. He'd thought finding her the most difficult part of his task. Next to that, convincing her he would keep her safe when she traveled to London would also require effort.

Well, he'd found her, but he hadn't counted on the complication of her son. He hadn't expected a destructive storm to maroon them. And he certainly hadn't anticipated the man who'd knifed him. So much for convincing her he'd keep her safe in London. His attacker might have been acting alone, but Jasper didn't put it past Withernsea to have him followed and then dispatched when he'd led the man to the prize. He couldn't be certain, but it was possible Withernsea now knew where Miss Carlisle was hiding. The duke wouldn't be able to reach her at the moment, but when the trail was passable, he'd send someone for her.

Which was yet another reason Jasper couldn't leave. Even if his attack had nothing to do with the duke, clearly Miss Carlisle was not safe here. All in all, taking this job was turning out to be the worst decision he had made in a long time. Not only would he not be stuck here if he'd stayed home, Miss Carlisle would be safer too.

He had often acted recklessly in the past. He touched his mask where it covered his scar as a reminder of that moment of rashness. Now he had a hole in his side and a woman and child in danger to show for this incidence of foolishness.

He heard a gasp and turned. Miss Carlisle stood behind him, clearly startled to see him standing there. The cottage wasn't visible from the trail, which meant anyone climbing it would not see the house until he walked a little further. But it also meant she had to round the same bend before she spotted any intruders.

She lowered her eyes, away from his bare chest, and pretended it was normal to see a half-dressed man standing on the side of the cliff. "How does it look?"

"Not promising. Half the trail has washed away, and what's left is steep and muddy. Come see for yourself."

She did, and he moved to the side to give her more space. It was impossible not to notice how skittish she was around him. Her movements were jerky, and her eyes darted everywhere but his face. Jasper focused on her tense shoulders as she stared down the trail. He imagined if he reached out and touched her, she'd leap like a coiled spring. "I've never seen it this bad," she said.

"How long have you lived here?"

Her gaze skidded to him and then back again. "Long enough to remember several heavy rains, but none like the past few days. It could be weeks before we can get down."

Jasper would climb down with rope before he'd stay here for weeks. He didn't want to make anyone uncomfortable, especially not a woman he found attractive. More than that, he didn't want to be reminded that every time he imagined kissing her she was thinking of what a monster he was. "That might be a problem. I don't remember seeing a well. And your garden is waterlogged."

"We don't have a well, but there's a spring on the other side of the cliff. Sometimes it's little more than a trickle, but I imagine it's quite robust now. And we can always drink rain water. I'll take care of the garden, but even without it, I have provisions enough."

He crossed his arms. She might have enough food and water for a boy and a woman, but he probably ate as much as the two of them together. "Let me take a look," he said.

Her brows shot up, and belatedly he realized he would have done better not to phrase it as an order.

"My lord, you had better worry about how much longer you can stand. You must be freezing, and though you're obviously feeling better, you shouldn't be walking around so much until your injury heals."

Apparently, she could issue orders as easily as he. The galling thing was that he would do well to listen to hers. He already felt tired and shaky.

"You need to eat and change your bandage," she said.

"You're probably right."

She raised her brows in surprise, though he knew there was no *probably* about it. She was absolutely correct. No sense in denying it, though he had enough pride to add the qualifier.

"Mama! Come and look at this!"

Jasper wasn't surprised the lad was awake and about. The boy was full of spirit. Jasper followed Miss Carlisle back toward the cottage, where the lad hefted a long stick and pretended to jab it at some unseen foe.

"I found a sword, Mama!" the boy called. Then, spotting Jasper, "Look, my lord. I'm dueling a dragon."

Jasper didn't see any dragon, and he wasn't certain if he was expected to pretend he did see a dragon. He didn't understand children's imaginations. Did they really see imaginary beasts or did they know nothing was there? Did one treat them like a madman in Bedlam, placating them so they didn't become unruly, or did one announce the obvious?

"And what does this dragon look like?" Miss Carlisle asked, giving Jasper at least one answer. He did not need to pretend he saw the imaginary beast.

"It's a big dragon with green scales and red wings and a yellow tail."

"He sounds very colorful."

"He breathes fire! If I'm not careful, he'll toast my sword, won't he, my lord?"

At this second attempt to engage him, Jasper deduced he had to make some comment. Miss Carlisle hadn't told the boy there were no such things as dragons, so that probably wasn't the way to go. And she hadn't pointed out that her son held a stick, not a sword. He was supposed to treat the boy like the Bedlam inmate then. "You should watch out for the flames," he said. It didn't seem like enough. "That dragon can roast your skin until it crackles and turns as black as charred ashes."

The boy lowered his stick in surprise and Miss Carlisle whirled on him, her mouth tight with disapproval.

"What did I say?" Jasper asked.

"I think we'd better go inside, my lord."

"Wait!" Her son raised his sword again. "Do dragons really do that? Have you ever seen a man roasted like that?"

It was a question Jasper didn't want to answer. "We can talk more when we break our fast," he said, following Miss Carlisle into the cottage. She stomped rather than walked, and he expected her to round on him as soon as they were out of her son's hearing. She didn't disappoint.

"What sort of thing is that to say to a child? He'll have nightmares of burning men after that."

Jasper shrugged. “You asked him about the dragon. I thought I was supposed to play along.”

“Not by giving him gruesome descriptions.”

He rubbed the stubble on his chin. “I’m new at this. I don’t spend much time around children.” And the children he did encounter in the rookeries had seen things that would probably have appalled Jasper.

“You aren’t a father then?”

“No!” The thought shocked him. “I’m barely an uncle. My oldest brother has a child now, a girl. But she’s only a couple months old. She doesn’t talk, only cry.”

“I can see why, with you as an uncle.”

He stiffened and moved past her. His head throbbed with anger and exhaustion, and Jasper knew he had better sit or the combination might fell him.

“I’m sorry,” she said. “I didn’t mean that how it sounded.”

“I know what you meant.” He sank down on the bed, blowing out a breath. “She’s too young to understand gruesome stories, but my mask is terrifying enough.”

“No—” She stood in front of him now, an arm outstretched as though beseeching him to understand her.

“But I didn’t wear my mask to her christening,” he said, not sure why he told her. Perhaps he wanted to hurt her as her unthinking comment had lanced him. “My brother didn’t want it in the church. Believe it or not, she didn’t seem to care about my wreck of a face. She cried no matter what I did and wouldn’t even be comforted in her mother’s arms. But the rest of those present…” He shook his head ruefully. “I think I can safely say I disgusted or terrified all of them. One lady had to leave before the service was even completed.”

"No." Miss Carlisle shook her head. "I'm certain it couldn't have been because of you."

He looked up at her. "You haven't seen it."

"I wouldn't be disgusted. I'm not so silly as that. I assume it's a war injury."

He nodded.

"Well, then. You're a war hero. Your scars are badges of honor." Her voice was matter-of-fact and practical.

He laughed and tapped his face. "This is no honor."

"If you don't believe me, then take off the mask and show me."

"Is that what you want? You haven't even eaten your breakfast yet. So eager to lose your appetite?"

"Eager to prove you wrong," she challenged, still standing in front of him and looking him directly in the eye as though she had nothing to fear.

He almost reached for the ties. He was tired of wearing the damn mask and would have relished the cool air on his tender skin. But he didn't want her look of revulsion haunting him. He couldn't escape her and God knew he didn't want to be trapped with her pity. "I don't want to scare the child."

"Richard won't—"

"I said no, Miss Carlisle."

She stepped back and out of reach at his harsh tone, and he immediately regretted raising his voice to her.

"I'll start on the morning meal." She hurried away, no doubt eager to distance herself from him. But then to his surprise, she spoke again. "We must speak at some point, I think."

He braced himself. He'd only told a handful of people how he'd received his injury. If that was what she wished to discuss, hell could freeze over first. "About?"

"About why you are here. I didn't want to press you when you were fevered and…" She had her back to him, but he watched the way she lifted the pan and paused with it in mid-air.

"And dying?"

She glanced over her shoulder. "And in pain. If you recall, I asked why you'd come looking for me. Can you tell me now?"

He should have told her long before. "I was sent by Viscount Carlisle," he said. She started as though the name was a pistol shot that took her by surprise. She spun around, her hand gripping the handle of the pan like one might a shield.

"What does he want?"

"To see you. Your mother—"

"Whose mother?"

Jasper realized they hadn't shut the door, and now the boy stood in it, head cocked.

Miss Carlisle's face changed instantly. The creases in her forehead smoothed and she brightened with an obviously false smile. "No one, darling. We were speaking of nothing. Are you hungry? I thought to make baked apples with cinnamon."

"That's my favorite!"

"I know. Go outside and play. I'll call you when it's ready."

The little boy glanced at Jasper. "Do you want to come out and play too, my lord?"

He shook his head. "I'm not feeling strong enough to battle dragons. Maybe tomorrow."

"Really? Hoorah!" And he scampered back out.

***

"You realize he will hold you to that," Olivia said, turning back to her task of stoking the fire. "From now on, he'll talk of dragons without ceasing."

Lord Jasper grunted. She couldn't see his movements with her back turned, but she imagined he was examining his wound. It must pain him after all his activity this morning.

"I don't mind," he said. "I don't say things I don't mean."

She paused in the act of gathering apples from a sack. "Then you do intend to play at battling dragons with him?"

He was indeed examining his side, and she had to remind herself to breathe, not stare at his bare chest. "I don't know how to battle dragons, but I'm generally a quick study." He looked up and she colored, realizing despite her intentions she had been staring at his chest. "But to return to our previous conversation. Your parents—"

"Shh!" Her head snapped up and she darted a look at the open door. "We'll speak of it later." She couldn't speak of London, couldn't think of what had happened there and the man who had done it, with Richard nearby. She didn't trust herself to control her emotions. And she certainly couldn't cope with so much emotion with Lord Jasper sitting shirtless just a few feet away.

She couldn't see his brows under the mask, but she imagined they drew together. Still he didn't say another word, honoring her request without question. But they'd have to talk at some point. Her parents had sent him and found her. She wasn't safe any longer.

She washed the apples and began to slice them, her fingers shaking slightly at the feel of his gaze on her.

"Can I help you with that?" he asked.

She almost laughed. If she was nervous with him across the room, she would probably slice a finger off if he was beside her. What if he touched her? What if she accidentally touched his bare chest? She let out a shaky breath. "No. Rest. You must be tired."

"I'm embarrassed to admit that I am. I used to march for days, and now a walk around the yard leaves me weak as a babe."

She finished slicing apples and began to coat them with cinnamon and a little sugar. "Your strength will return." Privately she thought he already had remarkable strength. She'd been perplexed when she'd awakened this morning to find her bed empty. She had the fleeting thought that she'd dreamed him. She opened the curtains in time to see him pass by, on his way to the trail down to the sea. In a panic, she'd rushed after him, half afraid he would leave without saying farewell. She was not thinking clearly. How would he leave without a shirt or coat and in enough pain that he winced whenever he walked? Still, she'd gone after him. A quick look around showed his footprints all over. He'd obviously surveyed her property, perhaps even walked out to the stable and the garden. A few days ago he'd barely been able to stand.

She should probably congratulate herself on her nursing skills except she doubted she had much to do with his survival. He was not an easy man to kill.

"If you're right, I'll be battling dragons tomorrow morning."

She imagined looking out her window and watching Richard and Lord Jasper wave sticks at invented beasts. It was the kind of game Richard loved and she rapidly grew tired of. But she knew Richard would relish playing such a game with a man. It hadn't occurred to her until now that her son had spent very little time around men and might crave interaction with a…well, not a father. Lord Jasper was not that, but Richard might certainly see him as such. Lately Richard had asked more and more about his father, and Olivia had avoided answering the question. The boy would likely have more questions after time spent with Lord Jasper.

And what would she say? *Your father is a monster? You were conceived in terror and hate? You are a bastard who should have been heir to a dukedom but will now never be accepted into Society?*

Was it better to tell the boy the truth, some version of it, or better to lie? So many times it had been on the tip of her tongue to tell Richard his father was dead. She could pretend Richard's father was a sailor whose ship had been lost at sea. He would hear that story at some point anyway as that was the part she played when she went into Penbury.

But how much longer would she be traveling to Penbury? She supposed she had hoped her parents had forgotten about her, or at the very least, given up. But clearly they would never leave her in peace, and even if she could convince Lord Jasper to keep her whereabouts a secret, she would no longer feel safe here once he left.

She sighed and took a wistful look about her cottage. Over the years she had done so much to make what had been basically a very rustic building cozy and inviting. She'd wanted a home for her son, and now she would have to leave and find a place to start all over. How she wished she could go home to her mother and father again. But that would never happen, and she could not allow herself to waste time on nostalgia.

"Mama, is it time to break our fast?" Richard asked, sticking his head in the door.

"Almost." She eyed the mud on his boots. "Take off your boots and wash your hands"—his face had mud splatters as well—"before coming in."

"I'll do the same," Lord Jasper said, rising. Olivia had almost forgotten him. He'd been so still and quiet, his head leaned against the headboard of her bed. She thought he'd fallen asleep. But now he rose and walked to the doorway. He looked back and frowned. "I'm sorry about the mud. I didn't think to remove my boots earlier. I'll clean the floors after we eat."

Olivia gave him a stern look. "You will not. I'll be happy to put you to work when you've healed, but until then you mustn't overtax yourself."

He nodded. "Yes, Miss Carlisle." His voice was obedient, but it was an attitude that didn't fit him. He was a man used to giving orders and commanding. He wouldn't be obedient for long. She heard Richard and Lord Jasper splashing in the water just outside the door, and then the two of them came in with a burst of the cool morning air. She served them apples and tea and then took her own seat. Since Lord Jasper had seated himself beside Richard, she was across from both of them. She made the mistake of looking up and staring directly at Lord Jasper's chest. After that, she stared at the food on her plate, her appetite seemingly forgotten.

"Why don't you wear clothes?" Richard asked suddenly, and Olivia, who had just put a bite of apple in her mouth almost spit it out. She would have chastised her son, but her mouth was too full.

"I am wearing clothes," Lord Jasper said.

"But only on your bottom half. Your top half is naked."

Olivia swallowed around the lump of embarrassment in her throat and felt her face burn. "Richard," she began.

"The most important part of me is covered," Lord Jasper said.

Richard wrinkled his nose, something he did when he didn't understand. "Mama says we have to cover our top and our bottom."

Lord Jasper's eyes met hers, and Olivia flushed harder. She might as well explode at this rate.

"That's true," Lord Jasper said slowly, seeming to choose his words carefully. "But my shirt and coat were ruined, and since I'm a man it's not wholly indecent of me to go about shirtless."

"What's indecent?"

"Uh…" Lord Jasper looked at her and she merely raised her brows in expectation.

"And why does it matter for men and not women?"

Lord Jasper made a show of chewing his food and slowly swallowing, but Richard kept his attention focused. "My lord?" he prodded before Lord Jasper could put more food into his mouth.

"Because…because men and women are different, of course." His mouth twisted triumphantly.

"How?" Richard asked. "How are men and women different?"

Lord Jasper seemed to realize he'd blundered into yet another ambush. His eyes pleaded with her, but she merely placed a small slice of apple into her mouth and chewed thoughtfully.

"I'll let your mother explain that to you," Lord Jasper said, rising and taking his empty plate with him.

"Traitor," she hissed.

Lord Jasper stacked his plate where she usually put the dishes needing to be washed. “I think I’ll step outside and get more fresh air.”

Richard jumped up then promptly plopped back down again. “Mama, may I be excused?”

“Of course.” If he stayed she’d have to explain the biology of men and women.

“Thank you.” He chased after Lord Jasper, and as the two males stepped outside, she heard him say, “Tell me more about what dragon fire can do. Can they really roast a man? Does skin really crackle?”

Six

She waited for the end of the day like a condemned man waits for the morning of his execution. As she put away the supper plates, she felt like Marie Antoinette as the tumbrels rattled in the streets outside her cell.

Richard hadn't taken a nap, but she hadn't expected him to. Her son had been far too excited at having Lord Jasper up and about to be talked into resting midday. Lord Jasper probably needed a nap as well. He'd kept Richard occupied while she'd mucked out Clover's stall and dug trenches to drain the standing water from the garden. He'd insisted on helping her half a dozen times, but she'd refused. She knew if he felt stronger tomorrow he would ignore her admonishments to rest and pitch in with her.

Finally, it neared Richard's bedtime and though the boy protested that he was not tired, his eye lids drooped and he could not stop yawning. She took as much time as she could reading to him and tucking him in, but he was asleep within moments. She could put off the inevitable discussion a little longer, but she might as well get it over with. All of her emotions and fears would be just as strong later as they were now. And she would have to face the uncertainty of her future at some point.

Olivia climbed down the ladder, dismayed to find Lord Jasper still seated at the table. He'd moved closer to the fire, but he sat, a blanket draped over his bare shoulders, as though waiting for her. Her last hope had been that he would fall asleep while she tucked Richard in. But he was awake, and she would have to speak of what had happened and not fall apart. She had to be strong, no matter how it sickened her to think back on the night she'd run away. No matter how much she wanted to lock all of those memories away and never think of them again.

"You must be tired," she said, trying not to sound hopeful. "If you wish to go to sleep, I can blow out the lamps and—"

"I can wait. I'd rather have this discussion now when we won't be interrupted."

Olivia's legs felt weak, and she clasped the edge of the table and seated herself across from him. She was glad he wore the blanket over his shoulders. No matter how many times she saw his bare chest, it still stirred something in her. And if it wasn't his chest it was the dip of his waist or the muscles in his back or the breadth of his shoulders…

"I can sew," she blurted out. "The clothing I make is practical, not fashionable, but I could make you a shirt and perhaps a rudimentary coat."

His mouth opened in surprise. "You have the fabric for that?"

That was a good question. She had an old dress she could remake into a shirt, but she didn't have enough heavy material to fashion a coat. Not for a man his size.

"I have enough for a shirt, though it won't be white linen."

He waved a hand. "I've worn homespun as often as linen. I'm no dandy."

"Then I'll start on it right away." She rose to find her sewing basket and the fabric she had folded and put away.

"You can look for fabric after we discuss why I came here. It's past time."

It was past time, but that didn't give him leave to order her about. "You're right that it's time I heard what you have to say, but don't ever presume to tell me what to do, my lord. I don't take orders from anyone—not you, not any man." Anger would help her be strong. She would hold onto it as long as possible.

He nodded once. "Understood. My apologies."

She narrowed her eyes, certain he would add more. Certain he would make a comment about her knowing her place, but he remained silent.

"Thank you," she said. "I prefer to stand. Go ahead."

"Several months ago, Viscount Carlisle approached me. He had been searching for you for some years without success. Time was running out, and he came to me."

"Why you?" she asked. Despite her claims she preferred to stand, she sank down across from him. Her legs shook at the mention of her father, and she needed firm ground beneath her.

"Because I'm the best. I can and do find anyone and anything."

"You work for Bow Street? I thought you the son of a marquess."

"I am, and I don't work for anyone but myself. Some might call me a bounty hunter."

"A bounty hunter. That isn't exactly flattering."

He shrugged. "Not everything I do is clean and tidy. More often than not I find criminals with a price on their head. When I give them over, I collect my bounty."

"And I have a price on my head?"

He opened his mouth but did not speak for a long moment. "Your father has not put a price on your head, and he's not the sort of man who would typically request my services. I imagine he heard about me because of my activities during the war. I have something of a reputation among my troop."

"You fought against Napoleon."

He gave her a wry smile. "In a manner of speaking. Suffice it to say, my skills are widely known. Your father came to me and offered to pay me to find you."

She jumped to her feet. "Won't he ever leave me in peace? Is he still trying to marry me off to that—" She couldn't speak his name. Bile rose in her throat at the thought of it. "That odious man?"

She'd put her hands on her hips defensively, expecting to have to declare that she would never go home, never become Withernsea's bride, never forgive her parents for coercing her into agreeing to the engagement…but something in the way Lord Jasper looked at her made her pause. She dropped her hands.

"It's your mother. She's not well."

Olivia sat heavily. Her mother. No, not her dear mother. "She's dying."

"I didn't spend much time with her, but that is my understanding, yes."

Olivia dropped her face into her hands. She didn't want him to see the tears pricking her eyes. As angry as she was at her mother for the viscountess's role in the debacle with Withernsea, Olivia still loved her. She'd thought of her often since becoming a mother herself and wondered if her mother had sat up with her when she was ill, as Olivia did with Richard, and if her mother had felt the same joy and poignancy when she'd taken her first steps as Olivia had watching Richard at a year of age. Somehow, in the back of her mind, Olivia had always imagined Richard meeting his grandparents. She didn't know how it would happen or when but she entertained a reunion fantasy sometimes when she daydreamed or couldn't fall asleep.

Now it appeared her mother would never know her grandson, and Richard would never know his grandparents. As she was her parents' only child, they would never have the experience of knowing a grandchild, of knowing Richard.

Olivia sighed and wiped her eyes. "Thank you for telling me."

"I didn't come to merely tell you. My mission is to bring you back."

Olivia gave him a steely stare—at least she hoped it was. Her eyes felt heavy and bloodshot. "I am not a mission, my lord. And I won't go back. Return to my father and tell him you were unable to locate me." She was proud that her voice had not shaken.

He shook his head. "No one will believe it."

"You're certainly not short on arrogance."

"It's not arrogance." He leaned forward and pressed his palms on the table. "It's the truth."

"Then go back and tell them I won't come. Or tell them whatever you like. It matters not to me."

"And when they tell me to come back and try to convince you, I won't find you here, will I?"

She didn't answer.

"You can't hide forever, Miss Carlisle."

"Oh, really? This coming from a man who wears a mask every moment of the day."

"I have my reasons," he snapped.

"So do I." She glanced up at the loft. They weren't speaking loudly enough to wake her son, but she still had the urge to make sure he was safe.

"If Withernsea mistreated you, then you should go back and expose him," Lord Jasper said.

She let out a bitter laugh, her entire body shaking now at the very idea of seeing the duke again. "What world were you raised in? The *ton* doesn't blame men for their indiscretions. It's always the woman who is ruined. And what is the solution to a ruined woman? Marriage.

"Well, I won't marry my rapist, my lord. And if I have to run and hide for the rest of my life, I'll do it." With that, she rose, ran to the door, and burst outside. She needed the darkness of the night and the cool of the sea air. She needed to get away. She wasn't safe here any longer. Somehow in the last few days her refuge had turned into a trap.

***

Jasper rose to go after her, then thought better of it. Even if he made it outside—and he was doubtful he had the strength at this point—what would he say? She was right. She, not Withernsea, would be blamed. Even though Withernsea had a reputation for vice, it would be assumed that Miss Carlisle had put herself in a compromising situation or allowed the duke to take liberties. As for the rape, it would be her word against his. Considering they were betrothed, there was no doubt in Jasper's mind that she would have been forced to marry the man as to erase any further scandal.

No wonder she had fled.

But she was no longer a young girl at the mercy of her parents and Society. Jasper didn't think she realized her own strength and power. She had made a life for herself in a situation where many men would have failed. She was a mother now and past the age where her parents could command her. What if she went back and exposed Withernsea for what he was? She had nothing to lose, but if she was believed and if Society decided to punish the duke, might she not save other women from a fate like hers?

And who was he to expect her to have that sort of courage? She was right. He wouldn't even risk taking his mask off in her presence much less exposing his scar to the public. Her scar was not so visible, but it was a wound nonetheless.

Jasper rose, determined to use the last of his strength to rest for the night. He had done too much today. He could feel his knife wound aching and the pain made it difficult to think of anything else. He rose, but he did not move toward the bed. He'd slept in her bed enough as it was. Tonight he would take the chair and she could have her bed back. The first step made his head spin, but he steadied himself with his hand on the table. When he felt stronger, he took a second step and then a third. That was when the wave of dizziness hit, only there was nothing within reach to grasp. Jasper swayed and fell forward. He heard a cry of alarm and wondered if he'd made the sound, and then a small body darted under him, keeping him from falling to his knees. He knew that scent of sea air and femininity.

"What are you doing?" she cried, moving under him and propping him up on his uninjured side. "Are you trying to hurt yourself again?"

"I might have overtaxed myself today."

"Now you admit it? When you're falling over?"

He looked down at her and squinted. "Your face is a blur."

She led him stumbling forward. "Let's get you to bed."

Jasper dug his heels in. "No. Take me to the chair. You take the bed tonight."

"Don't be ridiculous, and don't argue. You're in no condition."

Jasper would have argued further, but she was correct. He was in no condition to even think of a rebuttal or remember what it was they argued about. Instead, he allowed her to lead him to the bed. Only when it was time for her to disentangle herself from him, something went wrong, and he ended up falling into the bed and taking her with him.

He wasn't aware at first that she'd gone with him, only that he'd fallen at an angle, his feet off the bed and his head on the edge. He might have closed his eyes and slept right then, but she pushed at him hard enough that he opened his eyes. He looked down at her, cradled against him, half under his body, and frowned. He didn't remember taking her to bed. Neither did she seem happy about it. Her body was rigid, her face tight with fear.

"Let. Me. Up!" she said loudly, her voice rising at the end. She sounded almost panicked.

"Can't," he mumbled. "I can't seem to move."

She pushed at him again. "Roll over."

Ah, that was how it was done. His body felt heavy, like he no longer had control over it, but he finally managed to roll off her. She jumped up as though she'd been lying next to a snake. He tried not to take it personally, but he closed his eyes with the image of her frightened face seared into his mind.

When he woke, it was not yet morning. The room was still dark, none of the sun's rays piercing the curtains. He looked down at himself and realized that at some point Miss Carlisle must have tried to make him comfortable, pulling the covers up around him and laying his head on the pillow. His side ached, but it was nothing to the raw pain of his face. He peered at the chair, noting that Miss Carlisle slept curled in it. He didn't dare remove the mask when she could wake at any moment, but the pain was becoming almost unbearable. Wearing the mask for so long and not allowing his skin any respite had left the old injury inflamed. If he'd been home, he would have applied ointment and stayed inside until he could go out in the mask again. He didn't have his special ointment here, and he didn't have the luxury of giving his abused skin a respite from the mask now.

The pain from the chafed skin must have been what had woken him, and he could not go back to sleep. Instead, Jasper sat and watched the curtains for any sign of light. Unwanted as they were, he had his memories to keep him company.

He could close his eyes and feel the heat of the fire like it was before him now. When he'd been inside the burning building, Peter calling out for help because he'd been trapped under a fallen beam, Jasper had thought he would die. The heat was so intense that he had actually felt his skin blistering. But he'd refused to give up. He'd used every last ounce of strength to move that beam. And when Peter had started screaming at the pain of the fire catching his clothing, Jasper had begun to cry, but he hadn't stopped trying to free his friend. He would die trying.

He wished he had died trying.

Instead, he'd fallen backward when a burning piece of wood had fallen on his face, forever searing it and melting the skin on his forehead, temple, upper cheek, and ear. Then the sound of his own screams had joined those of Peter. He'd known death would not be slow, and he'd crawled toward Peter so at least they could die together.

He was awake and shivering when Miss Carlisle stirred. But he pretended to sleep in order to compose himself while she rose and went outside, presumably to attend to her body's needs at the outdoor privy.

When she returned he was sitting at the table. She started when she saw him, then straightened her shoulders. He spoke before she could. "Do you have any of that tea?"

Her shoulders relaxed. "The tea? Are you in pain?"

"Let's just say I don't feel quite as well as I did yesterday."

"Have your stitches opened? Are you bleeding again?" Without asking permission, she brushed aside the blanket he wore fastened over his chest and pressed her fingertips lightly across the bandages. He probably should have told her it wasn't his knife wound paining him, but he didn't want her to stop touching him. So he kept silent when she removed the bandage and inspected her handiwork. "It's a little red, but it looks as though it's healing." She'd placed one palm flat on his back to steady herself, and Jasper didn't even think she realized she was touching him there. He closed his eyes and kept his head high. If he looked down at her, he'd be tempted to touch her hair or her cheek. "I'll get you a clean bandage."

She moved away, and his body felt cold at the loss of her touch.

But before he could prepare himself, she was again on her knees beside him, wrapping the soft cloth about his middle. He tried not to shiver at her touch, but he couldn't quite suppress it.

"Are you cold?" she asked. "I'm almost done. I'll make you that tea."

He grunted in response, not certain he could trust himself to speak. It was ridiculous that he should find something so basic as a woman changing his dressing arousing, but clearly he had passed into the ridiculous.

She finished and moved to the hearth to stoke the fire, presumably to heat water for the tea.

"Miss Carlisle." Jasper had control of his voice again now that she was no longer touching him. "About last night."

She stiffened and did not turn to face him. "I won't go back to London, my lord."

"I understand. That wasn't what I wanted to apologize for."

She looked at him, her expression curious.

"I want to apologize for what happened in your bed."

"Nothing happened, my lord."

"I fell on you, and I want to assure you it was inadvertent. I wasn't attempting to take advantage of the situation."

"I never thought you were."

He should have allowed that to pass. He didn't. "I saw your face, Miss Carlisle. You were terrified."

"I think that's something of an exaggeration." She waved a hand and went back to her chore at the hearth.

"No, it's not." If she hadn't been afraid of him, he would have gone to her and touched her shoulder to reassure her. But touching her would not help matters. She didn't want to be touched, not by any man and especially not by him. "And I just wanted to assure you I had no ulterior motives. I simply tripped and you were below me when I fell." At least he thought that was what happened. "If I had not been so weak and exhausted, I would have helped you up, not crushed you."

"You didn't crush me."

"Nevertheless, I apologize. And I want to make a suggestion."

"What is that?"

"Once I am back to full strength—tomorrow or the next day—if the trail is still impassable, then I think I should sleep in the stable with the horse."

Her head snapped up. "What? Why?"

"Because I can see my presence here makes you uneasy. This is your home, and if I sleep in the stable, you can lock me out and feel safe again."

"You cannot be serious. I will not lock you out."

"Mama!" Richard's high thin voice floated down from the loft. "Can I sleep in the stable with Lord Jasper? I want to sleep outside."

She tossed Jasper a look that said I-blame-you-for-this. "No one but Clover will sleep in the stable, darling."

"But, Mama!"

"Come down and use the privy then I'll make everyone a meal to break our fast."

"But Mama!" The boy appeared at the top of the ladder, his lip stuck out in a pout. "I want to sleep in the stable."

"Your mother said no," Jasper answered gently. "To both of us. I guess we have to sleep inside like civilized men."

The boy cocked his head to the side. "What's a civilized man?"

Something Jasper hadn't been in a long time, and the past few days of pretending, of watching his speech and his manners, were beginning to wear on him.

Seven

The trail was still impassable and remained so for the next two days. Olivia was relieved as it meant there was no need to bring up the question of her going to London again. There were so many reasons she wouldn't go and shuddered to even think of it. She'd been attacked and violated and terrified in London and the man who had done it was still there, still looking for her. And even if Withernsea was no more, how could she look her parents in the face after what had been done to her?

What her parents had let happen to her.

She felt both angry at them for leaving her vulnerable to a man like Withernsea and ashamed at what he'd done to her. She couldn't stand the disappointment she knew she would see on her parents' faces when they met Richard and when they realized she'd been living like a peasant for the last five years.

And she was definitely feeling like a peasant today. She'd read books on gardening and that knowledge was proving useful. She'd finally drained the garden of the rain water and she'd been kneeling in the mud trying to trellis beans and dig holes for potatoes. She was covered with dirt and mud, her shoulders ached, and her knees were beginning to protest. She could hear Richard and Lord Jasper playing. Well, she could hear Richard. She assumed his shrieks and hoots of laughter were in response to something Lord Jasper had done.

She'd refused his offer of help again today, telling him to rest, but she didn't think she would be able to refuse him much longer. He was growing stronger. His fever had completely passed, and he didn't seem to need to nap any longer. He ate more and barely winced when he had to move his injured side.

This would probably be his last night in her bed. Then he would take the chair, or the floor, and she would take the bed. She didn't like the idea of lying down while he sat in a chair. It made her feel vulnerable, but what choice did she have? If she admitted her feelings, he'd insist on sleeping in the stable. She couldn't allow that. The man was the son of a marquess. How could she make him sleep in a stable? Not to mention, if he slept in the stable, Richard would want to, and she wanted Richard where she could see him and be certain he was safe.

She went back to work, ignoring her protesting muscles, and must have worked for another few hours because when she looked up again, both Richard and Lord Jasper were standing on the side of the garden. Richard had a mischievous grin on his face.

"What did you do?" she asked, immediately suspicious.

"Nothing," Richard said. Then, seeming unable to hold in his excitement any longer, Richard danced to her and grabbed her hand. "Come and see!"

She allowed him to tug her out of the garden. "I'm coming to see what you did not do?"

"You won't be disappointed," Lord Jasper said. No, she imagined he did not disappoint often. She shook her head to clear it of the thought.

Richard towed her into the cottage, where he pointed to the table, which had been set for supper. Rich, savory smells wafted over her, making her stomach growl. She was suddenly ravenous, and no wonder as she realized she hadn't eaten in hours. And that meant neither had Richard. What kind of mother forgot to feed her own child?

She looked at Richard and then Lord Jasper. "I lost track of time. You must be famished."

"We won't be once you sit down, Mama. Lord Jasper and I made soup and bread."

"We didn't make the bread. We merely sliced a loaf you had put aside," Lord Jasper amended.

"Time to eat, Mama!" Richard ran to the table and indicated where she should sit. The napkin by the plate had a flower on top. Olivia smiled at the pretty gesture. It had been years since anyone had given her flowers.

"Let me wash my hands and face first," she said. "I'll hurry." She went back outside and used the bucket of fresh water beside the door to wet a cloth and rub her face. She was dismayed when the cloth came back streaked with dirt. She must look a fright. She dipped the cloth into the water again, and a shadow fell over her. Olivia stepped back so quickly she almost knocked the bucket over.

"I didn't mean to startle you," Lord Jasper said.

"You didn't," she lied, retrieving the cloth and cleaning her arms. But now that she knew it was him, her heart hammered for another reason.

"I hope you don't mind that we prepared the meal. I'm no cook, but I've made my share of meals around a campfire. It seemed the least I could do, since you banned me from the garden."

"Because I wanted you to rest," she said, more sharply than she'd intended. She closed her eyes and blew out a breath. She had to calm her racing pulse. "What I mean to say is thank you. It's no small task to occupy a five-year-old all day and prepare a meal. I'm in your debt."

"Not at all. I am in yours." With a bow that seemed too formal for the situation, he returned inside. Olivia wondered if he knew just how close she'd come to leaving him for dead on that trail. If she had, he would most certainly be dead now. Of course, if he really considered himself in her debt, he'd leave her be. He'd go back to London and tell everyone she'd fled the country or was dead. That last option would devastate her parents, but at least she and Richard would be safe.

The meal was delicious, partly because she was so hungry and partly because she had not had to prepare it. It had been years since she had not prepared a meal. The vegetable soup and bread were simple but hearty and after she'd finished and insisted on washing the dishes so Lord Jasper would finally rest, she was ready for sleep. But she still had to cajole Richard into bed. She dried her hands on her apron with just that intention. Except when she turned back to the room, Richard was in Lord Jasper's arms, fast asleep.

"What are you doing?" she hissed.

"He would have fallen off the bench if I hadn't caught him. I thought I'd carry him to bed."

"Up the ladder?"

"You know another way to get him there?"

"But your wound—"

He rolled his eyes. "He doesn't even weigh as much as a sack of potatoes." And without waiting for her agreement, he carried the boy up the ladder, making the task she sometimes found difficult empty-handed look easy. She followed him up, removed Richard's boots then tucked him into bed in his clothes. She'd rather leave them on than risk waking him.

When she blew out the lamp, Lord Jasper gestured for her to descend the ladder first. She did so, and he followed her down. For whatever reason, she was now awake again. "Do you want a cup of tea?"

He shook his head, a movement which drew her attention to a faint trickle of blood on his cheek. "What happened to your cheek?" she asked, moving closer.

He stepped back, lifting a hand to touch it.

"The other side," she corrected.

He brought his finger away bloody then shrugged. "It's nothing."

Olivia stared at him. "It's not nothing. I finished your shirt and planned to give it to you tonight, but I won't let you try it on if you'll only bleed all over it."

"It's not from my wound."

"I can see that as your wound is much lower. Why is your face bleeding?"

His hazel eyes were almost gold in the firelight. "I told you it's nothing."

"And I told you that is nonsense. Will you tell me or must I see for myself?"

His voice turned hard. "I won't remove my mask."

She stared at him, working out what he'd said and the position of the trickle of blood. It must have come from under his mask. Was it possible he had an injury there she hadn't been aware of? "You are bleeding under your mask. Something is wrong, and I'd better look before it becomes infected."

"It's not that serious."

"My lord, forgive me for arguing, but you are bleeding."

"I'm not injured. The material from the mask irritates my skin. I don't usually wear it for such long periods of time."

She hadn't thought of that. Of course, such a fitted garment would irritate if not removed and if the skin below was not allowed to breathe.

"Then you had best take it off."

"No."

She'd been prepared for his refusal. "Do you think whatever is under there will shock me? I've given birth by myself"—her face reddened at having mentioned something so personal—"and tended your knife wound. I hardly think a scar will send me screaming in fear."

"It's more than a scar."

"Take it off."

"No."

"Then you force me outside. If you won't remove it in front of me, I'll leave. I won't be the reason you're in pain. Sleep without it tonight."

"Now you are offering to sleep in the stable?"

"Would you trust me not to look if I slept in the loft?"

He sighed. Deeply. "No."

"Then I have no other option." She removed her apron and began to gather her coat and a blanket to lay on the hay across from Clover. She would come back early and knock, so she would not surprise him.

"Wait," he said. "I'll go out."

She shook her head. "You'll need to treat your skin with a cool cloth." She pointed to a shelf. "You'll find clean cloths there as well as some ointment that might help. There's nothing like that in the stable. I am the one who will have to go." She clutched her blanket closer, looking down to make sure she had all she would need for the night, then lifted the latch on the door.

His hand came around her and pushed the door closed again. "Don't say I didn't warn you."

***

She turned slowly and looked up at him. His hand was level with her head, and her shoulder brushed his arm when she turned. "Don't say I didn't tell you it will make no difference to me what's under that mask."

Jasper gave her a rueful smile. He'd heard that enough times that he didn't believe it any longer. He knew no one could look at his ruined face and not feel revulsion. He felt it himself every time he looked in the mirror.

"Do you want me to ready the cloths and ointment?" Miss Carlisle asked.

Jasper nodded. She went to her task and he reached up to loosen the ties on the mask. Then he lowered his hands. If she was to see him, naked for all intents and purposes, he wanted something in return. "What's your name?" he asked.

She turned back to him. "What do you mean?"

"Only a handful of people have ever seen me without my mask. If you're to join that group, I'd at least like to know your Christian name."

She gave him a considering look then nodded as though she understood the significance of what he was asking, what he was giving. "You may call me Olivia," she said before going back to gathering cloths and ointment. Jasper was momentarily taken aback. He'd expected her to tell him her name. He hadn't expected to be given permission to use it. That was more intimacy than he thought she'd grant him. Perhaps she really did understand the implication of him removing his mask.

He reached for the ties again, and loosened the top half of the mask, that part that covered his forehead and hair. It disguised some of the damage the fire had done, but not nearly as much as the mask covering his eyes, temple, and upper cheek. Jasper loosened that as well and, wincing from the pain, he peeled the mask from his tender skin. Immediately, his skin burned from exposure to the air, but it was freeing to be rid of the material.

Jasper raised a hand, and it came away slightly pink. His scars hadn't bled too badly. Maybe this respite and some of the ointment would help the constant irritation. Miss Carlisle—Olivia, he reminded himself—turned around and started toward him without looking at his face. He watched her walk, keenly aware that she would look up at him and then her steps would falter. But their eyes met, and she didn't hesitate. The expression on her face was not one of revulsion but of concern.

"I was worried about the knife wound, but all this time it's been your face that pains you." She reached for his face, and he jerked back. No one but the surgeon had ever touched his scars. "I'm sorry," she said, lowering her hands. "I should have asked first."

"I'd rather tend it myself."

She held out the linen and ointment, her gaze never wavering from his face. It was as though she really did not find his scars grotesque. The only people who had ever looked at him as though he were not disfigured were the other survivors of Draven's troop. They'd been with him when it happened and had their own scars—visible or not.

"I don't have a looking glass," she said. "It might be easier if you allow me. I can see where the worst of the chafing is."

He took a deep breath. She wanted to touch his face, his scars. It was a liberty he'd never allowed. But he also realized that her reasons made sense. It would be easier if he allowed her to apply the ointment.

And, to his shock, a part of him *wanted* her to touch him so intimately.

"I promise to be gentle."

He shook his head. "That's not it. No one but the surgeon has ever touched me…there."

She pressed her lips together. "I understand. I'm here if you need assistance." And she stepped away, pretending to busy herself with the items to be mended in her sewing basket. But before she could sit down and begin her work in earnest, he cleared his throat.

"I'd like you to do it." He felt his cheeks flush and felt like a boy of seventeen again, attending his first ball and asking a girl if she might like to dance.

Her busy hands stilled, the only sign his words had surprised her. "Of course. If you'll sit here, that will make it easier for me to reach you." She gestured to the end of the bench closest to the fire.

He did as she asked, setting the supplies on the table beside him. She stood before him and lifted a linen strip then dipped it in a bowl of clean water. She wrung it out then placed it carefully over his ruined skin. The cool of the water felt so good, he couldn't help but blow out a breath of relief. After a moment, she removed the cloth and he saw it had tinges of pink blood on it. She repeated the gesture several more times until the cloth came away clean. Then she lifted the ointment and paused to study his face.

Jasper knew she was deciding where to apply it, but he could hardly hold still while she stared at him, seeing all of his flaws laid bare. He felt his neck redden further and then his cheeks flash hot as he imagined what she must be thinking. How he must disgust her.

He was about to lower his face when she slid fingers slicked with ointment across his wound. At first he felt nothing, but then, as it absorbed the medicine, his skin didn't feel as raw or as tight. She took hold of his chin with her other hand and applied more ointment where she thought it was necessary. When she was done, she set the pot of ointment on the table and washed her hands.

"It's probably best if you don't wear your mask for a few hours. I can put linen on the pillow so it isn't stained by the ointment."

"There's no danger of that as you'll sleep in the bed tonight."

She opened her mouth, but he held up a hand, indicating he wouldn't argue.

"Very well. Then before I retire, should I wash your mask? It will be dry by the morning if we hang it by the fire."

"I'd appreciate that."

She nodded and left him to gather the mask. He watched as she washed the parts carefully then hung them to dry. "It would really be best, my lord, if you didn't wear it for a few days. Your skin needs air to heal."

"I fear I will terrify your son."

Her brow furrowed in what seemed genuine confusion. "I doubt it. The mask is far more terrifying than your wound."

Jasper studied her face, but she gave no appearance of lying.

She looked back at him unflinchingly. "You really do think you look terrifying, don't you?"

"And you don't?"

She shook her head. "It's a serious burn. I can see that you were lucky not to lose an eye. I imagine it hurt beyond anything I've ever experienced, but you just look like a man who has been burned. You don't look like a monster. In fact, you're more handsome now that I can see your whole face than you were with only half of it visible."

Jasper didn't speak. He simply could not believe a word of what she said. He had been handsome once. He knew this, had been told he was attractive. But now—now he was as ugly as the devil.

"You don't believe me?" she said, as though she'd read his thoughts. "Don't you ever look in a mirror?"

"Not if I can avoid it." And when he did, he only looked at the half of his face that had not been damaged.

"Then you've no doubt built your scar up into something awful. It's not that at all." She reached out and cupped her hand over his cheek, cupping his wound as well. Jasper wanted to flinch back, but he didn't. And she didn't lower her hand.

"You don't think it's repulsive?" he whispered.

"No one would." That was not true. His own family had avoided looking at him at his niece's baptism recently. They'd forbid him from wearing his mask and then they all seemed horrified by the sight of him.

"I assure you, they do."

"Then they are blind." The way she looked down at him, the heat of her hand, the closeness of her body stirred Jasper. What would happen if he kissed her now? He hadn't kissed a woman in years, hadn't thought a woman would ever touch him again without being paid. But this woman, so pretty and tender, stood above him, looking at him with…appreciation. What if he kissed her? Then would she recoil?

"Or you are blind," he said.

"I'm not blind. I have—"

He reached out, cupped the back of her neck and pulled her to him. She stiffened in surprise, but she didn't protest when his lips brushed over hers. He pulled back and studied her. Her cheeks were flushed and her dusky blue eyes wide, but she did not look sickened.

"What was that?" she whispered.

"A thank you."

She lowered her hand from his face. "You're welcome."

He rose. "I'd like to kiss you again, Olivia. But that one would be…more than a thank you."

She shook her head and stepped back. "I don't think that's wise. I-I don't like to be touched."

Jasper stood rooted in place, unwilling to step forward and pursue her. He'd forgotten for a moment about Withernsea. "I overstepped. Forgive me."

She waved a hand and ducked her head to hide her flaming cheeks. "It's nothing."

"It was careless. I…" He paused, not wanting to bring up what the duke had done to her. "I had forgotten what it felt like to be touched."

Her head jerked up. "I can't believe that. Surely in Town they see you as a war hero. I can hardly believe a superficial burn scar matters to anyone."

He gave a low laugh. "I'm sure any number of mamas would be willing to sacrifice their daughters to me, being that I am the son of a marquess, but I'm unwilling, as yet, to accept their burnt offerings." Not that he had a chance to reject young ladies as he avoided all social engagements. But the few times he had been unable to avoid them, he had only pretended not to hear the whispers behind fans or not to see the way no young lady would meet his eyes, even though he wore his mask.

"And why should you? I forgot we were discussing the *ton*. Of course the ladies are superficial."

But she wasn't. Had she been, when she'd been younger, before Withernsea? Probably. But she'd grown out of it now.

Leave it to him to meet the one woman who found him handsome despite his scars but who was absolutely untouchable.

Jasper prayed the ground would dry quickly. The longer he was stuck here with her, the more unbearable it would become. He'd wanted her before, but that was in an abstract way. Any man would look at her and find her attractive, wonder what it would feel like to kiss her, touch her. But now the abstract had become concrete. She didn't find him vile, and she'd treated him kindly, tenderly even. He'd admired her appearance, but now he could not help but admire her character.

A dangerous thing when she was so unattainable.

He had no chance with her when she was so utterly and completely afraid of him, when she jumped because he moved without warning and trembled when he was nearby. That fleeting kiss was all he'd ever have of her unless…

He looked at her, his gaze roving over her lovely face.

Unless he could convince her that he was different than Withernsea. Unless he could persuade her to give him a chance to show her not all men were monsters.

Eight

Olivia could scarcely breathe from the heat of his gaze on her. It wasn't difficult to divine his thoughts. He wanted her, and she supposed she'd fueled that desire by touching him unnecessarily and allowing the kiss. The kiss had definitely gone too far. She should have stopped him. She could have. He hadn't grabbed her or forced himself on her. He'd given her time to stop him. So why hadn't she?

The short answer was that she wanted to kiss him.

She hadn't lied when she'd told him she found him attractive, even with the scar. She understood why he hid it. The wound hurt her to look upon because she could imagine the pain he must have felt. Whatever had caused it had all but melted the flesh on one side of his face. The skin on his forehead and temple seemed to slide down toward his brow, then miraculously cut away from his eye. His eye had been saved, but his ear and the side of his head were damaged. His golden-brown hair grew in patches on what was otherwise a bald section of skull. And then below his eye, the damage continued, though the burn there must not have been as severe. That skin was merely pink and smooth, highlighting his high cheekbones.

She'd had to clear the blood away on his temple. The mask probably rubbed him there, and that skin had taken the worst of the injury. He really shouldn't wear the mask again for a few days, but she doubted she could convince him to leave it off with Richard awake. She wasn't certain what

Richard's reaction would be. She did not think it would be fear, but he'd inevitably ask a thousand questions and be morbidly curious.

So maybe it was for the best if Lord Jasper wore his mask again. They'd already shared more intimacies than she was comfortable with, and she suspected Lord Jasper felt quite vulnerable tonight as well. That was probably why he'd wanted to kiss her again. Neither of them was thinking straight.

"You'll forgive me if I don't wish to discuss the *ton* tonight," he said, referring back to their earlier conversation.

"I will. No one should ever have to discuss the *ton.* And since it's late and we both worked hard today, I propose we go to bed." As soon as the words left her mouth, she wished she could take them back. They'd come out all wrong. "That is…what I meant to say—"

"I know what you meant, Olivia."

Oh, why had she given him leave to use her Christian name? That only made her feel more uncomfortable.

"I'll go to sleep in the chair. You take the bed," he said.

"Are you certain you don't need the bed?"

"I've occupied it long enough."

Olivia didn't argue. Her back ached, and she knew lying in her bed would feel much better than the rocking chair. Without another word, Lord Jasper moved the chair away from the bed and closer to the fire. Then he settled into it, taking the blanket he wore as a shirt and draping it over himself for warmth.

The blanket reminded her she'd wanted him to try on the shirt she'd sewn him, but that could wait until tomorrow. One more evening and she could finish the cuffs. She turned the lamps down and started for her bed then detoured to her changing area. She'd only used it when he'd been unconscious or outside, but there was no hope of either of those possibilities tonight and she did not want to sleep in her dress. She drew the curtains closed and even though she knew he could not see, she felt exposed as she disrobed and slipped on a nightrail and robe. When she opened the curtains again, he was in the same place she had left him, and he didn't look toward her as she tiptoed to her bed. Quickly, she removed her robe and laid it on the end of the bed. Then she slid under the sheets, determined to sleep deeply and forget all about Jasper Grantham.

But that was impossible.

She hadn't had the time or forethought to wash her sheets. She'd changed them several times when he'd been ill. She'd cleaned him and had made certain his bedding was fresh as well. But she hadn't changed it in a couple days and when she lay down, she could smell him. His scent lingered on the sheets and seemed to envelop her in its novelty. He smelled of man. She didn't know how else to describe it. She'd caught the scent on him tonight when she'd moved close to clean his wound. It was smoke from the fire, strong soap, and…man.

She'd feared men for the past few years and done everything she could to avoid them. But now she had a man in her house, one she couldn't escape. One—dare she admit it?—she did not *want* to escape. He was everywhere she looked and now his very scent touched her. She could practically imagine his hands on her.

Olivia shifted, trying to escape Lord Jasper and her own feelings. She didn't want a man's hands on her. She'd suffered through that once, and she'd sworn she'd never allow it again. Logically, she knew not all men were like Withernsea, but she had also heard and read enough to know what Withernsea had done to her was common among married people. She didn't ever want any man to do that to her again.

So why was her body rebelling against her mind and reacting to Lord Jasper's scent? Why did she have the urge to put her arms around him, allow him to kiss her, find ways to brush against him? She had thought those sorts of feelings were dead. As she rolled over again she promised herself she would manage to destroy them one way or another.

In the morning, she woke later than usual. She knew it was late because the sun was already in the sky, and she usually woke before sunrise. Not to mention, if she ever did try to snatch a few extra moments of sleep, Richard always woke her.

Richard!

She sat, glanced at Lord Jasper's chair by the fireplace and saw it was empty. "Richard?" she called.

No answer.

"Richard?" She was already up and on her way to the ladder. "Richard!"

She climbed the ladder faster than she ever had and then stared at the empty bed in the loft. Her head spun, and she barely managed to hold on to the ladder to avoid taking a spill. She didn't want to allow the thoughts to come into her head. She didn't want to even consider what she most feared had happened. She'd let her guard down, and now she would pay the consequences. Again. And not only her, but Richard as well. She started down the ladder, frantic to find Richard, when she heard a high-pitched giggle.

There was no mistaking the sound. It was Richard's. After it she heard a low murmur and then Richard's voice, quieter now but still audible. Olivia practically slid down the ladder in her haste. She ran across the cottage and yanked the door open. Lord Jasper and Richard were in the yard, just a few feet away, and clearly on their way toward the door she'd thrown open. Richard's face broke into a smile, but Lord Jasper's eyes widened. He'd donned his mask again, but it didn't conceal his hazel eyes. In fact, now that she knew what he looked like beneath it, she could easily picture his brows rising and his forehead creasing.

"Mama, you're supposed to be in bed."

"And you are not supposed to go outside without waking me."

Richard looked at Lord Jasper. "But I was with—"

"And you, sir"—she pointed to Jasper, who was looking studiously at the ground—"you should not have taken him out without waking me."

"We just wanted to let you sleep a bit longer. I was awake and so was the boy."

"And did you consider what I would think when I woke up and found the two of you gone?"

"We weren't gone long."

"We just went to feed Clover, Mama. We were coming back to make the morning meal."

Olivia's heart had ceased hammering so hard it hurt, and she was able to take a breath.

Richard, tears in his eyes now, rushed to her and threw his arms about her. "I'm sorry, Mama. I just wanted to help you."

Olivia clutched her son tightly. Sweet boy. She didn't know what she would ever do if anything happened to him. If she lost him, there would be no reason to go on living. He was everything to her.

"You are forgiven," she said, kissing the top of his head. He smelled of the sea air and fresh straw. "I might have overreacted just a little." She glanced at Lord Jasper who had closed the distance between them but looked down again when their eyes met.

"Can we still make the morning meal?" Richard asked.

Olivia frowned. "I don't know about that. What did you plan to make?"

"Lord Jasper can cook."

She looked at Lord Jasper again, but he was looking at Richard, who still held onto Olivia. "Perhaps we had better leave it to your mother. My skills are fairly rudimentary, and I can't promise what I make will be edible."

"What's *rudimentary*?"

Olivia tousled his hair. "It means he's still learning. Like you," she said. Lord Jasper was dressed in his trousers and belted blanket, but Richard still wore his nightshirt. He'd put shoes on, at least. "Now, you'd better go dress yourself while I start on the meal."

"Yes, Mama." Richard squeezed her again then scampered up the ladder. Olivia moved back, so Lord Jasper could enter. He closed the door behind him, eyes still on his boots.

"I really did only mean to help."

"I know." She almost reached over and touched his arm, but she couldn't quite find the courage. "But I don't want you taking Richard anywhere without telling me first."

"Understood," he said.

She would let that be the end of it. The gesture had been kind, and if she had awakened just a few moments later, she might have appreciated it more. "I suppose I will start on the meal." She headed toward the hearth to stoke the fire and move the large pot there into the flames to heat.

"Don't you want to..." Lord Jasper trailed off.

She glanced back at him, and he dropped his gaze again. He'd never been hesitant to look at her before. In fact, his direct gaze had made her catch her breath a time or two. Was he shy now that she'd seen him without the mask or...she looked down at the floor and noticed her bare feet. With a start, she realized she wore nothing but her night rail. It reached to her ankles, but the material was flimsy linen that tended to slide off one shoulder. She had nothing on underneath, and she couldn't be certain how much was visible. In her panic this morning, she hadn't thought about what she'd worn. Or rather, what she hadn't worn.

She flew to her bed, snatched up the robe, and slid it on over the night rail. But even that wasn't enough. She went to her dressing area, snapped the curtains closed, and dressed quickly in the same dress she'd worn the day before. She secured her hair in a long tail down her back, determined to pin it up later.

When she emerged, Lord Jasper was looking out the window. "I thought I might look at the trail again. See if the ground has dried out enough to try it."

"Good idea." She began gathering her supplies. She had porridge and tea. That would do until she could make bread later in the day.

"If you'll excuse me then." And he was gone.

Alone, except for the sound of Richard singing to himself in the loft, Olivia let her shoulders drop and closed her eyes. What was she supposed to make of him? A man who was considerate enough to try and give her a few more minutes of sleep. A man who averted his eyes when she was in dishabille. A man who challenged her with a kiss—time had given her perspective and she knew his actions to be a challenge now—to see if she would reject him. They were both vulnerable, in their ways, and he had shown her the same courtesy this morning that she had given him last night.

Either that or he really didn't see anything he found interesting when he looked at her.

***

The bloody trail was still muddy and wet. He'd go sliding right down and break his neck if he tried to descend from the cliff that way. And perhaps he liked that alternative better than the one currently facing him.

Olivia Carlisle, with her dark hair and her blue eyes, was driving him mad. She didn't mean to drive him mad. She probably didn't even realize she did it, which made it that much worse.

Jasper walked the perimeter of the cliff until he had a view of the sea, dark blue and choppy today. The brisk wind blew his hair off his neck.

He'd had a hard enough time sleeping last night when he could hear her sighing and tossing and turning. He'd not been able to forget touching his lips to hers, however briefly. She hadn't pulled away, hadn't reacted with disgust. Jasper hadn't thought such a thing possible, especially not with such a pretty woman. He didn't think a woman like her would ever look at a man like him.

And if that wasn't bad enough, this morning he'd awakened far too early and had plenty of time to observe her as she slept. He tried not to. It was ill-mannered, but how was he not supposed to look at her when she looked so lovely and tempting? Her loose hair swirled about her pillow like a collection of glossy mahogany ribbons. Her head was turned toward the fire, her hand tucked under her chin, and her cheeks pink. He couldn't see anything of her body. That was hidden under her bedclothes, but he could imagine where her breasts, hips, and legs might be.

And then this morning he had not had to imagine at all. She'd flung the door open dressed in little more than white gauze. That was an exaggeration, of course, but not much. The skirt was short enough that he could clearly see her trim little ankles, small feet, and pink toes. And the material was threadbare enough that he had no trouble making out the outline of the quiet flare of hips, a tuck of waist, and small but pert breasts. And all of it was creamy and smooth. He'd extrapolated this from the exposed shoulder he'd caught a glimpse of when her sleeve had fallen down her arm.

Jasper had tried not to look. Really, he had. It had been so long since he'd played the gentleman, but he did the best he could playing the part again. As he recalled, a gentleman generally ignored everything his body wanted and did the exact opposite. So when Jasper's body told him to move closer to her, he stayed where he was. When he wanted to look at her, to drink her in, he looked away. And when he wanted more time in her presence, he made himself leave.

Now he remembered why he'd stopped being a gentleman and preferred to live his life in the rookeries.

Being a gentleman was too much bloody work.

When he smelled food, he started back toward the cottage. As he neared, he could hear the boy chattering away. His mother was probably only listening with half an ear. Jasper was surprised to realize he liked the boy. The lad was curious and asked a lot of questions. Most of them were unanswerable—how many teeth does a dragon have, how long would it take to walk to China—but Jasper wasn't one of those men who minded a bit of conversation. When he'd been in the war, he and the other men of Draven's troop had routinely walked miles every day. Jasper had never minded some good-natured derision of the other men or telling a story or two to make the time go quicker. Anything was better than listening to Rafe prattle on or settling for Ewan's stoic silence. And though young Richard leaned more toward Rafe's side of the equation, Jasper had always liked Rafe. It was even easier to like the man now that he was in the Americas.

Jasper tapped on the door and entered. Olivia was placing the food on the table and nodded to him. "How are you feeling?" she asked, as though she hadn't run from him earlier in her haste to cover herself. "Does your wound pain you?"

He hadn't even thought of it really. There was still a dull pain, but he'd had far worse wounds that had pained him more. "I'm quite recovered," he answered, taking a seat at the place he'd come to think of as his. "In fact, I can work in the garden today if you'd like."

She stopped ladling porridge into the bowls and stared at him. "There's no need for that, my lord."

He blew out a breath. "I may have grown up as the son of a marquess, but I haven't lived that way for some time. I can pull weeds and shore up waterlogged vegetables."

"Can I help, Mama? Can I?"

She cut her gaze at Richard, and from the look on her face it was clear the boy hadn't been eager to help *her* in the garden.

"You might be able to do some chores inside the house if you have a mind to," Jasper said. He'd known that would be the mortal blow, and he'd been correct. Her gaze lifted from Richard and slid over what Jasper imagined to be all the tasks she felt absolutely needed attention. "And the fresh air is welcome after all the days inside due to the rain."

She narrowed her eyes at him—a warning. "You have to promise to stay where Lord Jasper can see you," she told the boy.

"I will!"

Jasper smiled. "It's settled then."

After the morning meal, he left for the garden with the boy following closely behind. He'd meant what he said about the fresh air. He could breathe again outside, could breathe now that he was away from her. He wished it were possible to avoid her for the next few days and then leave and not look back. But to do so would leave her and the boy vulnerable. That was something Jasper wouldn't do even if he hadn't been attracted to her. And so he'd have to speak to her again tonight, when the boy was sleeping. She wouldn't be safe here. If Withernsea knew her parents had hired him, then he could track Jasper to Penbury. He could find Olivia and Richard. Perhaps he already had. Jasper wasn't quite ready to write off the knife attack as random.

He stopped at the garden and handed the boy a spade from the garden implements he'd brought with him. The boy had been speaking continually as they walked to the garden from the house, and Jasper had pretended to be interested as the lad pointed out birds and insects. "Time to get to work," he said, stripping off the blanket he'd been wearing as a shirt. He knelt to begin weeding and the boy knelt beside him, copying everything he did.

"Is this right, Lord Jasper?" he asked, decapitating a weed.

"Try to get the roots too." Jasper showed him how to use the shovel to get under the weed and remove the entire plant. The ground was soft from the rain, so the boy wouldn't have to struggle. "And call me Jasper."

"But Mama said—"

"I know what she said, but it makes me feel like an idiot. I'm in rags, digging in the dirt, and you two won't stop milording me. If your mother objects, I'll take the blame."

"You're brave."

Jasper smiled as he pulled another weed. "Only with your mother. Can I tell you a secret?"

The boy nodded.

"My own mother was even more terrifying than yours. I never dared disobey her. She could have burned me up like one of your dragons with just a look."

"No, she couldn't!"

"Just consider it a warning. If you ever meet her, you'd better behave."

The boy set his spade aside. "Is she still alive?"

Jasper made an affirmative sound.

"What about your father?"

"Both of them."

"Do they look like you?"

Jasper raised his eyes. He glanced at the boy's red hair and knew he had to tread carefully here. "There's a family resemblance. My father and I have the same eyes, but I'm taller than he. As far as our features, I've been told I look more like my mother."

"They wear masks too?"

Jasper almost burst out laughing. He managed to restrain himself just in time. Of course the boy didn't understand why he wore the mask. And he was young enough to assume it was part of his appearance.

"No, they don't wear masks. I'm the only one who does, and I didn't wear one when I was your age."

"But why do you wear it now?"

Because I don't want to scare the hell out of you. But Jasper knew that wasn't the whole truth. He also wore it because he couldn't stand to be looked at, to have his scars on view. "I was hurt in a fire," he said simply. There was no point trying to explain war to the child, and his mother wouldn't appreciate that at any rate. "My face was burned, so I wear the mask to cover the wound."

"What do you look like under the mask?" the boy asked.

"Like any other man, except I have scars from the fire."

"Oh." The lad was silent for a long time, and Jasper began weeding again. Richard didn't pick up his spade, but Jasper hadn't really expected him to do much work. He just wanted to give Olivia a little space to complete her tasks in peace. He'd just settled into a routine of dig, push, pull, toss, repeat, when the boy spoke up again. "Do you have a son?"

Jasper shook his head. "I'm not a father." He doubted he ever would be.

"Do you want to be a father?"

Jasper paused, his spade stuck in the earth. "I don't know." He looked up at Richard. The boy was sitting on his knees, his face turned to Jasper, his eyes so hopeful.

"Because you could be my father."

Jasper felt all the breath whoosh out of him, as though he'd just been punched. He hadn't seen this coming. He should have. All the questions about whether he looked like his parents, what he looked like under the mask, whether he had children. The boy was looking for a father, and Jasper had fallen into the trap.

Except when he looked at Richard's hopeful expression he couldn't see it as a trap. He simply saw a boy who had love to give and wanted love in return.

"When I go to the village I see other boys with fathers, and since I don't have one, I thought maybe you could be mine."

Jasper released his painful grip on the spade's handle and put his hand on the boy's slight shoulder. "I would be honored to be your father, Richard. Any man would be lucky to have you as a son. But your mother is the one who makes that decision, and"—he closed his hand on the boy's shoulder before he ran off to ask his mother—"rather than troubling her with this at the moment, why don't I become something I know your mother would approve of?"

Richard's face fell. "What's that?"

"Your friend."

"I want you to be my father." His voice was petulant and just a bit whiny.

"Wanting something doesn't make it so, and friendship is a rare and important thing. The men I hold as my friends would die for me, and I would die for them. We've seen each other at our worst, and we try to bring out the others' best."

"You would die for them?" Richard asked.

"If you would accept me as your friend, I'd be a loyal friend. You could count on me."

"You could count on me too."

"Are we friends then?"

The boy nodded. Jasper stuck out his hand, but Richard just looked at it.

"We'll shake on it."

Richard took his hand, shook it, then threw himself into Jasper's arms. Jasper sat rigidly for a long moment, then closed his arms around the boy. He didn't want to admit it, but it wasn't just Olivia Carlisle he was beginning to care for.

Nine

Olivia didn't move from her spot on the side of the house. She'd stepped out to toss out dirty water and thought she'd peek at the progress the men were making in the garden. She'd heard most of the conversation, her heart breaking into tiny pieces so painful she had to put a fist against her chest. She'd known Richard wanted a father. She'd known he had questions, but she didn't know the answers to give him. And now he'd asked Lord Jasper to be his father. Lord Jasper had pivoted gracefully without saying anything that might allude to the boy's real father. She'd approved when he'd offered friendship, smiled when he'd held out a hand, and then couldn't hold back the tears when Richard hugged Lord Jasper.

And Lord Jasper had hugged him back.

Watching that scene had made it all so painfully clear. She'd given Richard all of her love, but she was deluding herself if she thought that would be enough. Of course, the child needed others in his life. Keeping him here, hiding him away, protected him but also deprived him of grandparents, cousins, friends, teachers. He was almost five years old. She couldn't stop his questions for much longer. She couldn't rob him of a normal childhood.

Leaving Lord Jasper and Richard as silently as she'd come upon them, she returned to the cottage. But instead of sweeping or beginning the noon meal, she sat in a chair and stared out the window.

She couldn't deprive herself either. For over five years she'd been running and hiding. She'd given up everything and everyone she loved. She didn't regret it because it had kept Richard safe. She'd die before she allowed Withernsea to touch her or her son. But perhaps it was time to stop allowing the duke control of the field. How many other women had he hurt while she hid away in silence? How many balls and dinner parties and days in the park had he enjoyed while she'd fought just to keep food on the table for herself and Richard?

She missed her parents. She missed her cousins and friends and aunts and uncles. And she didn't want to allow Withernsea to take any of it away from her or Richard any longer.

But if she returned to London, she'd need help. Withernsea would try to make her his again. He'd claim Richard was his and try to take him away. She had to show everyone what the duke really was. She had to stand up to the scandal of returning unmarried and with a child. Her parents hadn't been able to protect her before.

But she knew someone who could.

***

After dinner, Olivia tucked Richard into bed and kissed his forehead. All the time in the sun had tired the boy and she hadn't even needed to read to him before his eyes drooped. She climbed down from the loft and took a deep breath, not certain where to begin.

And then she forgot all about what she'd wanted to say because when Lord Jasper turned to face her she saw he'd removed his mask. He trusted her. He trusted her enough to remove it in front of her again. And she'd forgotten how very handsome he was.

"I can put it on if looking at my face offends," he said.

Olivia realized she'd been standing there speechless, and he'd taken her reaction the wrong way. "Please don't. I was surprised you felt comfortable enough to remove it, that's all. I promise, your face is far from offensive, *my lord*."

He winced. "You overheard us. I didn't mean to gainsay you, but it seems ridiculous to call me *lord* when I'm mucking out the stable."

"Not to mention you are such good friends."

"I'd like to be your friend," he said in a way that made warmth spiral into her belly. "I'd like for you to use my name, *Olivia*."

He was probably right. What she would ask of him tonight was an act of friendship. "Very well, Jasper. We'll be friends."

He smiled, but the smile was wary. She turned away from him and reached for the shirt she'd hung on a peg. "I finished your shirt. I thought you might want to try it on."

She held it out to him and he took it, holding it out to inspect it. "I'm impressed."

"I didn't learn much as the daughter of a viscount, but I did master embroidery and from there I taught myself to sew. It won't be the quality you're used to—"

"You have no idea what I'm used to. This is perfect." He stripped off the blanket, and she had to remind herself not to stare. More heat pooled in her belly. He pulled the shirt over his head then paused and flinched.

"What's wrong?" She went to him.

"I can't reach up on the wounded side. I'm not certain how to get my arm in." He started to slip the shirt off again, raising the arm on his good side, but she put her hand on the garment, holding it in place. He was remarkably warm underneath the fabric.

"I'll help you." She moved before him and helped guide his arms into the sleeves. She took each cuff and secured it, noting goosebumps where her fingers brushed. Was he merely cold or was he attracted to her? Did she even want him to be attracted to her?

Not certain what she should do and a bit flustered, she began to tie the neck closed, but he caught her hand. "I'm sorry. I always do that for Richard."

"I'm not a child." He didn't release her hand nor did he hold it tightly. She could have pulled away.

"I can see that."

"I told myself to stay away from you." His finger stroked the inside of her wrist, making her tremble.

"Why?"

"Because I knew if I was close I'd want to kiss you again." His gaze moved from her mouth to her eyes, and she knew he was judging her reaction to that. She wondered what he saw—not disgust, as he probably expected—but perhaps a bit of the fear that leapt into her heart.

She should move away, snatch her hand back. But he didn't tighten his grip, didn't move to force her. "You want to kiss me?" she asked, pressing her luck.

"Can't you tell?"

She shook her head. "I don't understand men."

The corner of his mouth lifted in a smile. "I don't understand women, and since I don't want a misunderstanding between us, I'm telling you I want to kiss you. That doesn't mean you have to allow it."

Her head swam at his touch and his words. "Why?" she blurted. "I mean, why do you want to kiss me?"

He looked puzzled, as though he hadn't expected that question. "I suppose I first wanted to kiss you because you were pretty and smelled…" He looked at the fire then back at her. "I liked how you smelled. But after that it was because you were kind."

"And now?" she whispered.

He looked back at her and released her hand. "Now?" He touched her cheek briefly, and her breath hitched in her throat. Seeing she didn't object to his touch, he tucked a curl behind her ear. "I suppose because I like you. You're brave, resourceful, intelligent, and on top of all that, a brilliant mother."

She shook her head. She was a coward. "I'm not brave." And she'd made so many mistakes in her life. "And I'm not smart."

"You're both, although if you allow me to kiss you, I'd definitely not call you wise."

She shivered when he touched her cheek again. "Because it wouldn't be wise to kiss you?"

"Not at all. If you kiss me, then you'll want more."

She laughed nervously. "*I'll* want more?"

He nodded. "And we should remain friends."

"And what if I want you to kiss me?" her voice sound low and husky, and she couldn't quite believe she'd said the words aloud. Blame it on her racing heart, that heat in her belly, and her shaky legs.

"Then put your arms around me, and I'll oblige."

Her arms felt heavy and almost impossible to lift. Fear rippled through her, but there was curiosity too. She'd liked the kiss they'd shared the night before. Would this be the same? And what if she kissed him and he took it as a license to go further?

She cut her gaze to him, and he looked steadily back at her, his head turned slightly so the scar was in shadow. So he felt unsure and vulnerable as well. Somehow knowing that erased her fears. She could trust him.

Her arms lighter, she raised them and placed her hands on his shoulders.

"May I?" He lifted his own hands and gestured to her waist. She nodded, cutting her gaze up to make certain Richard hadn't awakened and decided to spy on them. If he was confused about his relationship to Jasper now, he would be more so if he saw his mother kissing the man.

Jasper's hands settled on her waist, light but warm.

"And now?" she whispered.

"Close your eyes."

She let her lids drift closed, and when his grip didn't tighten, she relaxed slightly. One hand rose, and she felt his finger under her chin, notching it up. Then there was the slightest brush of his lips over hers. She waited for more, and when nothing else happened, she opened her eyes. "Is that all?"

"Do you want more?"

She had to smile. He'd said she'd want more, but he'd given her so little that she *needed* more. "Yes."

He touched her chin again, this time taking it between two fingers, and lowered his lips to hers. She closed her eyes, feeling a tingle when his lips brushed hers once then twice. Before he could pull back, she tightened her hands on his shoulders, and pressed her own lips against his. She mimicked what he'd done to her, lingering a bit longer.

When they parted, she didn't open her eyes.

"More?" he murmured.

She made a sound of assent and his lips slid over hers again, tasting her this time, seeming to learn the curves of her mouth. Her heart beat faster as heat pulsed through her body after each of his touches. Her hands slid from his shoulders to his neck, bringing their bodies closer. At the same time, his kiss deepened as he parted her lips and slanted his mouth over hers. The kiss was gentle, but it woke something primal in her, a sharp need she hadn't felt before. She made a low sound in her throat she would have sworn she'd never made before and his hands slid to her back and pulled her against him.

His body pressed to hers felt delicious. He was all muscles and hard edges, the feel of him hot and solid against her softness. Her head spun and she was dizzy with what she knew must be desire. In the back of her mind, she realized the kiss had gone on for several minutes and she should put an end to it, but she couldn't conceive of ever ending it. She couldn't imagine not touching him, not kissing him, not basking in his warmth. And then he slid his tongue across her lips and she froze, her heart skipping. She'd liked the sensation, but it also stirred up old fears. A memory of Withernsea forcing his tongue between her lips flashed in her mind, and she stiffened.

Immediately, Jasper stilled, his hold on her slackening. "What's wrong?"

She opened her eyes and pushed him back. He released her without hesitation. "I want you to stop."

"Then I'll stop." And he stepped back, giving her room. She put her hands to her flushed cheeks and turned her back to him, embarrassed that she had allowed the kiss to go on so long and also embarrassed that she had ended it to abruptly.

"I'm sorry."

"You have nothing to be sorry for. I'm sorry for whatever I did to upset you. As I said earlier, it might be best if I kept my distance."

She didn't want him to blame himself. He'd done nothing wrong. He'd been the perfect gentleman.

She turned, hands still on her warm cheeks. "It wasn't you. I…I liked the kiss. Very much."

He raised the brow on the unscarred side of his face. She'd imagined the expression before, but seeing it now made her wish he still wore the mask. He was almost irresistibly roguish when he did that. "Let me know if you'd like to try it again sometime."

"I thought you planned to keep your distance."

"I could be talked out of that."

Her throat went dry, and she had to clench her fists to keep from going to him. She wanted to be in his arms again. She wanted him to kiss her again. But when she remembered Withernsea's cold, wet lips on hers, she felt ill.

Olivia looked at the supper dishes. "Well, these won't clean themselves." And without another word, she went to work. Keeping busy would distract her from the man nearby. She wouldn't have time to think about how his shoulders had felt under her hands or the softness of his lips or the way his breath had smelled of tea and sugar.

"The shirt fits well," he said, his voice surprising her. "I appreciate it."

She nodded. She hadn't made it for thanks or even out of kindness. She did it because looking at his bare chest was too tempting for her.

"Can I do anything to help?"

"No. I'm almost done with these and then I have some of Richard's clothes to mend."

"I can keep you company while you sew."

"If you like." Wouldn't that be cozy, the two of them chatting by the firelight? But not kissing. Because he'd been right. If she kissed him again, she'd want more.

Much more.

***

Jasper watched her dry the plates before he went to stoke the fire to add another piece of wood. He should collect more tomorrow. The supply was low. He didn't like fire, preferred to keep well away from it, but he didn't want his weakness to mean more work for her. And when he had the fire poker in his hand, it kept him from reaching for her waist again. She might be petite and slender, but he'd felt the flare of her hips when he'd put his hands on her. She had curves where a woman ought to.

He poked at the fire again, trying not to think too hard about the softness of her breasts when he'd pulled her to him. They were small but firm, and since he'd only worn the thin homespun shirt, he'd been able to feel her pressed against him.

And then she'd stiffened. He'd done something wrong; that much was obvious. He'd used his tongue to trace her lips, and that must have upset her. He considered the action more of a prelude to a real kiss than anything else, but he understood he had to move slowly with her. She was like a newly lit fire. One had to coax the flame and make it grow into something hotter and brighter.

But *had* it been his kiss or was it something else? Had she opened her eyes and seen his scars close up and then lost her appetite for his mouth on hers? There was a reason he'd told her to close her eyes. If she didn't look at him, perhaps she could imagine she kissed someone who didn't resemble a child's nightmare.

And yet, she had looked at him before the kiss. She hadn't balked at kissing him, though she'd certainly seen the scar and more than once now. She was the first woman he'd kissed since he'd returned from the war. She was the first woman who had been willing to look past that scar and touch him. He'd forgotten the simple pleasure of kissing. He'd forgotten how much it could stir him, how much a kiss could make him want.

There had been women before the war, but he hadn't kissed them as he'd kissed Olivia tonight. Then a kiss had merely been something to push through on the trail toward more stimulating terrain. Now he wondered if all of those years he was actually missing the best part? He smiled—or perhaps since the path to anything more than kissing was closed with Olivia, he was making the best of the options available. But somehow kissing her didn't feel like settling. Kissing her felt like a rare privilege.

He glanced over and saw she had finished with the dishes and now sat with her sewing basket beside her. He sat across from her at the table. "Do you ever rest?"

She looked up. "Not often. There's much to be done here, especially if…" She trailed off, looked up at him, then back down at her sewing.

"If?"

"If I'm to restore everything to the condition it was in before the storm."

He thought about mentioning that she could not possibly think it would be safe here after he left, but he didn't want to raise such a contentious issue tonight. Her cheeks were still pink from their kisses, and he didn't want to see her face drain of color or the lines appear at her eyes that came when she was afraid. Tomorrow would be soon enough. And perhaps she'd come to that conclusion on her own. Unless he was mistaken, she wasn't saying all that was on her mind.

"Tell me about the war against Napoleon. I heard so little about it when I was in Town, and then I"—she glanced at the loft where the lad slept—"I was otherwise occupied. Did you serve under Wellington?"

He didn't like to talk about the war. Most soldiers who'd seen real battle didn't, but she likely hadn't been around any of them to know this. "Not under him directly, but yes, we were under his command."

"Did you fight at Waterloo?"

"No. My troop didn't fight any battles, not that sort, at least. We were more of a—" He might say *suicide squad*, but he opted for another explanation. "A special troop, carefully selected by Lieutenant Colonel Draven for our talents and skills."

She looked up at him, her blue eyes wide with interest. Clearly, she hadn't heard of Draven's troop or the Survivors. "We had special missions—reconnaissance, sabotage, ambushes. We spent time all over the Continent, going wherever Wellington needed us. I didn't see any major battles, but I fought plenty of smaller ones. Sometimes it was a matter of ascertaining the strength of the enemy. Other times we stole arms or passed along misinformation. Sometimes we engaged the enemy in order to prevent them from joining forces with their comrades and thereby attacking the British in greater numbers."

"It sounds dangerous."

Jasper glanced at the fire. "All war is dangerous. Besides, as the third son of a marquess, it's expected of me. I could be a soldier or a clergyman. I never really liked sermons or sickbeds."

She nodded as she examined her stitches and turned the small shirt she worked on over. "How many are in a troop?" she asked.

"We had thirty in ours." Before she could ask, he said, "Twelve of us came back."

She looked up sharply. "You lost that many?"

"We would have lost more, if we hadn't had so many with specialized skills."

She swallowed. "What was your skill?"

"I find things—people, objects, even information. It's a natural ability, I suppose. I've had it as long as I can remember."

She frowned at her work. "What sorts of things?"

He tried to think of something not related to the war. He didn't want to tell her how he'd found a French captain in a whorehouse or a cache of rifles in the basement of an orphanage. Then he might have to say what had happened to the captain after he'd been found or how they'd terrified the orphans by stomping in at night to confiscate the weapons.

"When I was about three my mother lost a brooch she loved. It was a family heirloom, something passed down from generation to generation. I'm told she searched everywhere for it to no avail. I suppose I saw how distressed she was and decided to find it on my own. I don't remember any of this. I was too young, but it's a story my family likes to repeat." Or at least they had when he could still bear to spend time with his family, before his mother's eyes filled with tears every time she saw him in his mask. "No one knows how I did it, but apparently I toddled up to my mother one afternoon when I was supposed to be napping and told her I'd found the brooch. Of course, I couldn't say *brooch* clearly, and she thought I said *coach*. She tried to send me back to the nursery, promising to take me in the coach later, but I wouldn't go. Instead, I took her hand and led her to the servants' wing. I stood outside a chambermaid's room, pointed, and said *coach, coach.*

"My mother didn't know what to make of all this and was about to have me carried back to the nursery when the housekeeper suggested I might be saying *brooch*. She asked if I'd found the brooch and I nodded, opened the door, and took my mother to a dresser."

"And the brooch was in the dresser?" Olivia asked. She'd dropped her sewing and was watching him with unabashed interest.

"Yes. The chambermaid was sent packing without references, and I was a hero. But that wasn't the last time I searched and found what seemed impossible for others to find. I can't describe exactly how I do it, but I seem to have a knack."

"And what sorts of things did you find during the war?"

"People, locations, weapons, maps—anything you can think of. I'm good at finding signs and asking the right questions. That's how I found you." He expected her to ask for details, but she picked up her sewing again. He would tell her them before she left. Maybe she could avoid leaving signs for the next person who came looking.

"The war is over, but you're still searching for the lost."

He shrugged. "It pays well, and I enjoy it. I find a missing ring, a stolen horse—"

"A missing woman."

He inclined his head. "And I'm paid for my efforts." The *Bounty Hunter* had been his sobriquet among the Survivors. They knew he didn't like it, and they didn't use it freely in his presence, but Jasper accepted it. He was a hunter and he took his bounty for what he found.

"And do you always give the item found back to the person who hired you?"

"I always have before."

"And this time?"

"This time is different." How could she think she was the equivalent of a brooch or a criminal?

"And if I asked you for a favor?"

His brows went up. "I'm listening."

"Thank you." She put her sewing back in the basket and rose, apparently not willing to raise the topic yet. "Good night, my l—Jasper."

Jasper watched her walk away and knew he wouldn't sleep much. That kiss was still on his mind. He'd said she'd want more, but he was the one dying for her to touch him again.

Ten

Olivia knew she had put the discussion off too long when Richard came to her the next afternoon and told her Jasper had inspected the trail and thought he might try it the next day. Trying it was not the same as leaving, but she doubted if the path was navigable that he would stay much longer. He'd already as much as promised he wouldn't reveal her location to anyone, though she knew she couldn't stay without fear of discovery. And she would be a fool to believe that a few shared kisses meant anything to him. They might be an awakening for her, but she certainly didn't expect him to pledge his undying devotion and stay with her forever.

Not that she wanted him to stay.

Or kiss her again.

Or touch her…

So when Richard declared he was weary of gardening and needed an adventure, which generally meant he would play at being a jungle explorer in the sparsely wooded area behind the garden and stable, Olivia found Jasper in the garden. He'd made substantial progress, and the garden looked much as it had before the hard rains. Perhaps she would be back in a few weeks to see what could be harvested.

He looked up at her approach, his eyes shadowed by the mask he wore. She wished he wouldn't wear it all the time. She liked how he looked without it so much better. The scars he thought so disfiguring were shocking at first but then just became a part of his features. And the scar certainly didn't take away from his attractiveness. It was just part of him, a visible reminder of his heroism.

There was no point in hedging, so she came right out with it. "I want to go with you."

He didn't react. He didn't even blink.

"To London," she added in case he hadn't understood her.

"Very well."

And then he dug the spade into the ground and extracted another weed.

Olivia crossed her arms. "That's all you have to say? Very well?"

He shrugged.

"Aren't you surprised?"

"Not really. You're an intelligent woman. You know you can't stay here after I go. You'll be found. And I have to assume you'll grow tired of running at some point."

"I am tired of running, and I can't justify dragging Richard away from the only home he's ever known to some place where I have to start all over. If, as you say, my mother is ill, this may be his only chance to meet her."

Jasper stood and dusted his hands on his trousers. He wore the new shirt she'd made him, and somehow he'd managed to avoid dirtying it. "And what about Withernsea?"

She bit the inside of her cheek to keep her lip from trembling. "I've thought about that. He has no claim to Richard. We never married, and he can't prove the child is his."

"And when he confronts you? When he spreads lies about you?"

She braced her feet and put her hands on her hips. "I'll hold my head high and ignore him. I want my parents to meet their grandchild. I want

Richard to have a home. If I suffer some embarrassment, it's a small price to pay."

"Legally you are still betrothed to Withernsea."

That was a point she hadn't considered. "I'm over twenty-one. No one can force me to marry him."

"He can make life difficult for your family."

"My parents haven't seen me in five years. I don't think he can make it more difficult."

Jasper's lips thinned, and she knew he disagreed. She wouldn't argue with him, and it reinforced her need to ask for his protection. But she'd never asked such a thing before, and to ask it of a man was doubly difficult. Just then Clover wandered toward the garden, lowering her head to nibble at some lettuce planted toward the edge. "Clover!" Olivia started for the horse. If she'd planned to stay, she would have started repairing the fence. "I'll put her in her stall for a little while," Olivia said as she rubbed the horse's neck and led her into the stable. The stall was clean, but she could tell Richard had not done a thorough job of mucking it out. He was only five, and she should have come earlier to complete the task. "I need to—" She began, calling over her shoulder to Jasper, but he had followed her inside.

"—muck out the stable," she finished, lowering her voice.

Jasper took the shovel leaning against the wall. "I'll do it."

She released the horse. "You've already done too much."

"You saved my life. It's the least I can do." He set the shovel back and stepped closer to her. Olivia felt that heat in her belly again, and the tingle of anticipation all along the skin of her arms and neck.

"I need to ask you for one more favor," she said.

"Ah, the one you mentioned last night?" He put one hand on the wall behind her. Before she would have felt trapped. He stood in front of the exit, and he blocked her way. But she liked the way he'd moved closer to her. She liked that his arm almost touched hers and that in angling his body this way, he shielded her from Richard's view should he pass the open door.

"Will you…if we go with you, we might need protection. I don't know what will happen when Withernsea realizes I've returned. He may not care. If he does, I'll decline to see him, of course, and I should be safe at my parents' home, but…I should be safe except…before…my parents couldn't…Withernsea took advantage—"

"I'll protect you," Jasper said. "He won't touch you or the boy."

"It's a lot to ask. I'm sure you have other work, obligations."

"You're not an obligation."

"Then what am I?"

"I don't know yet." He bent to kiss her, but she stopped him with a hand on his chest.

"Not with the mask on. I want to see you."

He reached up and loosened the ties in the back so the eye mask fell away. Olivia couldn't have said why, but the act was incredibly arousing. When he reached for the silk that covered his forehead and hair, she grasped his hand, lowered it, and took hold of the silk herself. She drew it off slowly, revealing his dark gold hair. She dropped the mask to the floor and threaded her fingers through his hair, tangling her hands in the thick strands. She tugged his head down, and he went willingly. This time it was she who brushed her lips over his first. The second time she did so, he kissed her back, his lips meeting hers more insistently. The kiss was dizzying, and she moved closer to him just as he caught her about the waist and held her steady.

This was where she wanted to be. Here. In his arms with the scent of the sea and clean straw and man all around her. She drew back and looked into his eyes.

"Close your eyes," he said, moving to kiss her again.

"But I want to see you."

His look was one of disbelief. "No, you don't."

"But I *do*. I like you much better without the mask."

"You don't have to say that."

"It's true." She slid her hand from his hair to his temple. He jerked back as she traced the worst of his scars. "Does it hurt?"

"No, but don't touch it."

"Why? It's part of you. I like touching you." She ran a hand over his shoulder and along his back. But he caught her hand before she could trace his scar again.

"I give you leave to touch me anywhere else."

Her throat went dry. "Anywhere?"

Instead of answering, he kissed her again. The kiss was deep, and she returned it. She didn't even mind so much when he traced her lips with his tongue. She rather liked it this time. She even liked when he coaxed her lips open and licked inside her mouth. She touched his tongue tentatively with hers and felt his hand tighten on her waist. But he didn't move to touch her elsewhere. Instead he allowed her to tease him with her mouth, to taste him, and trace his lips. But when he reciprocated, sliding his tongue between her lips, warring emotions swept over her. Part of her wanted more, panted for more, begged for more. And part of her couldn't forget Withernsea's invasion of her mouth.

That part won, and she pulled back. "I'm sorry!" she stepped out of his arms. "I just…I can't."

She moved toward the door, needing to get away, to escape her embarrassment.

"No, I'm sorry," he said, and his words stopped her.

"You did nothing wrong."

"I did something you didn't like. I made that same mistake yesterday."

She stared at him. She'd never met a man who so readily admitted fault, especially when he was not at fault.

"I'll probably keep making that same mistake, unless you tell me what I'm doing wrong." His gaze on her was steady.

"There's no point in correcting it. We shouldn't…meet like this anymore."

"Maybe we shouldn't, but just in case we do, enlighten me."

She didn't know how to say it, didn't know if she should even say it. How could she tell him?

He took her hand and held it lightly. "Just tell me. What am I doing wrong?"

She tried to swallow the lump in her throat. "When you kiss me…"

"You like it at first," he said gently prodding.

She nodded. "But when you…" She could feel her cheeks flaming. "With your tongue," she whispered. "It reminds me of…something unpleasant."

He squeezed her hand. "Then we won't kiss with tongues."

"We shouldn't kiss at all. Richard could return at any moment."

Jasper nodded and released her. "He'll play half the day, but if you don't want to kiss me, I won't argue."

She turned to leave the stable, pausing only because she'd forgotten to secure Clover in her stall. The mare was happily snoozing there as it was, but the door needed to be closed and locked. Jasper watched her complete the chore and as she walked past him, he said, "There are other things I can do with my tongue."

Olivia stumbled. "W-what did you say?"

"You heard me."

She shook her head, but she wasn't certain if she was denying she'd heard him or refusing his proposal.

"You're not even a little curious?"

Oh, she was curious. She was terribly curious. Especially when just looking at him made her breath come short and her knees feel weak. "What sorts of things?" She felt wicked for asking.

"I'll show you."

That was a tempting offer, but she was not about to give in. Not yet.

"I'd rather you tell me."

He blew out a breath, the first sign of frustration she'd seen in him. "If only I were Rafe."

"Who is Rafe?"

"A friend of mine with a talent for words." Jasper ran a hand through his hair, and she wondered if that was a gesture he'd made often before he wore the mask all the time. "Let's see, what would I like to do to you with my tongue?"

She caught her breath, but she didn't walk away. She didn't have to let him do it. She could just listen. He propped one shoulder against the wall of the stable and folded his arms across his chest. "If the skin on your neck is sensitive, I might use my tongue there. I could trace a path down to your collarbone." His gaze roved where his tongue might, and even though her collarbone was covered by the modest dress she wore, she could almost feel his eyes and his tongue there. "And if that makes you shiver," he continued, "I could make my way, slowly, to your ear lobe."

"My ear lobe?"

He nodded. "I'm told the ear is one of the most sensitive parts of the body. Your ears are small and delicate. I think you might like it if I brushed my lips over them."

She couldn't catch her breath now, and she knew he could see the way her breasts rose and fell with her rapid gasps. But his gaze didn't flick to her chest. Instead he glanced at her hands, clasped tightly together. "I could push your sleeves up and bare your wrists." He made this sound incredibly scandalous, though she rarely wore gloves and had long ceased to think of her wrists or hands as anything to protect. Now she looked down at her sleeve and imagined him pushing it up to reveal the pale skin beneath.

"I would kiss you there, lightly, on the inside of your wrist where your pulse hammers. I'd like to taste your skin, press my mouth against that beating pulse, kiss a trail up your arm."

"No more," she said, putting a hand to her heart. She feared it might jump from her chest if it beat any harder. "I don't know this Rafe, but I'd say you have a facility of words equal to, if not better, than he."

"Then I've done what you asked." He pushed off the wall. "Would you like me to show you now?"

She should say no, but she'd never felt such longing before. She swallowed. "Maybe you could give me a small example to better illustrate." Her cheeks went hot at her bold words.

"I could do that. Perhaps I should close the door, so we're not surprised." He moved past her, almost brushing against her, to take hold of the large door and swing it shut. She readied herself for the darkness and then the feel of his body against hers, but it didn't come. When she looked, he was bent by the side of the stable, examining the ground.

"What is it?" she asked, following him outside.

"Let me see your foot." She raised her brows, but he waved a hand, indicating there was nothing sexual in the request. "I want to see your boot."

She lifted the hem of her dress slightly so he could see the worn half boots she wore.

"Your feet are too small."

"For?"

"To have made these prints." She moved closer, examining the footprint in the mud next to the stable door. Several more led around to the side. They followed the prints to where they stopped at the window. Clover's bowed head was clearly visible. Now Olivia's heart hammered for another reason.

"Those are too big for Richard. Are they yours?"

He put his own booted foot beside the print. His foot was larger, the mark his boot made in the soft ground different. She stared at the ground then gasped. "Richard!"

And without a word, she ran.

***

Jasper followed her. He wanted to examine the prints more, trace the path whoever they belonged to had taken, but he had to make sure Olivia and Richard were safe. What if the man was still nearby?

His legs were longer than Olivia's, and he easily caught up with her. She knew the area better than he, so he allowed her to lead. She called Richard's name several times, and it took only a moment for the boy to answer.

"I'm here, Mama!"

"Thank God!" She rushed toward the sound of the boy's voice. Since the lad had sounded unconcerned, Jasper followed more slowly, looking for any signs the intruder might be watching and, though he wouldn't admit it, catching his breath. His knife wound hurt like bloody hell from the exertion of running. If the intruder was still around, Jasper wouldn't be much good in a fight if he didn't conserve his energy.

Ahead of him, Richard walked through the clearing, wielding a large stick like a sword, and his mother swept him up in her arms. The boy tolerated it in a way he wouldn't in another year or so, and then she set him down and checked him from head to toe.

"What's wrong?" he asked. "Why isn't Lord Jasper wearing his mask?"

Jasper started. He'd completely forgotten the mask. And now he stood in the open, his scar openly on display. And yet the boy didn't scream or run or even looked upset.

He glanced at his mother then back at Jasper. "I like you without the mask. You don't look as scary."

Jasper almost laughed. That was the last thing he'd expected the child to say.

"Thank you."

Richard studied his mother again. "What is it, Mama?"

"Nothing is wrong." She glanced over her shoulder at Jasper, giving him a meaningful look.

He nodded. He hadn't planned to tell the boy of their fears. He might not have much experience with children, but he wasn't an idiot.

"I wanted to make certain you weren't hurt. The ground is still slippery."

"It's mostly dry, Mama."

Obviously, that was true. Whoever had made those footprints had managed to climb up here, a feat that wouldn't have been possible even a couple of days ago.

"Come play near the house," she told him.

"But Mama!"

Jasper put his hand on the boy's shoulder to soften his disappointment. "I'll play knights and dragons with you."

"You will! Hoorah!"

Olivia threw Jasper a grateful look. It almost made up for losing the opportunity to kiss her neck. "Richard, you fed Clover this morning and mucked out the stable?"

"I did it all by myself!"

"Did you notice anything unusual when you went into the stable?"

"What's *unusual* mean?"

"Something that isn't how it should be?" his mother clarified. "Something out of place?"

"No." He looked at Jasper again. "Can I wear your mask?"

Jasper ruffled his hair. "No."

"Awww. Please?"

"What about it the woods?" Olivia asked. "Was anything different in the woods?"

"Why can't I wear the mask? Can I just try it?"

"Richard! I asked you a question." They were in sight of the house now, and she paused and turned Richard to face her. "Was anything in the woods different?"

He nodded. "Lots of tree limbs fell down." He brandished the one he still held, and Jasper caught the end before it smacked him in the face. "And I found a puddle with tadpoles. You should come and see!"

"I will," Jasper said. "I'll want you to show me later." He looked at Olivia over Richard's head. "Is there a way to reach the top of the cliff besides the trail?"

"Not that I know of. That's the only way we've ever taken. The southern side is surrounded by water and the northern side is too steep."

"Can we play knights and dragons now?" Richard asked impatiently.

"Yes. Since you have the sword, I'll be the dragon." He pointed at Olivia. "Stay where I can see you."

Jasper tired Richard and himself out playing in the sun. But though he might have liked to nap with the boy after lunch, he made his way back to the stable to examine the footprints again. He'd left Olivia at the cottage, keeping watch, so he was surprised when she appeared a few minutes later. "I didn't think you'd want to leave him alone."

"I don't," she whispered. "But I also want to know who has been skulking about my home. I set up a trap that will alert us if anyone goes in or out of the cottage."

Jasper looked up at her from where he kneeled beside the footprints. "You set up a trap?"

She nodded. "I made it when Richard was about two and would sometimes get out of bed. I couldn't always stay inside. I had laundry to collect or herbs to pick for dinner, so I would leave a pot filled with metal utensils above the door on the outside. A rope holds it in place, but if the door opens, the rope slackens and the pot turns over, dumping all the utensils on the stones outside the door. It makes an awful clatter."

Jasper considered. "We could have used you in the fight against Napoleon."

"England probably would have won much more quickly if women had been running the war."

Jasper smiled. She was so clever and confident, and she looked lovely with the sun glossing her dark curls. He wanted to kiss her, but now was definitely not the time. "It looks like whoever came up the trail made his way around the cottage and then to the stable. It doesn't appear he went into the woods, and I think he left the same way he came. I can't be certain. Richard and the two of us walked over much of the same ground. I'm a decent tracker, but it will take me time to piece it together. That time might be better spent packing to leave."

He saw the way her eyes went wide with fear. "When?"

"At first light?"

"That's too soon."

"You told me you wanted to go to London."

"But I meant in a week or so. I'm not ready yet."

"That was fine when the only concern we had was one attack on me that might or might not be related to you. But at this point we have to assume we've been found. *You* and Richard have been found."

"You think whoever hurt you and made these footprints was hired by Withernsea?"

Jasper stood and wiped his hands on his trousers, considering his next words carefully. "I don't know. I don't even know if it's the same man. It's possible your parents hired another man to track you in case I was unsuccessful, and the footprints are not made by the same man who attacked me." The idea of it annoyed him, but he wasn't ready to rule it out. "But we cannot rule out the possibility that whoever wounded me on the trail has come back or that he was sent by the duke."

She grabbed his arm, an action that surprised him because she'd so rarely initiated contact with him. "You think we could be in real danger?"

"I don't want to wait and find out. We leave in the morning, stopping in Penbury to arrange transportation to London."

"There's a mail coach—" she began.

He waved a hand. "The mail coach will be crowded and slow." And the last thing he wanted was people gawking at him. "I'd like to arrive in London quickly and quietly. If we take the coach we either have to lie about who we are or else word will spread quickly you're back. Even if we lie, there's a good chance I'll be recognized. Not that many men wear masks when not at a masquerade."

Her hand dropped and he quelled the impulse to take it in his own. "I don't have the funds to afford a coach and four. It would cost…I don't even know what it would cost to travel to London that way."

"I have coin enough."

Her brow furrowed, most likely because he hadn't had any blunt on him when she'd found him. He'd left his belongings and his money at Penbury's inn. He could retrieve them and if he needed more blunt he'd whisper a few names and receive credit easily enough. "Don't worry. I'll handle the travel. That will be the easy part."

She sighed and glanced back toward the cottage. "What should I tell him? This is the only home he remembers. Do I lie and say we'll be back? Do I tell him about his father? How do I explain why I've been hiding all these years?"

"I don't have those answers." He hardly knew what to say to the boy at any given moment. "Whatever you say will be right."

"That isn't very helpful."

He shrugged. "I'm more concerned he'll tell everyone he meets every detail about us. I'll try to avoid public places, but we won't be able to stay away from people entirely. We'll need to pretend you are someone else."

"Your wife?"

Jasper shook his head. That would have been an easy ruse if he wasn't so recognizable. There were times when being a scarred war hero and the son of a marquess did not work in one's favor. "Let's say you're the widow of one of my fellow soldiers." He thought of the men he served with. "You'll be Mrs. Peter Collins."

"Who was he?" she asked when they were only a couple yards from the cottage.

"A good soldier and a good man. He was the fourth or fifth son of a baron, so he's not well known."

"How did he die?"

"In a fire."

He heard her inhale sharply as he walked away.

Eleven

She couldn't sleep. She should have been exhausted. Between Richard's unending questions and the unending tasks to be completed before morning, she hadn't gone to bed until well after midnight. Jasper hadn't gone to bed at all. If she turned her head, she could still see him. He sat with his chair angled toward the door, keeping a silent, watchful vigil. He'd keep watch all night, she knew. He would keep them safe. She hadn't trusted a man in so long that it was strange to be able to trust one now. It was strange to know that she could sleep and he would make certain no harm came to her.

She only wished she *could* sleep because now they would both be exhausted on the morrow and they'd probably both be impatient at Richard's new onslaught of questions.

She allowed her gaze to roam over the shadowy room. The banked fire gave it a warm glow and produced enough light so that she could see far more than she wanted. There was the piece of wood where she had marked Richard's height every few months. She'd have to leave that behind, of course. And if she opened the door and looked out into the yard, she'd see the spot where Richard had taken his first steps. It had been only a few days after she had found this place. They'd spent hours and hours outside, enjoying the sunlight after over a year in the small, dark flat where she'd hidden previously. Richard had taken to the fresh air and before she knew it he'd stood on unsteady legs and then walked in faltering steps into her waiting arms.

She glanced toward the loft and thought of the books they must leave behind. They didn't have many, nothing compared to the library her father had, and even that was small compared to some. But she'd read them all to Richard. She'd spent hours up there, reading, singing, and rocking him.

Before she could stop it, a sob escaped her lips. She pressed her fist to her mouth to try and stifle it, but the scrape of Jasper's chair told her she'd not been successful. "I'm fine," she said, turning away from him.

For a long moment she thought he might believe it. She managed to tamp down the other sobs welling up inside her, but then he was before her, crouching beside the bed and taking her hand in his.

"I'm fine," she said again.

"You're crying."

She wiped her eyes with her free hand. "Nothing more than sentiment. I'll be fine. I should sleep."

He nodded. "I'll go back to my chair."

She closed her eyes and really did try to sleep but a few minutes later she heard what sounded like the crack of a pistol. She sat upright. "What was that?"

Jasper was still sitting in his chair, looking at ease. "A tree branch. The winds are strong tonight."

She rose and pulled her robe on. "Are you certain no one is outside?" She padded to the window and peered out of the curtains. All she could see was darkness. There wasn't even a moon to shed some light.

"I can go outside and check if you'd like." He stood.

"No!" she hissed quietly. "If someone is out there, it's safer inside." She crossed the room.

"If someone is out there, I want to know who the devil it is." He reached for the latch, and she grabbed his wrist.

"No!" She couldn't explain the irrational fear that seized her. "Don't leave!"

"You won't go to sleep unless I investigate, though I don't think there's anything to worry about. It was only a tree limb falling."

"Then stay inside." She dragged him back from the door. "Stay with me." She put her arms around him and pressed her cheek to his chest, thankfully covered by the white shirt she had made him. He stood stiffly for a long moment then put his hands gingerly on her back, patting her tentatively.

"You're shaking," he said. "You should go back to bed."

"I'm not cold," she murmured. "I'm scared. Just hold me for one minute." How long had it been since she'd been held? How long had it been since she'd given in to this small bit of comfort? For years she had been the one to comfort and calm. Tonight she wanted to feel safe.

A minute or two passed, and then he said, "You should go back to bed now."

"Come with me." She winced, glad he could not see her face, which she could feel was red as a flame. "Just to sleep," she said to his chest. "We can barricade the door."

"That's not a good idea—sharing a bed, I mean."

Now she did look up. "I know I can trust you."

He blew out a breath. "What about him?" He glanced at the loft. "What if he wakes and sees us lying together?"

"I'll tell him you were scared." Jasper barked out a laugh, and she couldn't help but smile too. "I hold him while he falls asleep when he's scared."

She took Jasper's hand and led him to the bed before she could reconsider what she was doing. Then she slid under the covers and held them up for him.

He shook his head. "I'll sleep on top. I want my boots on." He didn't have to say more. She nodded and moved over to make room for him. Jasper raised a finger and circled it. "You face that way, and I'll lay behind you."

She frowned. She'd rather liked burying her face in his chest, and she wanted to do that again.

"Olivia." His voice was quiet. "Even a man with a great deal of self-control has limits."

A slash of heat knifed through her. He wanted her. That had to be what he meant. Lying with her would tempt him and possibly arouse him. She, on the other hand, really had only wanted comfort. But now that he'd introduced the idea of more…

"No," he said, almost as though he could read her mind. "You need sleep, and I'm too tired to trust myself to stop at mere kisses. I'll hold you and nothing else. Agreed?"

She nodded and turned her back toward him. When he lay down next to her and pressed his body to hers, though, the feeling was a revelation. Her body instantly flashed hot and parts of her she rarely thought about tingled and ached slightly. He laid a hand over her waist, lightly and casually, and she wished he would hold her tighter, caress her hip, her belly, lower…

She let out a choked gasp at the throb between her legs.

"What's wrong?" He immediately lifted his hand. "I apologize."

She took his hand and put it back where it had been, too afraid to put it anywhere else. "Nothing is wrong. I'm just relieved you're here."

His stiff arm gradually relaxed. She lay with her eyes open for a long time, waiting for her heightened sensations to fade. Was this desire? Was this what it felt like to want someone so much it was almost a yearning? And how could she feel that way about a man she barely knew? A man she didn't love, though she could see herself falling in love with him. He was the sort of man she'd always imagined she'd fall in love with and marry. Lord Jasper was honorable and brave and handsome. Yes, the scar marred what must have been, at one time, a perfect face, but it didn't make him any less handsome to her. Now that he'd stopped wearing his mask, she might not have noticed the scar at all except to worry if it pained him.

Olivia could tell from the tension in his body, Jasper was still awake and on watch. Gradually, she was able to fall asleep, safe in his arms.

She woke early and opened her eyes. The cottage was still dark and all was quiet. Jasper's arm was still over her body, but it was heavy and lax now. His breathing was slow and even. She listened to him for a few minutes and then because her arm had fallen asleep, she wriggled onto her other side and snuggled into his chest. His arm tightened on her, pulling her close against him as his breathing resumed that slow, even pattern.

Gradually, the room turned charcoal and then pewter, and Olivia looked up at the stubble on Jasper's chin. Adjusting her position, she propped herself on her elbow and peered down at his face. His head was turned toward her, and the uninjured side lay on the pillow. This was the first time she'd had time to look at his scar without being observed. The skin of the scar seemed thinner and pulled tighter over the bones of Jasper's cheek and temple. She could imagine that as much as the initial injury had pained him, the healing and stretching of that raw skin had also hurt. How had he withstood the pain? She'd burned herself seriously while cooking three or four times, mostly when she was first on her own and trying to teach herself, and she remembered crying at the pain and doing all she could to numb it. But nothing seemed to help. The pain lasted several hours and continued, in milder form, for several days.

And while she might have burnt two fingers or the skin of her forearm, it was a small area compared to what he'd injured. His burns were so much worse than any she'd sustained.

Olivia reached out and lightly brushed her hand over the raw area of the scar, where it had been chafed by the mask. She should apply more ointment, especially as she couldn't take it with her. She wished she had known him when he'd been injured, wished she could have been there to ease his pain. She ran her fingers over the shiny skin near his temple and he reached up and caught her wrist.

She hadn't even known he'd awakened. His eyes, browner now than green, opened. "What are you doing?"

"I was thinking I should put more ointment on since I don't have room to take it with me."

He moved his head, tilting the damaged side away from her. Her chest tightened at the defensive gesture. She wanted so much for him to believe that he was not a monster, that she did not see him that way.

"You don't have to do that, you know. It doesn't bother me. I was just wondering how you endured the pain."

"I didn't have a choice." He kept his good side toward her. "How long have you been staring at me?"

"Not long. It's still dark outside."

"Not for long." He pushed himself up on an elbow. "We should get up and—"

She put her arms around his neck, holding him in place. "Not yet. Let Richard sleep a little longer."

Reluctantly, he lay back and she released him, lying beside him again. He was quiet for only a moment. "What should we do while we wait for him to wake?"

"You could tell me more about the war. How did you get your scar?"

He shook his head. "I don't want to talk about that."

"Then tell me about before the war. Did we ever dance together at a ball? I think I would have remembered."

"I can't talk about that either."

"Why not?"

"Because I can't think right now," he said, almost angrily. "I can't concentrate on anything but how warm you are and how much I want to bloody well kiss you."

She shrank back, dread making the hair on the back of her arms prickle. "You're angry."

"Not at you." His tone softened. "I'm angry at myself for having to struggle so much for control."

"I should tend the fire."

He grasped her wrist before she could flee. "Olivia, there's something you need to know about me. I don't beat men weaker than me. I don't kick dogs or throw rocks at cats. I don't poison rats or backhand children. And I have never, never touched a woman in anger."

She appreciated the words, but it was hard to feel the same sense of trust she had before. His anger frightened her. "I shouldn't have forced you to lie with me."

He laughed. "You didn't force me. There's nothing I wanted more, and now I'm dealing with the consequences."

"What consequences?"

"I want you," he said, his low voice making her heart thump. "And I know I can't have you."

"You want…like Withernsea…"

"No. Not that. But I look at your lips and I want to taste them. I see that little pulse beating here." He touched her throat below her jaw. "And I want to lick it."

She inhaled sharply.

"That feeling there." He pointed at her. "That's the consequences."

She felt her cheeks redden, but he'd been honest with her. "I want you too," she whispered.

"I know. That's what makes this all the more difficult. You don't really know what you want."

"I know I liked what you said you would do yesterday."

He raised a brow in question. He'd turned his face toward her again, apparently no longer self-conscious of his scar. "What was that?"

She ducked her head. "With your tongue?"

He made a low sound in his throat. "Should I try it now? You can tell me whether you like it or not."

"But won't that make it more difficult for you?" She thought of her own feelings of longing the night before and at the present moment. "Won't you have to struggle more?"

"It will be torture," he admitted, lifting her chin. "But it's the sort of torture I welcome."

"That makes no sense."

"True enough. Can I kiss you?"

She glanced up to the loft, but she saw no sign of movement yet. She looked back at Jasper, her gaze colliding with his. She couldn't breathe when she saw the look in his eye. She didn't even know how to describe it. It reminded her of the way Richard looked at a sweet on the rare occasion she bought him one from the village.

"Yes."

His lips brushed hers gently, carefully, and she knew he was holding back. He didn't want to frighten her, but she wasn't frightened anymore. He wasn't the kind of man who would hurt her or anyone except in self-defense. And all the pent-up desire she had felt the night before rushed out. She tangled her fingers in his hair and kissed him more deeply.

He groaned and pushed her onto her back, his lips taking hers in the way she wanted. And yet as passionately as he kissed her, his hands remained on either side of her body, not touching her, and his tongue did no more than taste her lips.

And then his mouth was gone from hers, and she felt his lips on her chin. He kissed a path to her neck, where she felt his tongue dart out and flick the spot where her pulse thrummed. Now she was the one who groaned. His hands closed on her shoulders as though he must hold on to something for support. His mouth moved higher, tickling and tantalizing her flesh, until it paused at her earlobe and he tasted her there. Her breath hitched and caught then hitched again when he lightly bit her earlobe then teased the sting away with his tongue.

She was panting now, her body on fire, her mind reeling. She wanted to pull him closer, touch his bare skin, but she tried to remember where she was and why she should hold back. It became increasingly difficult to remember as his tongue slid to her shoulder. With his teeth, Jasper pulled the loose neck of her night rail aside, baring her shoulder and kissing it. She had no idea she would like having her shoulder kissed and licked so much. She didn't want him to stop.

But he rose on his elbow and looked down at her. His eyes locked on hers and then slid to her bare shoulder and then down. She followed his gaze and saw the hard point of her nipple visible against the thin fabric of the night rail.

“I know somewhere else you might like me to taste,” he said, his gaze still on her nipple, which hardened at the attention. “Shall I draw down the neckline and show you?”

Her body screamed *yes*. At this point she would have believed she’d enjoy the way he kissed her elbow, but then the memory of Withernsea ripping her bodice and grabbing her breast and squeezing made her shudder.

“No.” She shook her head. “I—"

But Jasper had already pulled back, perhaps having felt the shudder. “You don’t have to explain,” he said. “‘No’ is sufficient.”

She slid her hands from where they’d wrapped around him, and he caught one of her hands in his and threaded his fingers through hers. His eyes were almost green now in the soft morning light. He looked down at her face. “I thought you were pretty the first time I saw you,” he said.

She braced herself, half afraid he would punish her for her refusal with harsh words.

“It’s not very often I’m wrong about my first impression. You’re not merely pretty. You’re beautiful.”

***

He rose and left the bed then. He’d known the words would soften her, but he hadn’t said them to try and take advantage of her. He’d said them because they were the truth. And he’d made himself disentangle from her because she’d said no, and if he stayed where he could feel her curves cushion him and smell her light feminine scent all around him, he might be tempted to try and change her mind.

She’d tasted better than he’d imagined. The sea was nearby and her skin held a slight saltiness, but under that it was velvet soft and so warm. Every inch he touched made him want more. The more he touched her, the more he wanted to touch her.

And then she'd put her arms around him. He doubted she'd even noticed, but he couldn't help but notice. Her touch awakened every one of his senses. When she wrapped her arms about him, her small breasts pushed against his chest and the points of her nipples scraped enticingly against his shirt.

He'd forgotten what it had been like to want a woman so much. He'd been so young when he'd gone to war, but he liked to think he'd cultivated some finesse when it came to bedsport. He liked to take his time, but with Olivia he found it increasingly difficult. Here was one woman who demanded he take his time, who would probably never have allowed more than she already had, even if they hadn't been leaving, and all Jasper could think was how much he wanted to plunge into her and rut like some sort of randy beast.

And so he stood and walked to the door, determined to step into the cool of the morning and douse his passion and his erection. But he was not so blinded by desire that he forgot to look about him, searching for signs anyone had been at the cottage. He'd wet the ground outside the door and by the windows so he could see footprints easily enough, but it was undisturbed. After seeing to his body's needs, he'd walked to the stable and the garden. All was undisturbed there as well.

Jasper didn't consider this turn of events promising. The fact that whoever had been spying on them two nights ago hadn't come back meant the man had found whatever he was looking for. He'd returned to report to whoever had hired him—Withernsea? Someone else?—and soon others would come to collect what they wanted.

He definitely had to take Richard and Olivia with him today. London hardly seemed like a safe haven, but Olivia's parents were there as were Jasper's friends, who could provide him information and Olivia protection.

"What are you doing?" came a small voice.

Jasper turned around to see Richard approaching, rubbing his eyes.

"Waking up. You?"

"Waking"—his sentence was interrupted by a yawn—"up. You're not wearing your mask."

"I'm not. I'll put it on again today, since we're going into the village. I don't want to scare anyone."

"You're not scary. I wish I had a scar like yours."

Jasper wasn't certain what to make of that statement. "No, you don't."

"I do. Can you cut my hair here so it looks like yours?"

"No." Jasper shook his head in disbelief. "Your hair looks fine the way it is. Let's go back before your mother comes out looking for us."

"Yes, sir. I mean, my lord." He took Jasper's hand, which surprised Jasper but seemed to be something the boy did without thinking about it. "Did it hurt?"

Jasper was still looking at the small hand in his. "What?"

"When you were burned? Did it hurt?"

"Yes, it hurt." Jasper began walking back to the cottage.

"Does it still hurt?"

"Not most of the time."

"I'm scared of it hurting."

Jasper paused outside the cottage then he knelt and took the lad's shoulders. "Nothing like this will ever happen to you. Your mother won't allow any harm to come to you, and neither will I. Do you know how I received this scar?"

Richard shook his head.

"I was protecting my friends. I'll protect you too."

The boy leaned close and Jasper thought he intended to hug him. He opened his arms, and the boy went into them but instead of hugging him, he moved close and spoke conspiratorially. "The one you really need to protect is Mama. She's scared."

Jasper froze. He and Olivia had both thought they'd hidden their concerns about the trip, instead speaking to the boy about all the fun and excitement to be had. But he hadn't been fooled at all. "Do you know what she's scared about?"

Richard shook his head. "Do you?"

"Yes. Don't worry. I'll keep her safe. Nothing will happen to either of you." He strove for the light tone they'd tried to adopt with the boy yesterday. "Think: in just a day or two you'll see your grandparents. They'll be so pleased to meet you." At least he hoped they would be pleased.

That made the boy smile. "Mama says they have a big fancy house. Do you think I can have a dog? And a pony?"

"That's not my decision." And thank God for small mercies. But he knew the boy was upset at having to leave Clover behind. She was too old to make the trip to London at the pace Jasper planned. Olivia knew a family with three children and a large pasture who would enjoy caring for the old mare, and she'd suggested they give the horse to them. Jasper had thought they should sell the horse, but Olivia argued she was too old to fetch much. She obviously cared for Clover and wanted to see her live her last years in leisure.

"I prepared something to break our fasts."

Jasper looked behind him and saw Olivia standing in the door to the cottage. He hadn't even heard it open.

"You eat," he said, guiding the boy to his mother. "I'll ready Clover so we can depart right after the meal."

She nodded, her eyes appraising him. He hadn't lied when he'd said he thought her beautiful. In the golden rays of the rising sun, she was so lovely he wanted to take her in his arms. He half wished he'd never touched her because now he knew what it felt like and he would miss it when they returned to London and went their separate ways.

"I'll pack something for you to eat on the way," she said.

He gave her a nod of thanks and went to ready Clover.

***

The trip down the path from the cottage to the seashore was as bad as he'd anticipated. He'd gone first with the horse, allowing the animal to pick her way down the steep, often precarious path. About halfway down, the trail evened out, and he left the horse and went back for Olivia and Richard. They had waited at the top, and Olivia smiled when she saw him. "Did you make it to the bottom?"

He shook his head. "Halfway." He stooped to catch his breath. "There's a spot you can rest there while I take the horse the rest of the way."

She nodded. Jasper gestured to the boy. "It's steep. Climb onto my back, and I'll give you a ride down."

"Like Clover does?"

"Yes. Since you're a brave knight who fights dragons, I have to be a noble steed."

"Let's go!" He climbed onto Jasper's back and Jasper started down, angling his body sideways to leverage against the incline. He looked back to make sure Olivia was faring well on her own and saw that she hadn't yet started after them. Instead, she'd pulled her skirt through her legs and secured it at her waist. Her pale calves were visible above her ragged half boots, and he didn't have to work hard to imagine the shape of her thighs.

He quickly turned back to the path. Freeing herself from the encumbrance of her skirts had been clever. The last thing she needed was him ogling her.

It took several hours, much longer than he'd wanted, to make it to the base of the cliff. Jasper's back and shoulders burned like fire, but even worse was the pounding in his head. He hadn't considered the boy would chitter in his ear the entire way down.

He gave Olivia his back so she might arrange her skirts without an audience, and then the four of them started for Penbury. Jasper donned his mask and Olivia pinned on a hat with a short veil.

"Not much reason to hide your face now," he remarked.

"And no reason to show it, either. London will know I'm in Town soon enough. I'd like to arrive without advance warning."

"What are you talking about?" Richard asked.

"Nothing, darling," she said with a smile. "Ready to begin our adventure?"

"I'm hungry!"

Jasper sighed. At this rate, they'd never make it to London.

Twelve

It was late by the time they stopped for the night. Olivia had known Jasper was frustrated by the slow pace of their travels. It had taken longer than he'd wanted for them to conclude their business in Penbury. They might have made better time if she hadn't stopped to say goodbye to the few acquaintances she had there, but they'd been kind and helpful over the years. Olivia didn't want to leave without a farewell.

She didn't know exactly how much coin Jasper had brought with him, but it was far more than she'd expected. Since he insisted they stay together, she'd waited in the common room while he fetched his belongings at the inn. Then she'd followed as he'd inquired about a coach and horses. An hour or so later, all was ready for them. He'd procured a closed carriage and four horses he could change at posting houses along the way. She'd expected a cart and one horse, if that.

"How much coin do you have?" she asked as she looked at the conveyance.

"Not as much as all this, but it helps to be the son of the Marquess of Strathern. I have good credit."

"I'll pay you back," she said.

"I wouldn't accept payment if you offered." He gestured to the carriage. Richard was already climbing about inside, exploring every inch. "Your carriage awaits, Miss Carlisle."

"And are you to play coachman?"

He nodded. "Much quieter out here."

She'd laughed because she already dreaded Richard's constant questions.

Now at the inn where they'd stopped for the night, Jasper procured two rooms. Richard had fallen asleep hours before, and he carried the boy to her room and tucked him in. "I've ordered refreshment if you're hungry."

"I am." The movement of the carriage made her slightly nauseous and she had not eaten much on the road.

"I've asked it to be sent to my room." His look was apologetic. "Shall I tell them we'll eat downstairs?"

She shook her head. Jasper's room was across the hall and close to Richard. "I think my virtue, what is left of it, is safe with you, my lord."

He gave her a look she couldn't read since he wore his mask and gestured for her to follow him. In the hallway, they met the maidservant with the supper tray. Once the food was laid out on a table, Jasper sent the servant away, and Olivia sank into a chair with a cup of warm tea.

"I've forgotten how awful traveling by coach can be. I think I felt every rock and rut."

He sat across from her and rolled his shoulders. "I'm afraid the conveyance isn't well-sprung."

She shrugged. "Another day and we'll be in London."

"It may be a day and a night. I thought we'd make better time today."

"I'm sorry we slowed you down."

He broke off a piece of bread from the warm loaf. "I should have realized traveling in company is slower than traveling alone. You locked the door to your room?"

She nodded, holding up the key. "Yes, but I don't want to stay long. If Richard wakes, he won't know where I am."

Jasper laughed. "He's so tired I'll probably have to carry him out to the carriage in the morning."

She smiled. "This is the most excitement he's had…ever, I think."

Jasper ate silently, and it was a comfortable silence. "Richard is worried about you," he said. Her head jerked up.

"What do you mean?"

He ate a bit of his vegetable tart. "He told me yesterday that he knew you were scared. He asked me to protect you."

Her heart plummeted to her stomach, and she pushed her food away. "Children always know when adults are afraid. No matter how well we hide it."

"I'll tell you what I told him. I won't let anything happen to you. Either of you."

She pressed a hand to her chest because her heart clenched.

"I'll protect you." His hazel eyes were very intent as he spoke. "I promise." "Like you protected the men of your troop when you received your scar. I…" She swallowed at the emotion threatening to choke her. "I can't tell you what it means to me that you'd say that. Thank you."

To her surprise, he glanced away from her in anger.

"Jasper?"

"I think before you start thanking me you should hope I protect you better than I did my friends. If I had, you wouldn't be masquerading as Peter Collins's widow. Peter would be alive."

"He was the soldier who died in the fire." It wasn't a question. He'd given her enough information over the time they'd spent together that she'd worked it out.

"I went in to save him. I failed." He rose and walked away

"Not without a fight. I can look at your scar and know that the wound almost killed you."

"There were days I wished it had. The pain was so great." He stopped at the window and parted the curtains. "The pain and the guilt."

"Do you think Peter would wish you dead?"

"No," he answered without pause. "And he wouldn't want my guilt either. We went into every mission expecting to die, ready to die. But that didn't mean we went without a fight."

She rose and went to him. "You lived, and I can't regret that because if you hadn't, you wouldn't have ever found me."

"I also wouldn't have led someone to your cottage. You'd still be safe there."

"I'd still be in prison there. You've given me a chance to start again. A chance for Richard to know his family."

"The *ton* is not so forgiving." His tone held a warning.

"I may live the rest of my life as an outcast, a scandalous woman. But I won't hide away in fear anymore." But even as she said it, her voice trembled.

"I told you, I won't let the duke hurt you. You're not a child any longer. No one can force you to marry him." He stared out the window.

She nodded, tears filling her eyes. She'd been strong the past two days for Richard, but now her legs wanted to crumple and her resolve felt shaky. "There's just so much I can't control. What will my parents say when they see Richard? What about my old friends? What do I do if Withernsea comes to call on me?"

"Tell him to get the hell out," Jasper said.

His matter-of-fact tone made her laugh. "You make it all seem so simple."

"It *is* simple. As someone who has lived outside the confines of Society for years, I promise you, life without those rules and strictures is much easier."

"Even for a woman?"

"A woman whose parents were willing to pay my fees to see their daughter again? Yes. They want you back. They love you."

It should have reassured her. Perhaps she could finally stop running, finally make a real home for Richard and herself. But she had a new fear now. "I want to see them again, but I can't stop myself wondering—what happens between us when we reach London?" She wasn't ready to say goodbye to him.

She hadn't wanted him in her life, but now she couldn't imagine being without him.

He dropped the curtains and faced her. "I'll stay nearby to make certain Withernsea doesn't bother you, and you're safe with your parents."

"And then?" She looked up at him, into his eyes what were neither green nor brown at the moment.

"There can't be anything else. I'm not the sort of man who pays court to ladies. I'm the son of a marquess who has gone into trade. My services are for hire. Even if I didn't have this scarred face, no respectable father would want me for his daughter." His tone made it seem as though the matter was already decided. She didn't want to believe that.

"What if his daughter isn't exactly respectable?"

"Then she doesn't need me to complicate her situation further. It's best if once you're settled that I'll leave you alone."

All of the air in her lungs seemed to whoosh out and leave her deflated. She could nod and accept what he said. It was probably the best course of action. But if she didn't tell him how she felt now, she might never have another chance. She swallowed. "What if I don't want you to leave me alone?"

Jasper shook his head slowly. "You will once you return to London."

"I won't." She pressed on, determined to say it now. "I've come to care about you, Jasper."

"You're scared and vulnerable. You don't know what you're feeling." She smacked his arm and he jumped back. "Hey!"

"Who are you to tell me I don't know what I feel?" Her annoyance had given her courage. "I know what I feel when you hold me, when you kiss me, when you look at me, when I see you carrying my son."

"Olivia." His tone held a warning.

"You want me to change the subject? Then tell me you don't feel the same. Tell me you don't care about me, but if you say it, I'll know you're lying. I've seen lust. I've experienced it. There's more than lust between us." Her cheeks were as hot as the fire in the grate, but she didn't look away.

"There's plenty of lust," he said, and the look he gave her should have scared her. It would have terrified her a week ago. But now it made her breath catch with hope and need.

"Then maybe you *should* walk away from me when we reach London. Maybe I should go back to my room right now." *Please don't let me go.* "I should forget about kissing you, touching you." He closed his eyes, his face the image of a man in pain. Olivia stepped closer. "Or should I stay?"

"Stay." His arms went around her, pulling her against him. Heat shot through her where their bodies touched. Under the heat was an acute awareness of everything about him, from the solidity of his chest to the hardness of his forearms where they pressed against her lower back. He leaned down to kiss her, but she leaned back slightly.

"You're still wearing your mask."

"Take it off me."

She practically moaned at the low, teasing tone of his voice. Hands trembling slightly, she lifted them to the ties behind his head and pulled the strings. She pulled them off and allowed them to drop to the floor. "That's better."

He leaned in to kiss her again.

"Admit it," she said as his lips brushed over hers, sending tingles of pleasure racing through her. "Admit this is more than lust."

His eyes met hers for a long moment. "This is more than lust, Olivia." His gaze still locked with hers, he bent his head and kissed her until her knees were weak and she had to cling to him or crumple to a heap on the floor. He kissed her throat again, her earlobe, and then unbuttoned her spencer so he could tantalize her collarbone and shoulder. He used his mouth, keeping his hands on her back or waist, but she became aware that he slid them up from her waist over her ribs, resting them just below her breasts. Her nipples hardened at his closeness, aching for relief. She wasn't certain what would bring it.

"Can I touch you?" he asked. A finger swept upward, grazing the underside of one breast. "Here?"

She nodded.

"Yes?" he asked, repeating the gesture with the other hand.

"Yes," she breathed.

His hands slid up and cupped her breasts, his thumbs brushing the sensitive points. "Like this?" he whispered.

"*Yes.*"

His hands caressed her gently, but though she sought relief his touch only teased and inflamed, making her want more.

"You like when I use my tongue here?" he looked up from kissing her shoulder. "And here?" He whispered in her ear and kissed it, sliding his tongue along the edge. "May I use my tongue here?" One finger circled her nipple, causing her breath to hitch.

She didn't know how to refuse. Her whole body trembled with a need she couldn't name. All she could manage was to kiss him and whisper, "Yes."

He lowered her to the bed. She hadn't realized they'd moved to stand beside it, but she was grateful. Her legs wobbled and when she lay down her head stopped spinning. He leaned over her, unpinning the front of her simple dress. For a moment she looked up at his figure above her and thought of another time and another man towering over her.

As though sensing her distress, Jasper slid down beside her, propping his head on his elbow. "Better?"

She nodded.

"Where was I?"

"The pins."

He reached for the bodice again and held up a pin. "Last one." His fingers lowered the fabric of her dress, and she closed her eyes.

***

Her chest rose and fell almost as though she'd been running. Though her dress was modest, now that Jasper had the bodice lowered, he could see the swells of her breasts rising above her stays and chemise. Her skin was creamy against the dingy material of her underclothes. If she was his, he would buy her a soft new chemise and stays with pink ribbons so he could take his time tying and untying them. As it was, her stays were easy to open. They laced in front, which was a welcome change from those he remembered, which laced in back. But then she hadn't had a servant to help her dress. All of her clothing was practical. He would have dressed her in impractical lacy concoctions.

He'd never paid much attention to women's clothing before, but he would have liked to see something besides brown and gray on Olivia. She wasn't yet five and twenty. She should be wearing blue and yellow and green.

He pushed the stays open and slid them down slightly, leaving only the chemise blocking his access to her flesh. A string tied in a bow kept it cinched, and that was easily undone. Now it was simply a matter of tugging the thin material of the chemise down. He could already see the outline of her breast beneath, the hard points of her nipples straining. He lowered the fabric, revealing the swells of her breasts but pausing just above the aureoles. Looking up, he studied her face—eyes closed, lips parted, cheeks flushed. "May I keep going?"

She bit her lip, nodding. It seemed almost as though his actions pained her. Jasper vowed to have her crying out in pleasure before long. He kissed the soft roundness of her breasts, first one then the other. She was warm and smelled of the sea and woman. Her skin was impossibly soft, and he half feared to hurt her with his rough stubble.

And then he tugged the remainder of the material down, exposing her, and he forgot his reservations.

She was small, but firm and round. Her pink nipples were like blush-colored berries in the center of a dollop of cream. He couldn't stop himself from taking one in his mouth and sucking ever so lightly. Her hands slid into his hair, and he had no doubt she wanted him right where he was, doing exactly what he was doing. It was no hardship to tease and cup and suck the velvet flesh. He liked the sounds she made when he circled her aureoles. He liked the way she bucked when he took a swollen nipple into his mouth and rolled it over his tongue before sucking until her hips rose from the bed.

Her face was pink now, her eyes half-lidded. Jasper kissed her neck again, just behind her ear. One hand fondled a breast, unable to cease touching her. "I can give you pleasure," he murmured. She took a breath and exhaled shakily. "Can I show you?"

She turned her head, and her eyes, so large and dark he couldn't even discern her pupils, met his. "You'll stop if…"

"Whenever you want."

He slid the hand on her breast down to her ribs. Her eyes seemed to glitter and in the candlelit room, shadows danced on her skin and her clothing. His hand slid down further, into those shadows, brushing over her center. She made a small sound, but he kept going until he caught hold of her skirts. Slowly, he tugged them up, his gaze never leaving hers. Finally, his fingertips brushed flesh. He stilled, allowing her to become used to his touch on her thigh. "May I continue?"

Her eyes searched his. "Yes."

He cupped her thigh with his hand, the flesh warm and giving to his touch. "You are so soft." His fingers inched higher. "Like silk." He slid his hand between her legs, parting them slightly. The air whooshed out of her lips, and he kept his gaze steady on hers. "Do you like this?"

She bit her lip. "I don't know if I should."

He wrinkled his brow. "If you don't, I'm doing something wrong."

"I like it," she whispered. His hand skated up her inner thighs until he felt the soft curls of her center brush his knuckles.

"I think you'll like this more." He lowered his mouth to hers, kissing her gently and tangling his fingers in her hair until he found her folds. She was slick with desire for him, and he slipped between them to rest two fingers against the heat of her.

He pulled back and looked down at her, not moving his hand, allowing her to become used to the feel of it between her legs. "There's a little place here." He moved one finger up until he found the rounded nub he sought. When he grazed it, she made a choked sound. "And if I tease that little nub, touch it, caress it"—he tapped the bud with his fingertip—"it will bring you to climax."

"Does it hurt?" she asked.

He swallowed and stilled. "You've never climaxed before?"

"I don't know."

He let out a breath. "You would know. And, no, it doesn't hurt. It feels…better than almost anything. Can I show you?"

She nodded, and he began to circle her bud with his thumb, moving his fingers into her folds. Her breathing sped up and he couldn't help but glance down at the rise and fall of her breasts, her nipples peaking and red from his attentions and her arousal. Her legs relaxed, opened slightly, and then she realized what she'd done and clamped them closed again.

"You'll like it more if you open your legs," he murmured. "Go ahead. I can't see."

She hesitated and then her legs fell open. He slid a finger up and over her, wetting her until she was slick, and then he gently massaged her with his thumb. His finger dipped inside her, just a fraction of an inch, teasing her. Her hips rose, and he entered her to the knuckle, sliding in and out as his thumb continued its ministrations. Her breath was short and punctuated by moans now. Her hands clawed the bed as she strained. Her muscles clamped briefly around his finger, and he withdrew it, coming back with two fingers to stroke the heat and wetness of her. He wanted to kiss her, but her head twisted from side to side as he rocked his fingers inside her and kept up the relentless teasing of her nub.

And then she cried out and stiffened. Her body tightened, squeezing his fingers. She lifted her hips, grinding against his hand as she cried out again and again. He could see that she struggled for control, saw that it was beyond her, and enjoyed watching her give it up for the pleasure. She seemed to ride every last wave of it, arching her back so he could take a thick nipple in his mouth and suck. She cried out again before her body finally began to relax and loosen its grip on him. He'd stopped moving his thumb, pressing it against her instead, but not before he flicked it gently across her. She jumped and moaned, and Jasper looked up at her, mouth still on her breast.

"And now you know what it feels like to climax."

She looked down at him with eyes all but clouded over from pleasure. "You look like sin incarnate," she said.

"There's a reason people keep sinning. Even when they know it's wrong, it feels so very right."

He grazed her bud again, and she whimpered.

"More?" he asked, licking the curve of her breast.

"If I say yes, I'll never go back to my room. I've already left Richard alone too long."

If it she had been another woman, Jasper would have convinced her to stay and would have made it exceedingly worth the sacrifice. Instead, he pulled back, lowered her skirts, and with a last kiss, covered her chest. "I'll walk you back to your room," he said as she sat up, slowly straightening her clothing.

She nodded, looking dazed and flushed and thoroughly rumpled. "It's just across the hall."

"And I'll stand outside to make certain your door is locked."

She didn't argue. They still didn't know who had been behind the attack on Jasper and couldn't know whether they'd been followed when they left Penbury. Neither of them were taking any chances. Her fingers shook as she laced and pinned her clothing into place. It was badly done, but when she yanked her spencer on, the sad state of her bodice was hidden. It was too bad, really. He liked seeing her rumpled. She looked even more lovely to him when her hair was mussed and her eyes heavy-lidded.

He walked her back to her room, waited for her to unlock the door, then checked the room to be certain all was as it should be. It was, and he went back to the hallway to wait for her to lock it.

She'd half closed the door before he grasped it with a hand. "Olivia."

"Yes?"

"Next time I'll use my tongue." He released the door and pulled it closed on her shocked expression. It took a few moments, but he finally heard her fumbling with the lock. With a smile, Jasper went back to his room.

Thirteen

She could hardly look at him the next morning. Every time she caught his eye, she flushed, thinking of his mouth on her breast and his hands…

Finally, when she and Richard were in the coach and he on the box, she allowed her thoughts to roam. What had he done to her? How did he know how to do that? Probably better if she didn't try to find the answer to that question. Probably better if she didn't allow herself to keep thinking the next: when would he do it again?

He was a wicked man. She wasn't so innocent as not to understand his last comment. Surely the Church frowned on that sort of behavior. Just as surely, if it felt even half as good as his tongue on her nipple felt, she could hardly wait. She could think of little else, eager for the day to pass so they could stop at another inn and she could go to his room and—

"Mama, you are not listening at all."

"What was that, darling?" Olivia blinked at her son, who sat across from her, his face all but pressed to the glass as he studied the passing landscape.

"I said, there's a hare. You missed it!"

"Are you certain it was a hare? They don't usually come out this time of day."

"I miss Clover," he said, apropos of nothing. "Do you think she misses us?"

"I think she has lots of children to fawn over her and feed her apples and carrots. She's probably grown as fat as a house."

He giggled and jumped onto her lap. "Mama, it's only been one day."

"Oh, well, then tomorrow she'll be as fat as a house."

He rested his cheek against her shoulder. "What are my grandmother and grandfather like? Are they kind or strict?"

She smiled at his use of that word. She'd tried to teach him his letters and numbers and when he wouldn't listen, she'd told him she would have to act strictly, like her governesses had done. He loved hearing stories about her governesses and tutors. In his mind, nothing was worse than strictness. How she wished he would believe that forever.

"Your grandparents are…" How to describe them? "They are kind and loving." They had always been that way when she'd been a child. She'd been their only child and they hadn't spoiled her, but they'd doted on and pampered her.

"Then why did you go away?"

"Because…" How to explain to a child her parents' insistence she marry the Duke of Withernsea?

She'd always understood she would marry a man of their choosing, and she hadn't argued when they'd told her their choice. That was until she'd spent a little time with the duke. He'd scared her. At first it was the way he looked at her, as though she were a horse or a piece of art he was inspecting, not a person, not the woman who would become his wife. And then he'd begun to say things that disgusted her. She tried to avoid being alone with him, but she couldn't refuse when he asked her to dance at balls. He always chose sets where they would have time to converse, and then he'd make lewd comments and promises about what he would do to her when she was his.

At first, she'd told her parents she didn't feel comfortable with the duke and needed more time before the wedding. But as the months passed and the duke became more impatient, she was forced to admit she didn't want to marry him. When her parents insisted, citing the betrothal contract, she confided in her mother some of what the duke had said. The viscountess had looked shocked.

Olivia had thought that the end of it. But then her father had come to her and told her that when she was a wife, these things would not be so shocking. The viscountess had looked pale as her husband spoke, but she hadn't said anything. Later Olivia learned her father had spoken to the duke. Withernsea had been angry about it, and he'd taken that anger out on Olivia when he'd managed to corner her alone at a ball.

Now, she looked at her sweet son. "I ran away because there was a bad man, and I was scared of him."

"Is the bad man still there?"

She nodded. "Yes, but I'm not scared of him any longer."

"Jasper says he won't let anything happen to us."

She hugged Richard tighter. "He won't. He's a man of his word. You can trust him.

"Mama?"

"Yes?"

Richard hesitated. "Is my father in London?"

She knew she would have to tell him at some point, but how was she to tell him his father was the man she'd been fleeing? That was something she'd rather not reveal until he was much older. "No," she said. And it was true. Withernsea had never been a father to Richard. And she would be certain he never met his son. She didn't think he had any legal rights to the child, but she didn't want to take a chance.

"Mama, can Jasper be my father?"

She swallowed. She'd been ready for the question and even thought about what she would say. It would be something about how Jasper was only a friend, and any man who would be Richard's father would have to marry her.

But after last night, she couldn't pretend to herself that she didn't have feelings for Jasper. That she wanted more than friendship from him.

"I don't know," she finally answered, because it seemed the most truthful. "He would have to marry me."

Richard sat forward and looked at her. "Why don't you just ask him to marry you then?"

"It's not that easy," she said with a laugh. "And gentlemen are supposed to ask, not ladies."

"Oh." He slumped, and she rubbed his back.

"I know you want a father, darling, but let me introduce you to your grandparents first. You will be very busy getting to know them."

"Yes, Mama."

Richard had had so few people in his life that she could understand his desperation for more. She had begun to think that perhaps she and Jasper had a future, but nothing was certain and she didn't want to give Richard false hope.

She took her time when they stopped for lunch, arguing with Jasper that Richard needed more time to stretch his legs. Jasper, black mask in place, didn't seem convinced. He tapped his foot impatiently and paced before the carriage. Olivia didn't fear his anger any more. He might not like having to slow his progress, but she didn't think he'd take it out on her.

"At this rate, we won't reach London until afternoon tomorrow," he said, arms crossed over his chest.

"That sounds perfect." She smiled and waved at Richard who was romping in a field with a puppy who lived at the posting house.

"We could have made it tonight."

She gave him a sidelong look. "Perhaps I'd rather spend one more night at an inn."

"Are you nervous about seeing your parents again?"

"Yes, but that's not it."

"Then why?"

She started for the field to begin the process of cajoling Richard back into the coach. He really did need time to run and play. But she glanced over her shoulder as she walked. "I like the company in the inns."

A slow smile spread over his face.

***

Jasper was known at the inn they stopped at for the final night. She should have expected he would be as they were close to London now, and his mask was rather conspicuous. It meant she ate with Richard in her room while Jasper ate in the public rooms with his acquaintances. He'd introduced her as Mrs. Collins, a widow he was escorting to London. No one had looked at her twice. Perhaps it would be the same in Town. Perhaps no one remembered her.

She read to Richard for a long time before he finally fell asleep, and then because the room beside theirs, the one Jasper had taken, was still silent, she brushed her hair and changed into her night rail and robe. But she didn't go to sleep. If tonight was to be their last night on the road, she wanted to spend it with Jasper. Who knew what would happen in London? She might never have another minute alone with him.

Finally, as her eye lids were beginning to droop, she heard the door in the room beside theirs open and close. She glanced at Richard, but he was sleeping with his arms thrown over his head, like he had when he'd been an infant. She went to her door, reached for the latch, then hesitated. Did she really plan to go to a man's room? What did she think would happen if she knocked and he allowed her inside?

She knew what would happen. That was why she stood at the door. That was why she'd been waiting for him to come upstairs.

She knew Jasper wouldn't come to her. No matter what she'd intimated this afternoon, he wouldn't expect anything of her. He'd showed her not all men were like Withernsea. She'd known that, deep down, but she'd been so angry and so betrayed she hadn't wanted to trust again. But Jasper's patience and vulnerability had won her over. And even though she was eager to see her parents, something else she never thought she would feel again, she mourned each mile closer to London. She might very well lose Jasper once they returned to Town. He had a life there that might not have room for her or the scandal that accompanied her, and once she was under her parents' protection, she would have to respect their decisions. Perhaps they would not think Jasper suitable.

She opened her door, looked right and left, and stepped into the empty corridor. She raised her hand to knock on Jasper's door, but he opened it before she had the opportunity. "What are you doing out of your room?"

"I…" She didn't know how to answer him. All she knew was she wanted to see him.

"Come inside before someone sees you." He widened his door and stepped aside. She scooted inside and he closed the door behind her. Quite suddenly, she second-guessed her decision. He wasn't wearing his shirt or his mask, and he stood closer than she was prepared for. She stepped back, only to feel the door press into her. Jasper put a hand on the door's frame. "What's wrong?"

She shook her head. It was difficult to think of words when he was this close to her. His hazel eyes looked green in the dim light of the candles and though she could see his scar, it didn't detract at all from his handsomeness. His scent of smoke and clean soap enveloped her, and she closed her eyes and inhaled.

"You can tell me," he said, obviously misunderstanding her expression. "Is it Richard?"

"He's asleep," she said. "It was no easy feat considering how excited he is to arrive in London tomorrow."

"Why aren't you asleep? Too excited?"

She shook her head.

"Worried?"

"Of course, but…" She should just say it. She'd regret it for the rest of her life if she didn't say it. She looked into his eyes. "I'll miss you."

His brows actually came together in confusion. "I won't abandon you."

"I know. But it won't be like it has been. I won't have time alone with you."

His gaze traveled to her lips then he determinedly brought it back to her eyes. "As I've explained, that's probably for the best. They'll be enough talk without the *ton* assuming something untoward between us."

She fought the urge to view his words as a rejection. If she did so, she might as well walk back out the door she'd just come in. But if he'd meant them as a rejection why did he look as though he wanted to kiss her? Why did he not move away from her?

"It may be for the best, but it's not until tomorrow. Untoward as it is, I want to spend part of the night with you."

His eyes darkened, but he didn't speak.

"Should I go back to my room?"

He nodded. "Yes."

Without hesitating, she turned and reached for the latch. His hand covered hers before she could lift it. "Not yet," he whispered next to her ear.

She shivered. "When?"

"After I do this." He lifted her hair and brushed it over her shoulder, then lowered his lips to graze her neck. Her hand tightened on the latch at the rush of pleasure. His lips moved over her skin, creating delicious spirals of warmth. She curled her toes and let her head fall back to give him greater access. A soft moan escaped her lips, and it was a sound she knew she should have been embarrassed to make, but she couldn't quite make herself care. All she cared about was the feel of Jasper's lips.

When he pulled back, she turned her head to look at him, to look at his soft lips that gave her so much pleasure. "Shall I leave now?"

"After this." He repeated his ministrations on the other side of her neck, this time moving the collar of the robe to press his lips to the patch of skin where her neck and shoulder met. Finally, she couldn't resist any further and she turned to face him. He pulled her close, and she wrapped her arms about him and lifted her lips to graze his. He kissed her back and everything inside her seemed to melt until she wasn't sure where she ended and he began. The kiss deepened and she clung more tightly until suddenly Jasper drew back.

"I'm sorry."

She pulled his mouth back to hers, needing the connection between them. "Don't stop."

He kissed her again, and she returned his passion with her own. Her hands roamed over his shoulders, down his back, along his muscled arms. Touching him was amazing. His skin was sleek and muscled under her fingertips. His flesh was hot and the more she ran her fingers over him, the more fervent his kisses until finally he pushed her back against the door and pulled away, lowering his head onto her shoulder and breathing heavily.

"Why did you stop?" She slid her hands to his chest, and he grasped her wrists and stilled her.

"I need a moment." His breathing was ragged and harsh.

"Have I done something wrong?" She shrank back now. She'd felt so safe and free, but perhaps she'd gone too far. She'd done something she shouldn't have.

"No." He tightened his grip on her wrists momentarily then looked into her eyes. "You've done nothing wrong."

"Did I make you lose control?" That was what Withernsea had said when, after he'd taken his pleasure, she lay crying on the cold floor. He'd blamed her, said she made him lose control.

Jasper furrowed his brow. "No. No one can ever *make* someone else lose control. You're beautiful and—I won't lie—I want you. But I am in control of my own actions, just as you are in control of your own actions."

"But Withernsea said—" She clamped her mouth shut. She hadn't meant to say his name. "I thought men were different. I thought they could reach a point where they lost all power over their desires."

"That's a lie told by someone who wants to blame someone else for his bad behavior. Nothing you could ever do would force me to lose control of my own actions."

She took a deep breath, and it was almost as though this was the first deep breath she'd taken in a long, long time. She'd felt so guilty all these years, as though she had done something to cause Withernsea to rape her. But what Jasper said made sense. And he certainly proved it with his own behavior.

"Then why did you stop?" she asked.

He smiled. "You want me to kiss you again."

"Yes!" she answered truthfully.

"I stopped because the rules changed. Before you didn't want me to kiss you with my tongue. I made the mistake of doing so, but you told me to go on. You kissed me back." He ran a finger along her cheek. "With your tongue."

"I'm sorry," she whispered.

"Why? I liked it. But I want to be certain you like it."

"I do. Before…I couldn't. It's different now."

"Very well."

She wrapped her arms around his shoulders. "Can you kiss me again now?"

"Eager." He brushed his lips over hers. "I like that. But I have one more question."

She blew out a breath.

He seemed to be trying not to smile. "What do you want from me tonight?"

Her cheeks burned. Did she really have to say it aloud? "Nothing. I should go back to my room." She started to pull away.

"There's nothing wrong with desire, Olivia. I like that you want me. I just want to be clear as to what you want."

"What do you want?"

"I want you to feel pleasure. I want you to feel safe with me. I want you to think back on tonight and smile."

His words made her skin burn hotter. But he didn't look away from her. He gave her no reprieve from her mortification. "I don't know what to say," she whispered.

"Start by telling me what you don't want."

She swallowed. "I don't want…I don't want to do—" She waved her hand. "The act that produces babies."

"Then we won't do that. What else?"

"I don't want you to hold me down."

"Never." He brushed his lips over hers again, his touch light. "What else?"

"I don't know."

"Can I undress you?"

Lord, she would burst from the embarrassment. "No." She looked away from his intense hazel eyes. "You could do…like the other night."

"Can I undress?"

"You are undressed!"

"I'll take that as a no. Can we go to the bed?"

She nodded.

He took her hand. "Say the words, Olivia. I want to be sure."

"Yes."

With a gentle tug, he led her to the bed. When they were at the end, he toed off his boots and laid on the coverlet, head propped on his elbow. "Want to join me?"

Shyly, she sat on the edge. Then, when he didn't attack her—not that she'd expected him to—she lay back and looked up at him.

He smiled down at her, smoothing her hair from her brow. "I thought you were a rum-dutchess when I first saw you."

"What's that mean?"

"It means handsome. I look at you now and can't believe you're here with me.

She could only imagine as she probably looked disheveled from their kisses and tired from traveling. "You're a very handsome man. I'm sure you've known many handsome women."

"None as beautiful as you."

"You're delusional."

"No, I'm not." He kissed her brow then her nose then her eyes. She giggled. Her cheeks and her lips were next. "To me you are the most beautiful woman I've ever seen."

She cupped his face. He flinched but allowed it. Perhaps she too should ask what was allowed. "To me, you are the most handsome man."

He gave her a dubious look.

"You are, Jasper!"

He shook his head. "I have another question for you. The bed is fine. You want to stay clothed—mostly clothed." He winked. "Can I touch you?"

She wanted to point out they were already touching. His body was warm against hers. But she knew he meant could he touch her intimately, as he had the night before. And, of course, that was why she was here—not entirely, but she certainly wanted that feeling again. "Yes," she said. "I want you to touch me."

"Where can I touch you? Your face?"

She nodded.

"Your neck?"

"Mmm-hmm."

"Your breasts?"

Heat, part embarrassment and part arousal, shot through her. "Yes. Everywhere." Anything to stop him from detailing every part of her body.

"That's quite a lot of license."

I trust you, she thought, but didn't say. "Can I touch you?"

He grinned. "I'd be disappointed if you didn't."

"Everywhere?" she asked.

"Yes." His look almost dared her. Did she have the courage to touch him *there*? He didn't seem to think so. She wasn't so certain either.

"Are we done talking now? Can you kiss me again?"

"About that—"

She groaned.

"Where can I kiss you?"

Oh, Lord. Not this again.

"Can I kiss your lips?"

"Everywhere, Jasper. Kiss me everywhere. Just kiss me." And to end the conversation there and then she grasped his head and brought his lips to hers. He kissed her. He kissed her so thoroughly she was all but breathless. And he touched her. His hands were everywhere, warm and gentle and making her squirm with pleasure. It had been easy for him to part her robe and loosen the ties holding her night rail closed. She felt his lips on her breasts, and she arched her back in pleasure. When his hand moved up her leg, rubbing her knee, caressing her thigh, then stroking that juncture between her legs, she wasn't afraid. She parted her legs for him. She wanted this, wanted him.

She wanted to touch him. The thought surprised her, but she didn't dwell on it. Instead, she slid her hand from his hard abdomen to the waistband of his trousers. His mouth was still on her breast, but he paused in his sucking, obviously curious as to what she would do.

She'd thought she'd be afraid of his member. She knew the pain it could cause her, but she wasn't fearful. She dropped her hand lower and felt the hard length of him. In wonder, she drew back.

He looked up at her. "You don't have to touch me."

She knew he thought she'd been frightened or disgusted. "It's not that," she said. "I didn't realize it would be so hard or so big."

His mouth twitched. "If you were anyone else, I'd think you were trying to flatter me."

She gaped at him. "You take that as a compliment?"

"It's a compliment to you."

"How?"

"You have a son, so you know men don't walk about in this condition all the time. I'm hard and…er, big because I want you. I'm attracted to you. I like being with you."

"What will happen if I touch you again?"

"Nothing."

"What if I reached inside and touched it?"

"Nothing you don't want to happen will happen. No matter what you do."

She slid her hand to his waistband again. "May I?"

He closed his eyes as though reaching for control. "Yes. Do you want me to lay back?"

She shook her head. "You can keep…doing what you're doing."

He laughed. "You like it, do you?" She blushed, but before she could duck her head, he caught her chin. "If you like it, tell me. It's not wrong to like it. That's the whole idea."

"I like it," she whispered.

He kissed her breast again, and she slid a hand inside the waist of his trousers. He was right there, the head of his member lying flush with the waistband. She explored the head, the velvet skin that felt as though it had been stretched over steel.

"I like that," he murmured against her nipple.

Her hand slid down, feeling the hard length of him. He was hot, and she felt the blood pulsing against her palm where she touched him.

"You can stroke me, if you want," he murmured, taking her nipple in his mouth. She didn't have much room to move her hand, but she tried. He let out a slow, shuddering breath, making her skin pucker deliciously. She slid up and down his length again, and as she did so, his hand cupped her sex and one finger slid inside. She let out a soft moan.

"Yes?" he asked.

"Yes," she breathed. He stroked her, matching his movements to hers on him. She finally understood how the act that had produced Richard could have been. How it should have been. As her body reacted to his touch, she wished she'd told him to undress. She could change her mind now. What would it feel like to have his naked body pressed against hers?

"I made a suggestion last night," he said, his lips moving to brush against her earlobe.

She shivered. "What was that?"

"I think you remember."

How could she forget? "Your tongue," she said.

"That's right." His finger slid out of her then up and over that sensitive place. "Right here."

She gasped. "What's wrong with this way?"

"Not a thing, but if you agree, I'll show you the other way and you can judge for yourself."

She swallowed. It seemed rather indecent to allow him to put his mouth between her legs. Of course, if she had been acting in the way Society considered *decent*, she wouldn't be half naked, sprawled on his bed with his hand up her skirts and hers down his trousers. She'd enjoyed everything he'd done so far…

"Shall I?" he asked.

"If I don't like it?"

"Tell me to stop."

He slid down her body, and she withdrew her hand. He rose to his knees then moved between her legs, parting them wider. "I have to lift your skirts a bit more," he said. As he spoke, he ran a hand between her breasts, his gaze on her making her hot and excited. The way he looked at her was both full of desire and reverence. "May I?" he asked.

"Yes."

He pushed her skirts up, bending to touch his lips to her thighs as he did so. She grasped the coverlet with her hands to keep from wriggling. Finally, she felt the hem trail over her hips, and she knew she was exposed to him. He paused in his kissing and glanced at her face. "May I look at you?"

She nodded.

"The words, love. I want no confusion. Can I spread your legs and look at you?"

"Yes."

He nudged her legs open, his movements gentle but firm. Then she felt his hands on her sex, opening her. "You're perfect." One finger slid inside her again, and she tensed as the pleasure zinged through her. "Pink and wet."

The more he talked, the more he looked, the more the pleasure inside her built. He slid his finger out. "Don't come yet, love. If you wait, it will be even better."

She tightened her hands on the covers she'd clenched as he bent and pressed his lips to the curls between her legs. She jerked at first then settled as she became used to the feel of him. But then he moved lower, his tongue tracing her folds. She moaned and bucked as he licked her.

"Not yet," he said. She bit her lips, her body beginning to shake as he opened her with his fingers then licked his way to that small bud he'd found the night before. White hot pleasure flashed through her, and she couldn't stop the moan this time. She couldn't stop the way her hips rolled or her nipples ached.

"Patience, love," he whispered, his breath hot against her. He licked her, teased her, circled her, and she knew she was being too loud, but she couldn't control the sounds coming from her. He'd been right. This was better. She didn't know the words to describe how good this was. Her hands fisted in his hair as his head moved up and down then side to side as he pleasured her. Finally, he slid his hands under her hips, raised her to him as though she was a feast for his taking. She didn't have any patience left. She let go and felt as though she were flying. Her body shook and trembled and she knew she had to bite off a scream. It was so wonderful, so absolutely amazing.

She didn't know how she would ever stop herself from loving him now.

Fourteen

She'd completely unraveled in his arms, and he'd loved it. He loved the taste of her. He loved the feel of her in his arms, against his mouth. He loved looking at her. Her hard, rosy nipples had turned red as cherries and puckered right before she'd come. And the look on her face. God, he'd thought her beautiful before. He'd do anything to see that look again.

Now he slid up beside her. Her eyes were closed, her breath coming in gasps, her breasts rising and falling with each one. He cupped one, and she jerked, her eyes opening. "You liked that," he said, fondling her soft flesh. It wasn't a question. He'd known she'd like it. Though he hadn't expected her to come so easily. She'd been ready to climax from just his gaze on her.

"It was…I don't know."

"Yes," he said. He bent to take her cherry-red nipple in his mouth. When he sucked lightly, she moaned as though helpless to the pleasure of it. "Will you let me do it again?"

"Again?" Her voice was almost a screech. "I couldn't possibly…"

He slid a hand down and cupped her.

"*Oh.*" Her hips rocked slightly, pressing her center against his palm. He sucked harder on her nipple and she shuddered.

"Will you let me pleasure you again?"

She swallowed, and he thought she might refuse. But when she looked at him, her eyes were large with desire. "On one condition."

"Anything."

She sat and allowed her robe to fall from her shoulders then she pulled the night rail over her head so she was completely naked. She saw his look and her cheeks turned pink. She started to cover herself, but he grasped her hands.

"I like looking at you, and you like me looking."

She gave a slight nod and lowered her hands. "Before I said I wanted to stay dressed."

"You're allowed to change your mind. You're allowed to tell me *stop* or *more* or *yes, yes, yes*."

She closed her eyes at the echo of how she'd sounded just a few minutes ago.

"Lay back," he said.

She opened her eyes, and the dark blue irises glittered. She lay back. "Now what?"

"Your turn to give me an order."

"Kiss me…"

He kissed her, exploring her mouth for a long, long time. When he pulled back, she shook her head. "You're not done."

"No? You said to kiss you."

"You didn't let me finish."

"Go on then."

"Kiss me…everywhere."

He obliged her.

***

At some point before dawn she rose, dressed, and he made sure she was safely back inside her room with the door locked. He lay on his bed with the intention of sleeping for a few hours, but the bed smelled like her. It smelled like the two of them. His cock was still hard. She touched him again, stroked him, but she hadn't wanted to go further. He'd take whatever she was willing to give him. And if she hadn't even been willing to allow him to touch her, he would have still wanted to spend the night with her.

What did it mean? He had a suspicion it meant he felt a hell of a lot more for her than mere affection. And that was too damn bad because tomorrow they'd be back in London and that would be the end of these late night rendezvous. She'd be home with her parents. He'd watch over initially and stay as close as possible. It went without saying that he'd have a few words with Withernsea to ensure the duke stayed well away from her. And then eventually she wouldn't need him any longer. He'd go back to his life in the rookeries and she'd go back to raising her son. One day her father would probably find her an acceptable man to marry, and Jasper would read about it in the papers. Someone else would be touching her, kissing her, making her gasp. Someone without a ruined face and a scarred past and a profession that meant he spent an inordinate time in bawdy houses and flash kens and ended up talking like the rogues and doxies half the time. Olivia thought he was a gentleman, and he'd been born a gentleman, but he'd long since forgotten how to be one.

Except with her. It had been easy to slip back into the formal speech and the proscribed manners with her. But that wasn't who he was. And when she realized that, she wouldn't want him.

He must have dozed off at some point because he awoke to a pounding on his door. Jasper rose, hastily donned his mask, and stumbled to the door. He opened it, a harsh word on his tongue, but bit it back when he saw Richard bounding on the threshold.

"It's morning!" Richard hurled himself at Jasper, giving him no choice but to catch the lad. "Can we go now? Can we?"

"I have to dress first." Jasper set the boy down and pulled his shirt over his head. His wound still gave a twinge of pain once in a while, but he largely ignored it.

Richard grabbed his hand and tugged. "Let's go."

"Where is your mother?"

"Dressing. She said to fetch you."

He didn't doubt it. She'd probably sent the boy out and crawled back under her covers. They were close to Town, and there was no hurry. He'd give her time to sleep. "Have you ever eaten in the public room at an inn?"

The boy shook his head. "No."

"You can't go to London without having done so at least once. Are you hungry?"

The boy nodded vigorously. Jasper pulled on his coat and boots. "Let's go then."

After a hearty breakfast and a visit to the stables so the boy could see all the horses, Olivia was dressed and ready. She didn't look as though she hadn't slept, though she looked pretty. Her cheeks were flushed and her eyes bright. Jasper realized she was probably nervous to see her parents again after so many years.

It was an easy drive to London, and once they were a few miles out, Jasper allowed Richard to sit on the box with him so the boy might see all the city had to offer. He wondered what the capital must look like to this child who'd spent his entire life on a remote seaside cliff. To him she looked as dirty and squalid as always. Smoke hung around her buildings and streets, making the city look gray from a distance. It was gray inside as well. Limestone and marble buildings that had once been white had turned dingy and sooty over the years. The streets were muddy and packed closely with carts, carriages, and horses. Men and children weaved between the conveyances with seemingly little care for their lives. Others moved like ant colonies along the sidewalks. The sounds and smells were a dissonant cacophony to the senses. The scent of freshly baked bread mingled with the contents of the chamber pot thrown from a window. The city always hummed with the sound of wheels, horses, and low voices, and above it all rose the shouts of hawkers calling, "Juicy red apples!" and "Ha'penny for a posy!"

Richard's eyes were wide as he took it all in, but Jasper noted the boy had also slid closer to him and placed his hand on Jasper's leg as though needing to feel connected to someone or something safe. "My grandmother and grandfather live here?" he asked as Jasper turned down Piccadilly.

"Not far now. They live in Mayfair." Jasper might have taken a faster route to the town house, but he enjoyed pointing out the sights and shops he'd loved when he'd been a child—Green Park, the Serpentine in Hyde Park, the shops in Old Bond Street, Gunter's Tea Shop. Finally, he made his way to Brook Street and stopped the carriage before Viscount Carlisle's home.

The child looked at the whitewashed building with its flowers spilling from window boxes. "Is this another inn?"

"No." Jasper swung him down. "This is the residence of Viscount Carlisle, your grandfather." He opened the door to the carriage and helped Olivia stepped down. Her hand shook in his. "I'm right here," he said quietly.

She clutched his hand tightly. "You'll stay, won't you?"

He nodded, though the decision was her father's, not his. With a smile and cheeriness he knew must be forced, Olivia released him and bent to look Richard in the eyes. "Shall we go and knock on the door?"

But Richard had suffered a sudden attack of shyness, and he lifted his arms for her to pick him up. She did, holding him tightly, while he buried his face in her shoulder. Jasper walked behind them, and when Richard raised his head to peek at him, Jasper stuck out his tongue. The boy giggled. Jasper knocked on the door, sparing Olivia the awkwardness of knocking and holding Richard, and then the three of them stood in silence.

"What if they're not at home?" Olivia whispered.

"The knocker is on the door," he answered. "They're home."

She hoisted Richard higher, attempting to secure her hold. "Do I look well enough? I tried not to muss my hair in the coach." Her dark blue eyes were wide and concerned.

"You look like a rum-dutchess."

"I seem to recall that's a good thing."

He heard footsteps inside. "A very good thing."

Finally, the door opened, and an elderly butler blinked at them. He looked at Jasper, then Olivia, then Richard, whose face was still hidden. And then he almost crumpled.

"Oh, dear Lord."

***

Olivia would have recognized Dimsdale anywhere. She'd known him since she'd been Richard's age and he'd come to work for the family as an underbutler. Seeing him now made her feel every single year she'd been away. His dark hair had thinned so he had a bald patch on the top and his kind eyes seemed smaller. And though he was still taller than she, his shoulders looked thin and stooped. He staggered at the sight of her. "Is it really you?" he asked, hand to his heart.

"It is, Dimsdale. May we come in?"

"Of course!" He moved aside then fluttered his hands, apparently forgetting to close the door. "I should announce you. Your father…oh, but your mother—"

"Take a moment, Dimsdale," she said, trying to keep her voice calm. Funny how seeing his disorientation had relieved her of her nervousness.

"Why don't you show us to a parlor or the drawing room?" Jasper asked. "Then the viscount can come to us when he's ready."

"Yes." Dimsdale nodded. "That's right. Yes." He led them up the stairs she had scampered up and down a thousand times as a child. Olivia had to put Richard down because he was too heavy to carry upstairs. Her son went directly to Jasper who lifted him as though he weighed nothing. At the top of the stairs, Dimsdale opened the door to the drawing room and showed them in. "I will have the housekeeper send refreshments. You won't know her, Miss—er—Miss. She's new."

He left them alone, and Olivia turned to survey the room. "It looks different," she said. "It used to be done in the Grecian style, all white with gold braiding. I wasn't allowed to touch anything for fear my dirty little fingers would smudge something. I like this better." The furnishings had been reupholstered in bright colors—blues, greens, and deep yellows. She went to the window and pushed the heavy draperies aside. Still the same view of the street and the neighboring town houses.

"I'm hungry," Richard said, his voice beginning to take on that whiny tone that she knew meant he needed a nap. Jasper sat on a blue and white couch, and Richard sat on his knee. It was strange to see Jasper with his mask now that she'd grown used to seeing him without it. He felt like another person to her, not the man who'd lain with her the night before, teasing and torturing her until she dissolved into a puddle of satiated splendor.

"The housekeeper will bring tea and cakes in a few moments, darling." She tried not to look at Jasper for too long, but she wondered what he saw, what he thought when he looked at her. Did he remember her kneeling naked before him? Did he think about all the sounds she'd made when he touched her? She was mortified to think of it now, in her parents' home and in the light of day.

The door opened, and Olivia turned, expecting to see the housekeeper, but it wasn't her at all. Her father stood in the doorway. Olivia held her breath, staring at him with as much interest as he stared at her. She didn't know what he saw, but she saw a man who had grown old in five years. His hair was almost completely white now and the lines on his face had deepened. He still stood straight, his clothing tailored and crisp, but there was something defeated in his eyes. "It's you," he murmured. "You're really here."

Olivia blinked several times, surprised at the way his voice wavered. She'd always hoped her parents would greet her with open arms, the prodigal daughter returned home again. But now that her daydream was coming true, she wasn't certain what to do. Her father moved forward, his arms held wide. Olivia spared a glance at Richard and Jasper, but they were both watching her with interest.

And then she was in her father's arms again, her cheek pressed to his chest, and the familiar smell of his tobacco surrounding her. She couldn't help but let out a small hiccup as tears streamed down her cheeks. "Papa!"

"My dear. My darling. You're here. You're alive." He stroked her hair, his hands tender and light, almost as though he feared she might disappear at any moment.

"I'm here. I've missed you."

He pulled back and kissed her forehead. "Your mother has been ill. She isn't well enough to come down. You must come and see her." He took her hand, but she resisted. She looked at Jasper and Richard then took a shaky breath.

"Does she know I'm here?"

"Not yet. Come. Seeing you again is her fondest wish."

"Before we go, there's something I must tell you. It might be better if you don't tell her about me."

"But you're all she's talked about."

"Papa, I ran away because—"

"That doesn't matter, Olivia. Your mother and I made a mistake. We take the blame. We never should have tried to force you to marry the duke. You're home now, and that's all that matters. We have you to thank, my lord," he said with a nod at Jasper.

"But that's not all that matters." She looked at Richard and nodded to him. Jasper murmured something to the boy and gave him a little push toward Olivia. Richard walked slowly across the room, and as he did so, her father's eyes grew large. Finally, her son stood beside her. "My lord, allow me to introduce you to my son, Richard Carlisle."

She'd deliberately used the boy's surname, her own, to make it clear she had not married while away. This was her son, born out of wedlock.

Her father stared at Richard, and Olivia's heart clenched painfully. Richard's blue eyes met the viscount's, and the little boy looked so hopeful. *Please, God, don't let him say anything to hurt Richard.*

Slowly, very slowly, the viscount moved forward. He stood before Richard and held out his hand. "So you are my grandson?"

Richard nodded and whispered, "Yes, my lord."

"Your name is Richard?"

Richard nodded.

"We have something in common then."

"We do?" Richard smiled at her as if to ask if she knew what it could be.

"We do. My name is also Richard." The viscount held out a hand. "It is a pleasure to meet you, Richard."

Richard took the hand and giggled. "It's a pleasure to meet *you*, Richard!"

Olivia felt all the tension inside her float away, like a bubble on the breeze. But then she saw her father's face. He was close to tears.

She put a hand on her father's arm, and he took a breath, attempting to compose himself. "We will talk later. Now I want to take you to your mother."

"Shall I bring Richard?"

"Not this time," he said. He smiled at her son. "Perhaps later today or tomorrow when she's feeling a bit better."

"Mama?" Richard took her arm and held on tightly.

"I'll only be gone for a few minutes. Jasper will stay with you." She glanced at him, and he nodded. "And the housekeeper is on her way with treats. Don't eat them all before I return."

"Yes, Mama."

He ran back to Jasper and climbed on his lap. Olivia gave him a reassuring smile then followed her father out of the room. At the landing to the stairs leading up to the bed chambers, her father paused. "The boy is Withernsea's?"

Shame slammed through her. Her cheeks grew hot. "Yes."

"Does he know?"

"No. And I don't want him to know. I know you don't like lies, Papa, but I've told people I encounter I was married and my husband died."

He pressed his lips together. "I think it's best we stick to that story, though Withernsea is no fool. He can add and subtract."

"But he cannot be certain, and if he is kept away from Richard and me, it should not be a problem." She took a deep breath and forced her shoulders back. "If you can't support me in this, I will be forced to go."

She waited for his reaction. His gaze had slid away from her, and when it returned it was even more troubled than before. "He still wants you. I don't want you to leave again, Olivia, and I do support you. But if you're to stay, I will have to find a way to deal with the Duke of Withernsea."

Olivia grasped her father's hands and held them tightly. The love she felt for him in that moment warmed her throughout. She'd missed her parents and needed their love and support more than she'd wanted to admit. "I just want to stay away from the duke, Papa. If you will support me in this then I will stay. I'm done with running, and I'm not afraid of the duke anymore." Maybe if she said it enough it would be true.

"You have grown up," her father said with a smile. "I imagine you had no other choice. But I am here now, and I will take care of you. Leave the matter of the Duke of Withernsea to me." He didn't wait for her agreement but started up the stairs. "Your mother must be wondering where I am. Don't mention any of this to her. Not yet. You will understand why when you see her."

With a last look at the drawing room doors, Olivia followed her father up the stairs to the room that had always been her mothers. Even before she stepped inside she could smell death. She paused and grasped her father's sleeve. "Is she?"

"Not yet. You've come in time and seeing you might strengthen her." He opened the door and she followed him into the dark room. The curtains had been drawn and the lamps kept low, and it took her a moment before she could see the figure in the bed. When she did, she halted. Her mother was but a shell of the woman she'd been. Her once long, thick golden hair was now dull and brittle as straw. Her body had withered away so that it barely disturbed the bedclothes. Her eyes, dark blue like Olivia's own, looked too big for her gaunt face.

"My dear," her father began, moving closer to the bed. The nurse who had been sitting beside it stood and moved into a corner and out of the way. "I have a wonderful surprise for you."

"A new poem by that scamp Byron?" Her voice was weak and paper-thin.

"No, something even better. A visitor, actually." He motioned for Olivia to come closer. "Lord Jasper found her, my dear. He found our Olivia."

Olivia made her legs move, forced herself to stand beside what remained of her mother. She looked down and saw tears in her mother's eyes.

"Is it really you, Livvy?"

"Yes." She blinked back her own tears. "I'm here, Mama."

"Am I dreaming?" she looked at the viscount. "Is it our Livvy?"

"It's her. She's really here. She's come back."

The viscountess reached out a hand and Olivia took it. Her mother still had a great deal of strength, though her fingers were bony. "You will stay, Livvy? You won't go away again?"

"No, Mama. I will stay."

"And the duke? You will marry him now?"

Olivia tensed, her gaze darting to her father.

He shook his head slightly. "Let me worry about all of that, my dear. We have our Livvy back."

"Will you sit with my, Livvy? Will you read to me?"

"Of course." Olivia worried about Richard. She hadn't wanted to leave him alone so long immediately after arriving, but Jasper was with him. He would be fine. "Of course, Mama. What shall I read?"

"*Twelfth Night*, of course."

Of course. It was her mother's favorite of Shakespeare's plays. Olivia had been named after one of the characters. She took the seat beside the bed and lifted the book of Shakespeare's plays on the bedside table. She had to move various vials and medical implements to do so, but when she had it, she turned to the marked page. "'If music be the food of love,'" she began. "'Play on.'"

She continued through Duke Orsino's speech, but her mind was on her son, hoping Jasper was keeping him too busy to notice her absence.

Fifteen

"I'm not leaving," Jasper said, keeping his voice low so as not to cause a scene. Richard was playing with some toy soldiers one of the footmen had found, and Jasper didn't want him to hear. But the old butler wouldn't give up.

"My lord, the family appreciates your assistance, but his lordship has asked that I show the boy to the nursery the housekeeper prepared and see you out."

"I'm not leaving until I see Olivia."

"*Miss Carlisle* is with her ailing mother at the moment. They are not to be disturbed. Please do not make me fetch the viscount."

"This is not your day, Dimsdale. If you want me to leave, I need to hear it from the viscount's own lips."

"Very well." The butler turned on his heel and stormed away.

Jasper went back to the couch and sat. A plate of crumbs sat on the other cushion, the only remaining evidence of Richard's three tea cakes, and Richard played on the floor nearby.

When Dimsdale closed the door, Richard looked at Jasper. "Do you have to go?"

Jasper clenched his jaw. So the child had heard. "I'm sure your mother will be back shortly." She'd been gone far longer than he'd expected, but then what did he know of deathbed reunions?

Richard pushed the wooden soldiers away. "I don't want you to go."

"You are safe here, Richard. Lord Carlisle is your grandfather."

"But I want to be with you." He climbed into Jasper's lap. Why did distraction and changing topics work when Olivia tried it and not him? Was he doing it wrong?

"You know I don't live here. I can't stay."

"Then I'll go to your house."

"Your mother won't like that."

"She can come too."

Jasper took an instant to appreciate that idea. He rather liked it, until he remembered the sort of people he usually worked for and the visitors who often came knocking in the wee hours. Jasper often spent more time in the shadows of London than he did in his own rooms.

He'd never had a reason to want to be home before.

"Your mother belongs here. Besides, this isn't the last you'll see of me. I'm not so easy to be rid of." The night before he'd allowed himself to hope he would have more nights like that with Olivia, but now that he was back in London he saw those thoughts for the rubbish they were. How could he forget that he was a disfigured younger son who had gone into trade and sold his services? No decent noble family would want him as a suitor for their daughter.

The door opened again and the viscount walked in. He looked tired, and Jasper couldn't help but sympathize with the man. He'd had quite the day. "Lord Jasper," Carlisle said, his gaze lingering on Richard in Jasper's lap. It probably appeared strange to see a small boy clinging to a masked figure. "My butler said you wanted to speak with me before leaving. I'm certain you must want payment for your services."

Jasper's eyes narrowed. "I don't want payment."

The viscount's brows rose. "No?"

"Your daughter saved my life. I owe her more than I can ever repay."

"What's this? How did Olivia save your life?"

"I'll let her tell you, or we can ask her together. I won't leave without seeing her again."

The viscount shook his head. "She's with Lady Carlisle. The two haven't seen each other in years. I told her I would see Master Richard settled in the nursery myself. I'm certain you must be tired from your travels. Come back tomorrow and call on her."

Richard's hand tightened on Jasper's neck.

"I'd rather not leave the boy alone."

Carlisle's face tightened with impatience. "He won't be alone. I will be with him, and I have plenty of staff. Olivia will see to him as soon as my wife falls asleep. She sleeps a great deal these days."

"I'd rather—"

"Must I pull her from her mother's deathbed to ask you to leave? This is my house, Lord Jasper. I've asked you politely."

Jasper's jaw hurt from the effort at restraint. The viscount was correct. This was his house. Jasper had no right to be here. Olivia wasn't being held against her will. She needed time with her mother. The boy was fine. He might be a little frightened of the new place, but Jasper would not be leaving him without friends.

Slowly, he untangled Richard's arms from his neck.

"No!" the boy said, attempting to hold on.

"I have to go. I'll be back tomorrow."

"Don't go!"

Jasper set the lad on the floor and rose. "You will tell Miss Carlisle I plan to call tomorrow."

"Of course." Carlisle nodded.

Dimsdale appeared in the doorway, a smug smile on his face.

"Dimsdale will show you out."

Jasper had no choice but to follow the butler. He spared one look back for Richard. His grandfather was bent, speaking gently to the boy. But Jasper couldn't help but feel the child seemed very, very small.

***

Ten days later, he hadn't seen Olivia again. He'd come back to the townhouse every day and been told, every day, that she was not at home. He'd asked to see Richard and been told the boy was not at home. He knew they were both at home, and when he'd pushed his way in, the viscount had threatened to have his footmen throw Jasper out. Jasper could see now he'd misjudged the man. He'd thought him weak and easily swayed, but though he might be meek, he had an unbendable backbone. That must have been where Olivia inherited hers.

"Lord Jasper, I assure you the boy is fine. I've engaged a governess for him and his mother is with him as much as she is able. Right now she is with her mother. The viscountess is gravely ill. Surely you understand. I've sent payment to your solicitor. Our business is concluded."

Jasper had instructed his solicitor to tear up the payment Carlisle had sent. "I told you, I don't want payment."

"Then what do you want?" the viscount demanded.

What did he want? "I want to see Miss Carlisle and Richard again." He needed to see with his own eyes that they were well. Jasper hadn't suffered any additional attacks on his life since being back in London, but he wasn't taking any chances. Olivia might still be in danger. He'd promised to protect her, and, though he wasn't allowed inside, he'd kept a watchful eye on the town house. He just wanted to speak to her.

"And so you shall," the viscount said, his tone softening. "Today is not the best time. As I've said, my wife is very ill."

Jasper knew this was true. He'd spent hours each day loitering in front of the town house. He'd seen the doctor come and go. He'd even questioned the man and been told the woman only had a few more days, if that. The viscountess was dying. Who was he to take her daughter away from her in her last hours?

"You will tell her I called?"

The viscount nodded. "Of course. She knows you have been here every day. When all of this"—he gestured vaguely—"is over you shall come to dinner. You can tell me all about how you found them, and I can thank you properly for your service. If you won't accept payment, perhaps you will take that much as thanks."

Jasper knew this offer was made to appease him, but he also knew empty words when he heard them. There would be no invitation to dinner when the viscountess was dead. The man didn't want Jasper near his daughter. He might be the son of a marquess, but he was the third son and the black sheep of the family. No respectable father would want Jasper Grantham near his daughter. He'd expected that. But he had thought Olivia would fight it. She knew that he had called every day and he had not seen her. So perhaps, now that she was home, Olivia didn't want to see him. She'd certainly not written to him or made herself available when he'd called. He'd known that their time together would end when they returned to London, he just hadn't expected it to happen so abruptly.

"Tell her I called," Jasper said again. "And be on guard for anything unusual. I was attacked by a man with a knife when searching for your daughter. I don't know who was behind it or if I was the target or your daughter."

"Yes, well, knife attacks are not a concern now that's she's home with her parents." The clear implication being that Jasper's unsavory line of work made Olivia unsafe in his company. Dimsdale opened the door and without another choice, Jasper walked through it.

Outside, a cold drizzle had turned the city wet and miserable. Jasper pulled his greatcoat around him and stood looking up and down Brook Street. If *he* couldn't get in to see Olivia, surely whoever had attacked him in Penbury would have even more difficulty. Withernsea either did not know or did not care that Olivia was back. She and Richard seemed utterly safe and secure. Jasper could begin to retreat now. Could go back to his old life. Which was…where, precisely? But for a couple servants, he lived alone. He had no great desire to wander his empty rooms. He could have taken work. He had any number of men requesting his services. They would have paid handsomely for them too.

But Jasper didn't want to hunt for another lost person or thing—not when he couldn't have the ones he had found. The ones he wanted. The thought of spending the night in a tavern or wandering one of the rookeries did not appeal.

Which left only one place he did want to go—The Draven Club.

The club was not a long walk, but with the rain and the streets having been turned to mud it was bound to be unpleasant. Jasper didn't care. He needed the time to clear his head. Not that anyone would question him if he showed up and told them all to go to hell. It was the one place any of them—any of the Survivors from Draven's troop—could go and be accepted no matter what. They were brothers. They had a shared history, shared memories, shared horrors.

Perhaps Neil would be there. The leader of the troop was logical and level-headed. All of the men brought their problems to Neil and Neil, the

Warrior, more often than not, solved them. He was the sort of man who never gave in and never gave up.

Ewan was like that too. He didn't speak much, but Jasper had spent plenty of evenings with him in companionable silence. The Protector of the group, Ewan was fiercely loyal. If Jasper asked Ewan to break down the doors to Carlisle's house and clear the way for him to charge in and find Olivia, Ewan would have done it without questioning.

But Ewan and Neil didn't come to the club as much as they had before they married. Jasper didn't really expect to see either of them today. And he knew he wouldn't see Rafe, who had gone to the Americas. Rafe had been Jasper's closest friend, though with Jasper's ugly scar and Rafe's too handsome face, they were very much opposites in appearance. He wouldn't have minded drinking a glass of whatever Porter had open with Rafe tonight.

But perhaps Lord Phineas would be there. Or Nash. Jasper had heard the Sharpshooter was in Town. Perhaps Draven himself would be dining at the club tonight. Jasper reached the club on King Street in St. James's and knocked on the door. It was open less than a moment later by Porter, the Master of the House. He nodded at Jasper. "Good afternoon, my lord." Porter swung the door wide to admit Jasper into a wood-paneled vestibule. The gloomy weather meant the chandelier above had been lit, and light flickered off the large shield mounted on the wall opposite the door. A sword that reminded him of the sort Highlanders used bisected the shield. The pommel of the sword had molded into the shape of a fleur-de-lis, and a skeleton stared at him from the cross guard. Situated around the shield were smaller fleur-de-lis that marked the fallen members of the Survivors—those who hadn't returned from the war.

Jasper looked long and hard at the second to last fleur-de-lis. Peter had been the seventeenth man to die. Jasper knew he had almost followed.

"The dining room, my lord?" Porter asked.

"Is Wraxall here?" Jasper asked the older man who stood so erect, walking stick clutched in one hand and silver hair gleaming under the light of the chandelier.

"No, my lord. Colonel Draven is in the dining room."

"The dining room then, Porter."

"Yes, my lord."

Porter walked slowly, leading Jasper past the winding staircase carpeted in royal blue and into the all but empty dining room. Draven was the only man seated in the room, occupying one of the five tables, that closest to the fire. The room was paneled in wood with a low ceiling, crossed by thick wooden beams. The light in this room came from sconces on the walls and a cozy fire crackled in the hearth. The five tables had been topped by white linen and set with silver.

When Jasper walked in, Draven raised his head and his mouth curved in a half smile. Draven was perhaps fifteen years Jasper's senior. He had wild red hair and piercing blue eyes. He might be in his forties, but he was still in prime condition. Jasper wouldn't have taken him on in a fight.

"Where the devil have you been, Lord Jasper?" Draven asked, motioning to an empty seat across from him.

"Here and there, sir," Jasper answered, following Porter, who led him to the table. He sat and began to remove his mask as Draven asked Porter to bring another glass so he might share the wine in the bottle on the table.

Jasper had no inhibitions about removing his mask here. Every man who came to this club had scars. Jasper's were simply more visible than others. "It looks as though we're the only ones here today," Jasper remarked.

"Your friends don't come as much as they used to now that they've married."

Anger flared in Jasper. First Neil, Ewan, and Rafe had deserted him, now Olivia. "I'll never understand why a younger son would marry," he said bitterly. "He's not the heir or the spare, and when he's served his time in the army and come out a hero, why not enjoy life?"

Draven said nothing and merely sipped his wine.

"Why tie yourself to one woman when women are fickle creatures?"

"I know why Mostyn and Wraxall married," Draven said, speaking of Ewan and Neil. "I even know why Rafe Beaumont chased a woman all the way to America."

Jasper drank the wine Draven had set in front of him. "So do I. All three of them are daft. *Dicked in the nob*, as Rafe would say."

"So he would, and he might even agree with you. Love can have that effect."

"Love." Jasper sneered. "Love fades, just like passion."

"Not always." Draven toyed with the rim of his wine glass. "I was married."

Jasper almost choked, and he wasn't even drinking any wine. "What?" he sputtered.

"It was a long time ago." He had a faraway look, and his light eyes had turned darker.

Draven married? Jasper had never so much as heard the man mention a sister, much less a wife. Come to think of it, he'd also never seen the lieutenant colonel with a woman. He'd thought the man too busy for baser pursuits, but perhaps he was loyal to his wife. "I've not had the pleasure to meet Mrs. Draven."

Draven smiled ruefully. "She doesn't live in London. The marriage took place years ago. I haven't seen her in a long time."

"What happened to her?" Jasper asked, dreading the answer.

"I don't know. Duty called, and I always followed. Fool that I was."

Jasper didn't quite know what to make of his one-time commanding officer. He'd never heard the man speak of his personal affairs.

"Is she still alive?"

"I suppose she is alive somewhere. She's probably forgotten me by now."

"But you haven't forgotten her," Jasper said almost to himself.

Draven lifted his glass in a salute. "I didn't think I was in love with her," he said. "I sneered at love, much as you do. But I think I must have fallen in love with her and not even known it. Else why would I still think of her today? Why would I wonder if she was well, if she'd found another man, if she ever thought of me?"

Jasper stared, open mouthed. If Ewan and Rafe had said such a thing, he would have poked at the man mercilessly. He wouldn't take that liberty with Draven.

Draven drained his glass. "I'm foxed, Jasper, but not so foxed that I can't see your problem."

"My problem, sir?"

"Who is she?"

"I'm not following, sir."

Draven pointed at Jasper. "There's a woman behind the anger I saw earlier. And I, for one, say it's about time. You can't let your face dictate your life. You can't spend the rest of your life hiding in dark alleys and slipping into shadows."

"I'm good at slipping into shadows."

"I wouldn't have made you part of my troop if you hadn't been. But there's a time for everything, and maybe it's time you stopped hiding."

Jasper scowled. "Maybe it's time you stopped drinking."

Draven laughed. "Don't want my advice, do you? I don't blame you. I didn't want advice when I was your age either. I'll give you some anyway."

"Oh, good."

Draven leaned close, ignoring Jasper's sarcasm. "Don't let her go without a fight."

"Don't let who go, sir?" Jasper said.

Draven laughed again. "You keep telling yourself she doesn't matter. One day you'll be drinking alone, sitting across from a young man, telling him what a fool he is for throwing his chance at happiness away."

And before Jasper could object to being called a fool, Draven rose and stumbled away. Porter was at his side in a moment, and then Jasper was alone in the dining room. No reason to stay here. He could go home and be alone in his rooms. He could call on Neil…and watch the man give puppy dog eyes to his bride. He could take one of the cases hopeful clients had pressed on him since he'd returned to London.

Or he could step out of the shadows…

Jasper rose. His eldest brother didn't live far. If he left now, he could arrive just in time to interrupt his dinner.

Sixteen

Her mother had improved in the weeks since Olivia had been home. She'd gained a little weight and was able to stay awake for longer periods of time. Olivia had spent hours nursing her mother, spooning broth between her cracked lips or adjusting her pillows so she might sit.

When she wasn't with the viscountess, Olivia spent time with Richard. The new arrangement was certainly an adjustment for Richard who had been used to having his mother all to himself. But the housekeeper had a grandson close to Richard's age, and Olivia had encouraged the boys' friendship. And just recently she'd employed a governess for Richard who would begin his formal education. So Richard had much to occupy him. Olivia spent her free time with him, and when she was not with him he played with his friend, spent time in his studies, or visited with his grandfather. She was surprised at how accepting her father had been of her son. She'd thought he would balk at the idea of a bastard under his roof, but he seemed to genuinely like his namesake.

They had still not told Lady Carlisle about Richard, and if she had heard the sounds of the boys playing, she hadn't asked about it. Olivia's father said knowing about Richard, knowing the events that must have led to Richard's conception, would upset her mother too much. Olivia agreed. The viscountess's health was fragile. On the other hand, she felt like she was lying by not bringing up such an important part of her life.

But then what was important changed from day to day. Jasper had been important to her, and he'd all but deserted her. He hadn't come to call and hadn't answered even one of the letters she'd given her father to send to him. Her father said he thought he'd heard Lord Jasper was busy with his clients. She knew Jasper didn't think he'd be acceptable to her family, but she had thought she'd be able to convince him otherwise. He'd said he wouldn't abandon her, but he'd done exactly that.

And it hurt. Because she did feel abandoned, and she missed Jasper so much her chest hurt when she thought of him.

She told herself he hadn't been absent because he didn't care. He'd done it for her own good—or some other ridiculous notion. She told herself to fight for him. She wouldn't make disappearing from her life that easy. As soon as she had a bit more time, she would send for him or go out herself and find him.

Of course, the thought of going out was rather daunting. Withernsea was out there. Somewhere. Several times she'd asked her father if word had gotten out that she had come home, and her father had reassured her that her return to London was not widely known. Olivia almost wished she was important enough for her return to have made all the papers. She might have relished the chance to see her old friends, especially those prone to gossip, and say whatever she could to ruin Withernsea's reputation. She would certainly like to see him scorned by London Society, but more than that, she didn't want other girls to suffer what she had at his hands.

As her mother grew stronger and Olivia had time to reflect on her past and her future, she realized she wanted to expose Withernsea for the blackguard he was. Most people wouldn't believe her. Or worse, they would blame her for her own rape. But if she spoke out, her words might make other girls and their parents think twice before trusting Withernsea.

Olivia herself didn't know if she could ever truly trust another man again. She wanted to trust Jasper. She wanted to believe he would not abandon her. Deep down a part of her whispered that she was a fool. Of course, he'd left her. Why would he say with someone like her? That voice was growing louder and louder, especially when she was with Richard. Not only had Jasper deserted her, he'd deserted Richard. And Richard was the one who suffered.

"But Mama," Richard said as they ate their toast and porridge together in the nursery one morning. "Jasper said we would see him all the time in London. Why doesn't he come?"

She brushed a hand over Richard's unruly hair. "I don't know, darling. Perhaps something unexpected came up."

"Can't we go see him?"

"No. That's not appropriate," she said, though she'd been thinking along the same lines. "He must call on us."

Richard stuck his lower lip out. "Sometimes I liked it better in our cottage. There weren't so many rules, and I could run outside without shoes on. Nanny always makes me wear shoes. Even inside!"

Olivia gave her son a sympathetic look and rubbed his shoulder.

"And I miss Clover. Do you think she's being cared for?"

"Yes. I wouldn't have given her to anyone who wouldn't love her."

"Do you think she's forgotten us too?" The *too* was obviously a reference to Jasper. Olivia understood Richard's anger, but she didn't want to fan it. If Jasper wasn't to be part of their life, then she should encourage Richard to move on. She should probably do the same.

"I don't know," she said. "But would it be so bad if she had? I don't want her to spend her last years pining for us. I hope she's happy and doesn't give us more than a passing thought once in a while."

Richard smiled. "I want that too, Mama."

"Now you'd better finish eating because I hear your governess has a lesson on mathematics planned for this morning."

His face brightened. "Oh, good. I love mathematics!"

"I know. And later today you shall have to tell me all you learned."

"I will, Mama."

She left her son with his governess and made her way to her mother's room. She was stopped by Dimsdale before she could reach the viscountess's room. "Your father wishes to see you in the library, Miss."

With a nod, Olivia turned and took the stairs to her father's library on the ground floor. The door was open, and he looked up expectantly when she arrived.

"How is my grandson this morning?" he asked.

"Very well. He's enjoying his studies."

"Good." He lifted a stack of paper from his desk and flipped through what looked like invitations. "You've been home a couple of weeks now and your mother is doing much better. I wondered if you might be willing to accompany me to a few social functions."

Olivia stared at him. Then, seeing he was serious, she gripped the back of a chair before taking a seat. She clasped her shaky hands together firmly. "I hardly think you want me at your side, my lord. I've been gone five years, and I know there must have been a scandal when I disappeared."

"Your mother and I managed the scandal," he said. "We worried about you. You are home now, and you are our daughter. There's no reason you can't go about in Society."

"You can't be serious. You know I won't be accepted. Even if no one knows about Richard, and I pray they do not, my reputation has been ruined. I can well imagine the rumors spread about me." Feeling more confident in her argument, she stood. "Not to mention, I do not want to go out in Society.

I haven't missed the balls and the pleasure gardens and the theater." Very well, she *had* missed the theater.

"Livvy, is this about Withernsea? I told you I will deal with him. There's no need for you to live like a hermit."

Olivia wanted to trust him, to believe him, but she couldn't risk seeing the duke again. The very thought terrified her. "If I go out he will learn I've returned."

Her father leveled a serious look at her. "He knows you are home, Livvy."

Olivia sank back into her chair, her skin turning cold. "How did he find out?" she asked, her voice little more than a whisper.

"I don't know. He's never given up searching for you. Perhaps Lord Jasper went to him and—"

"No." Olivia shook her head. "Lord Jasper would never have told him."

"I suppose one of the servants might have been indiscreet, but we've had them for years. Those who gossiped were let go long before."

Olivia shuddered. "I don't think it was the servants or Lord Jasper." She looked up from her hands and into her father's eyes. "I didn't come home because I wanted to. Not completely. I'd intended to send Lord Jasper back to London and either stay in my cottage or move Richard somewhere we'd never be found. I came home because someone else had found us."

"What do you mean?"

"Lord Jasper found me weeks ago, but when he climbed the path to the cottage, he was attacked by a man with a knife and wounded. Richard found him, and I nursed him back to health."

"Yes, I know some of this. Surely it was a random attack."

"We can't know that. A storm moved in and it rained for days. I don't know that I've ever seen another storm like that. The path was washed out and we were trapped inside. No one could get to us, and we couldn't leave. Lord Jasper had no proof the attacker wasn't just someone hoping to rob him, but when we found footprints and evidence we had been spied upon, we suspected it was the same man or a man from Withernsea."

"And so you came back."

"I could have run again, but how long until I was found this time? And Richard is growing up. I can't hide him in a dark room all day. I can't deprive him of other children and an education. I came back to reclaim my life." She waved a hand. "Not what it was before. I don't want the balls and the musicales. But I don't want to live in fear, and I want to be part of a family again and for my son to know his grandparents."

"Then you should not live in fear. Come with me to a ball. I want you to enjoy your life."

"And what if Withernsea is there?"

"I'll make certain he is not on the guest list."

She'd wanted a chance to speak to others about the duke and expose him. Perhaps this was it. And yet the thought of seeing the duke terrified her.

"What do you say, my dear?" her father asked, smiling with encouragement.

Olivia rose. "My head is pounding. I can't think. We should discuss this later."

The viscount stood as she went to the door. "I need to respond to these invitations, Livvy. I can't wait any longer."

Olivia stopped with her hand on the casement. "I trust you, my lord. Pick one, and I'll try to make you proud."

***

"This is a first, little brother." Jasper's eldest brother, Martin, Earl of Shrewsbury, stepped into the drawing room. The countess, a pretty blond who had prattled on the last ten minutes about the weather and fussed over the tea cart nervously, rose. Jasper stood respectfully.

"If you'll excuse me, my lords, I'd like to peek in on Mary."

"I'm glad to hear she's doing well," Jasper said.

The countess blinked at him with wide blue eyes. "Thank you, Lord Jasper."

"I will see you at dinner, my dear." Martin watched her go then gestured for Jasper to sit again. Jasper hadn't ever paid much attention to his brothers' domestic arrangements. He'd been on the Continent when they'd married, and he'd only met their wives briefly. The ladies were from good families and came with sizable dowries. That was all that seemed to matter to his father, the marquess. But today Jasper had watched Martin with his countess. And he'd paid attention when the lady had mentioned her husband. There didn't seem to be any particular affection between them. They had married out of duty and obligation and produced a child as was expected. Since the child hadn't been a male, Jasper supposed they would have to produce another.

"You've never come to call before," Martin said. "What is the special occasion?"

"I've called before."

Martin raised a brow, looking very much like their father. "When you had no other choice. We used to be friends, Jasper. I always liked you better than Hugh when we were boys."

"Saint Hugh?" Jasper used the old sobriquet for the middle brother. "I should hope you like me better than that self-righteous prig."

Martin smiled. "And yet I see Hugh more than you these days."

"Yes, well, masquerades aren't the fashion, and I scare women and small children without my mask."

"The war changed you," Martin said, eyes narrowing.

Jasper gestured to his mask. "As we just discussed."

"Not only your appearance, but your personality. You used to enjoy the theater or a house party. Now you seem to prefer skulking in the shadows with thieves and prostitutes." Martin leaned forward. "If you wanted, you could become the most popular man in the *ton*. That mask gives you an air of mystery that would make more than one woman swoon."

"I have no interest in making women swoon." There was only one woman he wanted to affect in that way. "But I do seek information about a certain woman."

"And you came to me? Isn't finding out secrets your specialty?"

"And how is it you think I come by these secrets? I ask the right man or woman the right questions."

"Go ahead then." The earl looked mildly interested now.

"What do you know of Miss Carlisle, daughter of Viscount Carlisle?"

Martin shrugged. "Nothing. I don't think I've ever even seen the woman."

Just then the drawing room door opened, and the countess stepped inside. "I'm sorry to interrupt. Shall we set another place at the dinner table? Lord Jasper, you are welcome to dine with us."

Martin glanced at Jasper, who shook his head. The earl gestured to his wife. "Lord Jasper can't stay for dinner, but he has a question that I can't answer. Perhaps you can."

The countess smoothed her already perfectly coiffed blond hair. "Of course." She gave Jasper a nervous smile. "What is it, my lord?"

"Have you heard anything of Miss Carlisle, daughter of Viscount Carlisle?"

"Just rumors really."

Jasper nodded. "What rumors?"

"That she's returned to London. No one knows where she has been these past years. Some say the Continent, others speculate she ran away to Gretna Green to marry a secret lover." As she spoke, she seemed to forget about Jasper. Her face became more animated. "Of course the Duke of Withernsea refuses to speak of her or hear her name mentioned in his presence. His close friends say he still considers himself betrothed to her."

"I hope you aren't associating with Withernsea," Martin said, mouth curved down with distaste.

"I have more sense than that," she said. "But Lord Richlieu is part of his circle and Lady Richlieu and I are both members of the Ladies Society for the Betterment of Orphans and Widows."

Jasper almost rolled his eyes. If the ladies of the society did anything more than sip tea and gossip, he was the Duke of Wellington.

"And Withernsea hasn't been to see her?" Jasper asked.

"No one has seen her. Carlisle keeps her locked up tightly. His wife is ill, and the family isn't at home to callers."

The information was nothing Jasper didn't already know. Carlisle was obviously keeping Olivia safe. Jasper didn't need to continue watching over her. He could go back to his old life. The thought didn't fill him with any anticipation.

"But…"

Jasper had been about to take his leave. At the countess's drawn out word, he stilled.

"This is rumor, you understand. What I told you before is fact, but this is…well, I don't like to gossip."

Martin coughed, and when his wife gave him a sharp glance he mumbled, "Excuse me" and covered his mouth with a handkerchief.

"I don't gossip either, Lady Shrewsbury. I assure you, whatever you say to me will be held in the strictest of confidence," Jasper told her.

She glanced at her husband, and Martin nodded his agreement. Approval given, she looked about the room to ensure no servants were present and then gave him a shrewd look. "I heard," she said, voice low, "that Viscountess Carlisle is improved of late and Miss Carlisle and her father have accepted an invitation to a private ball."

"Whose?"

"That I do not know."

"But you know something else," Jasper said, recognizing the look on her face.

"Whichever ball it is, Withernsea will also be in attendance."

Jasper closed his hand tightly. "I need you to find out which ball it is."

Martin shook his head. "Lydia doesn't work for you."

That was her name—Lydia. And for a moment he'd forgotten she was his brother's wife and a countess. "My apologies. I shouldn't have asked."

"Oh, but I don't mind," she said, voice breathless. "It actually seems rather exciting!"

Martin looked at Jasper as though to say now-look-what-you've-done.

"I've delayed your dinner long enough," Jasper said. "I should take my leave."

"You're welcome to stay," the lady said, this time seeming to mean it.

"I'm needed elsewhere, but thank you."

Outside the town house, Jasper felt hopeful for the first time in days. He had no doubt the Countess of Shrewsbury would discover what he wanted to know. And if Olivia was planning to go out, he would be there to keep her safe from Withernsea, even if she no longer wanted to see him.

Two days later a note from his brother arrived at his rooms. Jasper opened it, but it wasn't Martin's handwriting. It was the pretty script of a lady.

Tonight. Lord Forsythe's ball.

Jasper didn't have an invitation, but he'd never let that stop him before.

Seventeen

Olivia's hands shook as she stepped from her father's coach and into the lamplight of the torches blazing before Lord Forsythe's town house. A dozen footmen stood before it, assisting guests departing their carriages. She and her father had waited in the line of carriages for a half hour, all the while her nervousness increasing.

She'd hadn't been to an event like this in years, and the last time she had, it had ended in assault. What would people say when they saw her? Would they cut her? Whisper about her behind their fans? Thank God she would not have to face Withernsea. Just the thought of him made her feel nauseated. She wanted to go home, but she had Richard to think of now. Her father had asked her to go to the ball, and he had been so good to her and Richard. How could she refuse him this small request?

Her father took her arm, and she lifted the hem of her dress, a midnight blue silk with silver embroidery on the hem and bodice. Her father had hired a modiste to come to the house, but since there was not enough time for her to make a gown for Olivia, she had modified another she'd made for a woman who had decided not to buy it. The modiste had said the color was all wrong for that woman, but with Olivia's dark hair and deep blue eyes, it would suit her perfectly.

She'd been too nervous as she pulled on her white gloves to really see herself in the glass. She supposed she looked well enough. Richard had stared at her when he'd seen her and then began to cry. "Where is my Mama?"

She'd bent down and gathered him into her arms, much to the disapproval of her maid who worried the dress would be wrinkled. "I'm right here, darling. I'm just dressed up."

He pulled back and touched her elaborate hairstyle and the light dusting of blush she wore. "I don't like it."

"Do you want to know a secret?" she whispered. He'd nodded. "I don't either. I'll kiss you when I return home. Listen to Nanny while I'm away."

He'd nodded again, his eyes still wet with tears.

"Are you cold?" her father asked now as he led her to the open door of the Forsythe town house. "You're shivering."

"Nervous," she said.

"Don't be. Lord Forsythe assured me you would be welcome."

They entered the vestibule, a semicircle with a high ceiling. Around the edges stood Lord Forsythe, his wife, and their children. Olivia passed through the line, curtsying as was required. Forsythe and his wife were pleasant enough, as were their daughters, who were cool but polite. Forsythe's sons, however, made her cringe. They looked at her too long, their eyes sliding down her dress until she felt as though she was wearing nothing. She moved quickly after her father and away from the men's eyes. But all too soon, she was in the ballroom, where the dancing had not yet begun but the gossip surely had. As soon as she was announced, the room quieted. All eyes darted from her to the back of the room.

And there stood the Duke of Withernsea, tall and handsome and powerful as ever.

***

Jasper's breath caught when Olivia stepped into the room. He'd turned and looked at the door to the ballroom even before she was announced. It was as though he'd felt her presence.

He stood off to one side, behind a group of people. It had been easy to slip over the wall of the garden then in through an unlocked French door. He'd entered the ballroom without anyone noticing and kept to the shadows. A few men and women had passed him, and those who knew who he was had nodded. Those who didn't looked quickly away.

No one spoke to him. No one would dare speak to him.

"So that's who you came to see," a voice said from beside him.

Jasper started in surprise and turned to see Lord Phineas standing beside him. Jasper blew out a breath. So much for no one daring to speak to him. Phineas was one of The Survivors. They'd called him The Negotiator because he could talk his way into or out of anything.

"Oh, it's you," Jasper said, slightly relieved.

"I'm well, thank you for asking. And how are you?"

Jasper scowled at him. "I don't have time for pleasantries."

"Oh, good. Then I might as well come right out and ask what the devil you are doing here without an invitation."

"Why do you think I don't have an invitation?"

"Besides the fact that you came in through the French doors a quarter hour ago—yes, I saw that—you don't know Forsythe from Adam. The man practically lives at the House of Lords and that isn't your usual set."

"But it's yours?"

Phineas waved a hand. "We are talking about you and your interest in Miss Carlisle."

Jasper glanced at her again. She and her father were making their way through the ballroom, stopping to speak to people here and there. Her face was pale and her eyes large. Knowing her as he did, it was obvious she was terrified. And yet, she still looked beautiful. She was small and willowy, but the dress hinted at her womanly curves. The upsweep of her hair highlighted her long, graceful neck, and the chandeliers made her dark hair gleam.

"She's pretty," Phineas said.

Jasper shot him an annoyed look. "What do you know about her?"

"Only what everyone else knows. She's been away for some years and now she's back. Withernsea says she's his—"

"Withernsea had better not so much as look at her."

"Too late for that." Phineas gestured to the other side of the room where the Duke of Withernsea watched Olivia with as much interest as Jasper had.

"I need to speak to her privately."

Phineas gave a short laugh. "I don't see how you'll manage that. Everyone is watching her. Once the dancing begins, she won't have a moment alone."

Phineas had a point. Jasper's only chance to speak to her would be if he asked her to dance, but the two of them dancing together would hardly be a private affair. But if someone else danced with her…

"I can't say as I care for the way you're looking at me right now," Phineas said.

"I need you to ask her to dance."

Phineas balked. "I haven't even been introduced."

"You can take care of that easily enough. Ask her to dance and then tell her I want to speak to her. She can feign feeling unwell. Lead her to the terrace where I'll be waiting."

"I should say no."

"Why?"

"Because I don't particularly want to make an enemy of Withernsea."

"But…"

"But I attend far too many balls and soirees and fetes—to say nothing of the routs. It's been an age since I had any fun."

"I'd hardly call this fun." Jasper waved a dismissive arm in the direction of the ballroom.

"It reminds me of the old days and our missions."

"Which were not fun."

"Speak for yourself. I always found them exhilarating. And I already have my dancing shoes on," he said, referring to the phrase they'd always repeated before missions because they expected to be dancing with the devil by the end of them. And yet here he was, and here was Phineas.

Phineas started away, but Jasper clapped him on the shoulder. "I never said thank you."

"It's just a dance, Bounty Hunter."

"That's not all I meant and you know it."

Phineas shrugged his hand off. "I never said thank you either." He started away. "I don't intend to start now."

***

"I want to go home," Olivia said for the fourth of fifth time since they'd arrived and seen Withernsea. The dancing would start soon, and she and her father stood on the edge of the dance floor talking quietly. "You promised he wouldn't be here."

"I was assured he would not." He didn't look at her when he spoke. He was watching Withernsea across the room. Olivia had tried to ignore the duke, but every time she spotted him he was watching her surrounded by men who also watched her then whispered to the duke. She knew they were talking about her. Were they plotting something? Some way to get her alone?

"You were obviously misinformed, Papa." Why would her father not let them leave? Why did he keep watching the duke? "I cannot stay here."

He glanced at her briefly. "We just arrived. If we leave so soon we risk insulting our host."

"Then say I am sick. Say we've had an urgent message from home."

But he ignored her, his gaze on Withernsea. She'd had enough. She would leave without him, if necessary. She turned and almost plowed into Lord Forsythe.

"Miss Carlisle. Lord Carlisle," Lord Forsythe said, bowing to Olivia and her father. A handsome man she didn't know stood beside him. "May I present Lord Phineas. Lord Phineas, Miss Carlisle and Viscount Carlisle."

Lord Phineas made a very pretty bow. He had straight honey-colored hair that was too long for convention but too short to pull into a queue. When he bowed, a section of it fell over his forehead. He rose, brushing his hair back and away from clear green eyes. "A pleasure, Miss Carlisle. My lord."

Her father made a non-committal sound and shifted nervously from one foot to the other.

"Lord Phineas is a younger son of the Duke of Mayne," Forsythe said.

"That's not my fault," Lord Phineas said, making her smile. "And I didn't beg an introduction to impress you with my titles. I hoped to claim your hand for the first dance, Miss Carlisle. Please tell me you aren't spoken for."

"I don't think so," her father said at the same time Olivia said, "That would be lovely."

Lord Phineas looked from her father to her, amusement making those compelling eyes bright. "Shall I leave you to discuss the matter?"

"No," Olivia said. This was her chance. She'd dance one dance and then her father would be mollified and allow her to leave. "I accept your offer."

"Then I shall return." Lord Phineas bowed, his hair sweeping down over his brow again. When he had stepped away, her father gave her a hard look.

"I thought you didn't care to dance."

She had said as much in the carriage, but that was before she'd seen Withernsea. Now she welcomed any chance to avoid speaking with him. And by the looks she had noted in the eyes of some of the men, she would have other offers. Her reputation was certainly in question. But she hadn't taken into account the men in attendance who weren't looking for a wife. They didn't care about the scandal associated with her, and she didn't think it would be long before they circled.

At least Lord Phineas looked at her face, not her chest, when he spoke to her, and he didn't seem to have an inflated opinion of himself. Truth be told, she didn't want to dance with any of these men. It had been so long since she'd danced that she feared she'd embarrass herself. But more than that, she had no interest in any of the gentlemen here.

She'd known Jasper wouldn't be here, but that didn't mean she couldn't wish for him. She needed him here tonight. He would have kept her safe from Withernsea and the eyes of the men around him. Not that he would ever attend a ball like this. He would not want to step onto the dance floor so everyone could gawk at his mask. She wondered what he was doing now and where.

The night before they'd arrived in London, she'd been almost certain he was in love with her. The way he'd touched her and spoken to her and kissed her had given her hope that he might feel something of what she did.

And then he'd walked out of her life, seemingly without a backward glance. Her heart squeezed painfully every time she thought about it. And that, she reminded herself, was the reason she disliked men. They couldn't be trusted. They lied and pretended to feel things they didn't feel. Jasper wasn't any different than other men except that she'd made her heart vulnerable to him. Thank God her mother and Richard had needed her. She hadn't had time to mourn the loss of Jasper, and she'd been too tired at night to lie in bed and remember the way his body had felt lying beside hers.

The orchestra finished tuning and the first strains of a quadrille began. Before she could look for him, Lord Phineas was before her, bowing with his gloved hand extended. She took her place with him and the other dancers in the middle of the floor. As they waited for their turn, she whispered, "I hope I remember all the steps. I haven't danced in years."

"I'll talk you through it if you like. I could dance this in my sleep."

He took her hand then and proceeded to do exactly that until he had to pass her off to another gentleman momentarily. Before long it had all come back to her, and she was smiling and dancing without thinking. She tried not to look for Withernsea, but she could all but feel his eyes on her, making her skin crawl. The half hour passed quickly, and when Lord Phineas led her off the dance floor, she hoped he would take her straight back to her father so she could depart.

"Why don't we step outside for a bit of air?" he said.

Olivia stiffened. She'd let her guard down too soon. Men were all the same. "No, thank you," she said clearly. She tried to pull away, but he held her arm firmly.

"I need to speak with you in private."

"I have absolutely nothing to say to you that can't be said in full view of the other guests."

"That may be true," he said, speaking close to her ear. She tried to shrink away from him. "But Lord Jasper is waiting outside, and I believe he prefers to converse without an audience."

She stopped walking abruptly. "Lord Jasper?" she whispered, whirling to face Lord Phineas. His hold on her arm loosened, and he nodded. "He's here?"

"On the terrace. He asked me to dance with you and then take you to see him."

"How do you know him?"

"We fought together on the Continent. Will you walk with me? I'd rather not attract attention."

She put her arm through his again and allowed him to promenade her about the side of the dance floor. As they neared the terrace doors, half open she saw now, she stiffened again.

"Miss Carlisle, I promise you have nothing to fear from me," he said, looking her directly in the eye. "I swear on my grandfather's grave, and if you know anything about the fourth Duke of Mayne, you know he would haunt me for a thousand years if I ever forswore a vow made in his name."

She did know something of Lord Phineas's ancestor. She might not believe in ghosts, but the fourth Duke of Mayne was just formidable enough to overcome the Grim Reaper and do as he pleased.

"Very well." She allowed Lord Phineas to lead her to the terrace doors and slip outside. He did it so skillfully, she could almost believe no one had noticed. But certainly her father had been watching and would come looking for her in a moment.

"If you'll excuse me, Miss Carlisle," Lord Phineas said, "I'll go delay anyone else hoping to sample the night air." And with another bow, he was gone.

She turned from the door, scanning the small terrace that overlooked Forsythe's manicured gardens. No lanterns had ben lit on this side of the house, and it was dark and chilly. Was she supposed to wait for Lord Jasper or—

"Olivia."

She shivered at the sound of his voice then turned slowly. He stood behind her, his form in shadow and his face covered by the silk mask.

"Why are you here?" she asked, suddenly very angry. He'd known how frightened she'd been to come back. He'd promised to keep her safe and he'd abandoned both her and Richard at the first opportunity. And now he showed up here?

"It was the only way I could think to see you." He didn't move from the shadows, and it was almost as though she spoke with a phantom.

"You might have come to the town house. Richard has been asking for you."

He moved with a quickness she hadn't expected, reaching for her and pulling her into the darkness with him. Now she shivered for a different reason. "You think I didn't come to your father's town house? I came every day. Your father or your butler turned me away."

She shook her head, glad for his arm on hers. Her legs felt suddenly weak. Why would her father turn Jasper away? Why would he lie to her about it?

"Did they tell you I called at all? Did they tell you I stood outside on the walkway for hours at a time, hoping to see you come or go?"

"No. I don't understand it. Why would my father lie?"

"I believe I mentioned before that no respectable man wants his daughter associated with me."

"But…" She didn't know what to say or what to think. Her head was spinning. She'd been lied to for weeks! Was else was her father lying about?

"I had no way to see you until tonight." His hands closed on her upper arms, the heat of his ungloved skin warming her. Suddenly she could breathe again. She hadn't even realized the tension and fear she'd carried these last weeks. It was as though she had been holding her breath and could now finally let it go and inhale again.

"You came for me," she said, leaning closer to him.

"Damn right." His arms went around her and she was pressed against his body, which was both familiar and mysterious to her now. Then his mouth was on her throat, his breath on her earlobe. "Can I kiss you? I've missed the taste of you."

Why had she ever doubted him? Of course, he had not abandoned her. She trembled and closed her eyes. "Yes."

His mouth was on hers before she'd even finished the word. His lips were cool and gentle, but that wasn't what she wanted from him. She fisted her hands in his hair and pulled his head down until she could feast on his mouth, tangling her tongue with his and deepening the kiss until she forgot where she was and why.

She didn't know how much time had passed, not nearly enough to satisfy her, when he pulled back, resting his forehead on hers. "I don't know how I'll walk out of here without you."

"Then don't. I don't want you to leave."

"If you stay out here much longer, you'll be missed. Phineas is skilled, but even he can only hold a worried father off for so long. You have to go back in."

"How will I see you again?"

"Which bed chamber in the town house is yours?"

She blinked at him. “Second floor, facing the back of the house. First window on the right. But Dimsdale will never allow you inside, and the servants can’t be bribed.”

“I think you’re forgetting who I am and what I do. I’ll find you. I just needed to know you wanted me to find you.”

“You’ll come tonight? I’ll be home soon. I have to leave. Withernsea is here.”

His hand on her arm tightened. “I know. Stay away from him, and leave as soon as is feasible. I’ll have Phineas look out for you. Now you’d better go inside.”

She didn’t move. It seemed almost impossible to step out of the safety of his arms. “You’ll come tonight?” she asked again.

“I’ll be waiting for you when you arrive home.”

She opened her mouth to tell him she loved him, then closed it again. “I’ll see you soon then.” Reluctantly, she drew away and slipped back through the terrace door and into the brightly lit ballroom.

***

Jasper let his head fall back to rest on the wall. His entire body burned for her. Touching her, tasting her, having her scent in his nose again was enough to drive him mad. He had half a mind to scoop her up and carry her out of the ballroom and never look back.

But he’d long since learned to think before acting. He had the scar to remind him daily of the folly of impetuousness. Not that he regretted going in after Peter. If given the chance, he would have done it all over again. But he might have been smarter about it next time. Found another of the troop to help him. Thrown a wet blanket over his head…

Perhaps nothing would have made any difference. Perhaps he wouldn’t have been able to save Peter no matter what he did. And perhaps no amount of watching and waiting would reveal the reason Olivia's father had lied to her or why he would put her in close proximity to Withernsea. But he had to try to find out. And this time there was more than himself to think of. Olivia had a son and a mother who was dying.

"So you're the reason she was out here so long," a deep voice said.

Jasper opened his eyes, not moving any other part of himself. He went completely still, glad he had the knife in his boot, fingers itching to use it. Before him stood the Duke of Withernsea.

"You're either a fool or an idiot for coming out here," Jasper said quietly. "I could kill you and no one would be the wiser." He wanted to kill the man. He wanted to do it slowly and watch as the duke died a painful death.

"So much venom. You and I haven't even been introduced, Lord Jasper."

"I never had any desire to be introduced to you. Your stench was foul enough even from a distance."

"Harsh words for a man you don't know. Don't tell me you believe the lies that little slut has told you about me."

"Which little slut, *Your Grace*? You forget I spend an inordinate amount of time in brothels and the dark alleys of rookeries. I've heard all about you and your...preferences."

The duke stepped closer, and though Jasper itched to wrap his hands around the man's throat and squeeze, he knew it wouldn't be that easy. The duke was a large, strong man. He might have a multitude of vices but neglecting his health hadn't been one of them. Jasper could kill him, but what good would he do Olivia in a jail cell? He might be the son of a peer, but there were a hundred witnesses just inside the door and they'd certainly notice two men struggling.

"At least I have appetites. They say the war took yours? Did your cock burn off with your face?"

Jasper didn't take the bait. "Stay away from her, Withernsea. She's under my protection now."

"She's betrothed to me, you deformed monster. That makes her mine. If you want to keep the half of your face that's untouched whole, then you'll stay away from Miss Carlisle and me. Good evening." He turned on his heel, dismissing Jasper and slinking back into the ballroom.

Jasper almost went after him, but that would only give the duke the reason he needed to have Jasper thrown from the ball. Instead, he waited in the shadows until Phineas returned. "I couldn't keep him out," Phineas said. "I was conversing with Lord Carlisle when I saw him head that way. What happened?"

"A lot of sword waving. I need a favor from you."

"More dancing? People will talk if I ask Miss Carlisle again."

Phineas was right, and the last thing Olivia needed was more gossip. "Just keep an eye on her. If Withernsea tries to get close to her, prevent it."

"And what do you have planned?"

Jasper went to the edge of the balustrade and threw a leg over. "A little climbing expedition." He jumped the short distance and looked up. Phineas saluted then disappeared back inside. Jasper headed for the shadows and made his way to Brook Street.

Eighteen

Her father continued to put off their departure. He begged her to remain only ten minutes more. Then after ten minutes, only another ten. No one else asked her to dance. Olivia found herself standing by the wall while other ladies were claimed for reels and waltzes and country dances. She didn't notice at first. Her thoughts were too full of Jasper. A dozen times she'd wanted to raise her hand to her lips to touch them. Had he really kissed her? Had she really been in his arms just moments before?

"Would you like champagne?" her father asked.

Olivia blinked and seemed to remember where she was. "I'd like to go home," she said.

"One more glass of champagne and we will go." He smiled at her, his eyes kindly and imploring. "I'll return right away."

She frowned as he walked away. How much longer must they stay? She wanted to speak to her father alone and ask why he'd lied to her. She needed answers and explanations.

But that wasn't the only reason she was desperate to leave. She imagined Jasper waiting for her in her bed chamber. The thought was scandalous—and exciting.

She'd been so certain when she arrived that men were interested in asking her to dance, but none had approached her. The reason became clear as soon as her father left her alone to fetch her champagne. They hadn't wanted to make her a respectable request.

The first man sidled up to her in such a way that she didn't realize he was beside her until she felt his breath on the back of her neck.

"Miss Carlisle," he said in a deep voice.

She was so startled she almost jumped. Only through sheer force of will did she remain calm. She turned, and seeing he was all but on top of her, stuck her folded fan between them, forcing him back slightly. "I'm sorry, have we met?"

"I've been wanting to meet you all night."

She recognized him as one of the men who'd been whispering with Withernsea. Had the duke sent him to harass her? "Then you should have asked my father for an introduction."

He gave her an oily smile. "We don't need formalities like that, do we, Miss Carlisle? May I call you Olivia? You may call me George."

"No, thank you. If you'll excuse me, sir."

"But I had hoped to take you for a breath of air. I hear Lord Forsythe has an impressive library."

"No, thank you," she said again, moving closer to another wallflower and her mama. The women turned their backs on Olivia, noses in the air. But at least George had given up. Except that he was almost immediately replaced by another so-called gentleman. Olivia had to put him off as well. How long did it take for her father to find a footman with champagne? Should she go to look for him? She dared not leave her position.

The longer her father was away the more panicked she became. Her heart began to pound hard and sweat beaded on her temple. The last time she'd been left alone at a ball, Withernsea had taken advantage of her. She tried to close her eyes, tried not to remember. She didn't want to think of his lips on hers, his hands ripping her clothing, forcing her legs open.

She swallowed the bile rising in her throat, closing her eyes to try and calm herself.

But when she opened them Withernsea himself stood before her.

He bowed, his smile tight and knowing. When he rose, his eyes traveled over her boldly, making her wish she had a shawl to cover herself. "Miss Carlisle," he said, his eyes finally meeting hers. "May I have this dance?"

She tried to speak, but her voice had deserted her. She couldn't breathe, and the blood rushed in her ears so loudly she couldn't hear the orchestra. Finally, she shook her head.

"Come now, Miss Carlisle. Do not be difficult." He held out his hand, demanding she comply. Olivia almost took it. She didn't quite know how to refuse. But she couldn't stand the thought of touching him, of dancing with him, of making *polite* conversation with him.

"No, thank you," she finally managed to squeeze out of her tight throat.

"You don't mean it. Dance with me or you'll make a scene."

"No."

He frowned at her. "You are making a scene. Do you want everyone talking about you more than they already are?"

She didn't move.

"You are my betrothed. You will dance with me." He grabbed her arm and began to pull her. She jerked back violently, almost losing her balance.

Withernsea towered over her, glowering. "Dance with me this minute, or you will be sorry."

"No," she said firmly. Then "No" even more loudly. "I will *not* dance with you."

"Lower your voice."

Heads were beginning to turn their way and a few ladies murmured from behind fans.

"I won't. I will not dance with you. Not after what you did."

The orchestra played, but those around them seemed completely uninterested in those dancing the waltz on the dance floor. Olivia could feel the heat rising in her cheeks.

"I've done nothing. I merely asked my betrothed to dance."

"Oh, you know what you did."

A few gasps and murmurs reached her ears, but she didn't look away from his face. She stared at him hard, her glare accusing. Where was her father? How could he leave her this long? He'd promised to stand with her.

"And I think you know what you did," Withernsea said. "I could ruin you and your father for breaking our betrothal agreement."

She flinched back at the threat. She had no doubt he could do so, but she'd rather be ruined than spend even a moment in his company. She almost said, *Then do your worst*, but the image of her mother lying at home in bed, thin, weak, and ill flashed into her mind. And then she thought of her son. What would Withernsea do if he knew about Richard? How could she protect her little boy? What did the duke want from her? A dance? An apology for breaking the betrothal contract? Would an apology make him go away? But the words stuck in her throat, making her nauseous when she thought about speaking them.

The silence between them continued, the tension rising, until finally it was broken when her father appeared at her elbow. "Your champagne, my dear. Duke, how good to see you," he said.

Olivia didn't know how her father could greet the other man so cordially when he knew what Withernsea had done to her. She took the champagne, clutching it tightly in trembling fingers. She wasn't shaking from fear so much as rage. Tears pricked her eyes, but she refused to cry. Everyone would see it as weakness, when it wasn't weakness at all, just pent up fury.

"I wish I could say the same, Carlisle. I asked your daughter to dance, and she refused me."

Her father turned his indignant gaze on her, and that was the moment she realized she was standing alone. Her father hadn't just been lying about Jasper. He'd been lying about everything. He wasn't on her side. She couldn't believe something so vile about her papa, but with the two men standing side by side and glaring down at her accusingly, she knew coming to London had been a monumental mistake.

Her father had been manipulating her since the moment she arrived home. He pretended to be her ally and all the while he'd been on Withernsea's side.

"Olivia, you have my permission to dance with His Grace," her father said, as though that had been the reason for her refusal.

"I'm not feeling well, Father. I fear I would be a poor partner. Would you escort me home?" she said loudly enough for those around them to hear.

Her father looked from Withernsea to Olivia.

"Perhaps if you had a sip of champagne you might recover."

"No." She glared at him. "I am returning home. With or without you."

Her father gave Withernsea a scared look then nodded. "O-Of course."

She looped her arm through his and turned away, but Withernsea stopped them.

"This is not over, Olivia. You belong to me. We are betrothed, and you will honor that contract or face the consequences."

Olivia turned slowly, gripping her father's arm for what little support he could give. "Good night, Your Grace."

Once in the carriage, Olivia let out a slow breath. She had made it through the ball, and that was a victory in itself. Jasper would be waiting for her back at the town house. She needed him to hold her after the encounter with Withernsea and her realization about her father. She felt vulnerable and scared. Withernsea had been part of her nightmares for the past five years. Seeing him here, in the flesh, was like facing her demons and realizing there was no waking up.

"That didn't go very well," her father said. "You could have danced one dance with him."

The rage she'd been keeping contained boiled over. "You all but abandoned me."

"I did not. I went to fetch you a refreshment, and when you wanted to leave, I agreed."

But they both knew that was a lie. He had put her off over and over again.

"One dance would not have hurt and might have even helped matters," her father said.

"How can you even ask that of me? He raped me, Papa. I cannot dance with him. I do not ever want to see him again." She spoke slowly, trying to explain, once again, to her father. Perhaps he simply didn't understand what must be done. "We can't acquiesce to the duke's wishes any longer. He must be made to realize that I will not marry him. We should cancel the betrothal contract and pay the penalty. I don't comprehend why he didn't marry in my absence."

"I don't either. I'm afraid…" He trailed off and rubbed the bridge of his nose. "I'm afraid he may have developed a somewhat unhealthy obsession with you."

Olivia felt the bile rise in her throat. "Then perhaps it's better to deal with it in a straightforward manner. No placating him."

Her father shook his head. "It's not that simple, Livvy. He could hurt us financially."

Her heart seemed to plummet into her belly. "The contract can't be worth that much."

"Your mother has been ill for some time, Livvy," her father sighed. "I haven't managed the finances as well as I might have. If it were just the cost of a lawsuit and the damages for breaking the contract, it would shake us but not topple us."

"But?"

"But Withernsea is a powerful man. He can persuade creditors to call in debts, woo my steward away from the estate, make certain my investments don't come to fruition. He will ruin us. He can do it."

"I am already ruined! Lord Forsythe and his family didn't want me at their ball. With the exception of Lord Phineas, I didn't receive a single decent proposal while I was there. I'm seen as a fallen woman and men think they can say and do what they want to me. I won't be treated that way. I haven't done anything wrong, and while I don't expect Society to believe that, I did think you would support me."

"I *do* support you!"

"How? By forcing me to attend an event where I am treated like a common light skirt and forced to speak with the man who raped me?"

"Keep your voice down!"

Olivia gawked at him. They were in a moving carriage. The wheels clattered so loudly on the streets she could hardly hear herself speak. "Why should I? Maybe it's time everyone knows what Withernsea did."

"And do you think if you accuse him anyone will believe you?"

"Why shouldn't they?"

"They'll say you are lying for attention or monetary gain. He'll call you a liar, and then it will be your word against his."

"And why should anyone believe the word of a woman?" She spat the last word as though it were an expletive.

"*I* believe you, Olivia. But accusing him publicly won't help us. He'll only work that much harder at ruining us."

She lifted her hands in surrender. "So if he will ruin us if I keep quiet and ruin us if I speak up, what other choice do I have?"

Her father didn't answer, and the silence went on for a long time. She stared at him, uncomprehending, but her father refused to meet her eyes. She went through the options over again, unable to think of another. Unless…

"You can't be suggesting I honor the contract?" she said on a gasp.

Her father flinched, but the look in his eyes was guilty.

"No! How could you even consider marrying me to him?"

"Livvy, listen to me."

"No! I'll never do it. Never!"

"Livvy, you are the mother of his child."

"Richard is not his child. Richard is mine. Withernsea's only role in begetting Richard was a few brief moments of violence. He doesn't know about Richard, and he never will."

"Be reasonable, Livvy. The boy needs a father. What better father than a wealthy, powerful man? And anyone will look at the child and know his parentage. He looks just like the duke."

"You're mad," she said, her voice shaking. "What have I ever done to make you hate me so?" Oh, she had been a fool, a great fool. She should have run as far and fast from London as she could. She should have never trusted her father.

"Don't you see? We have no other choice. Withernsea will ruin us, and it would kill your mother. I'm an old man, Livvy. It will kill me. Where am I to go, how am I supposed to afford to care for your mother if Withernsea sees to it that our credit is not accepted, our investments go bad, and we're evicted from our house?"

She stared at him, tears distorting her vision and making him look like a shapeless, spineless mass.

"It will be a temporary solution. Your mother won't live much longer, and I need six, maybe nine, months to secure our assets so that Withernsea can't touch them. Then you can divorce him, run away, whatever you like."

"And you think once he has me, he will ever let me go?" she said with a calm she didn't feel.

"I'll help you escape. We'll devise a plan."

She sneered at him. "Like you're helping me now, Father? Tell me the truth, was this your plan all along? When you hired Jasper to find me, was it to bring me back so Withernsea could marry me?"

"Of course not!"

But she saw the lie. His eyes flicked away from her for a brief instant, and she knew she had found him out. "Withernsea wasn't able to find me through his own means, so he had you hire Jasper. Jasper wouldn't have ever agreed to work for him, but he'd work for you, especially when you told him you wanted me back because Mama was dying."

"Your mother *is* dying."

"Convenient for you then. And now it makes sense why you told me Jasper hadn't called on me—yes, I know you lied about that. You've been keeping us apart because you want me for Withernsea."

"Because I saw there was more than there should be between you and that ruffian!" Her father exploded. "Lord Jasper clearly took advantage of you when all I paid him to do was bring you home. The man has no honor."

"He has more honor than you ever will. Did you know, Papa? When you signed the betrothal contract, did you know the kind of man Withernsea was?"

"No." He looked at her, and his expression was imploring. "I didn't know. I'd heard rumors, but I swear, they were only rumors." He sighed. "I made a mistake, but we're in too deep now. I've lain awake countless nights, trying to find a way out. You marrying the duke is the only way."

"No."

He slammed a hand against the carriage frame in a display of anger she'd never seen from him before. "Why not? Is it because of that deformed mercenary? Do you imagine yourself in love with him? He's using you, Livvy."

She clasped her hands tightly, so tightly her fingers hurt. "He is neither deformed nor a mercenary. He was wounded in the war. He fought under Lieutenant Colonel Draven. And he's an honorable man. But yes, I do love him. And I don't know if he loves me back, but even if he never wants to see me again, my answer to you does not change. I will not marry Withernsea."

The carriage slowed as they arrived at the town house. Olivia reached for the door before the footman could hop down and come around to open it. She jumped out of the conveyance and ran for the house.

"We will speak about this more tomorrow!" her father called after her.

Then I'll be gone tomorrow, she vowed, and ran past Dimsdale and up to her room.

***

The door flew open and Jasper rose from the chair near the fire. He'd been dozing, the comfort of the chair and the warmth from the fire making him drowsy. But he'd barely gained his feet when she launched herself into his arms. He almost toppled backward from the force of her embrace.

"Jasper," she said and buried her head in his chest. "Thank God you're here."

"I told you I would be," he murmured, keeping his voice low so as not to wake the nurse sleeping in the next room. Breaking into the house had been incredibly simple. Waiting for Olivia had been much harder.

"Yes, you did," she said and hugged him tighter. Her put his arms around her, holding her close and hoping that would still her trembling. After a few minutes, he lifted her and carried her to the bed, cradling her in his lap as he sat on the coverlet.

"Do you want to tell me what happened? Withernsea didn't touch you, did he?" He tried to keep his voice level, but if the duke had laid a finger on her, he would leave now, find the man, and kill him.

"No, that's not it. I just need you to hold me. I need to feel safe."

"You're safe with me, love," he whispered into her hair. It smelled of lemon soap and flowers. She had flowers pinned in her coiffure, sprigs of lavender, and he plucked them out and dropped them on the floor. Then he found the pins and removed them as well. Her hair tumbled down her back in a soft wave. "Better?" he asked.

"Yes. My head was aching. That's better."

"Why don't we remove your cloak? It's too warm in here for such a heavy garment."

She nodded and he reached for the ties, loosening them and letting the cloak drop from her shoulders and onto the bed.

"Why stop now?" she murmured, her eyes meeting his. The invitation was clear, and though he'd been hoping for it, he hesitated.

"We're in your father's house. The nurse is just in the next room with Richard."

"Then we should be very quiet." Her hand slid to the bodice of her dress and she pulled out one of the pins, then another, then another. Finally, the bodice was loose, and she slipped it down then moved off his lap to let the garment slide to her feet. Standing before him in her petticoat and chemise, her hair down about her shoulders, she looked very young and very beautiful. She reached for the strings of her petticoat, but he took her hands in his.

"What happened after I left? Did Withernsea try to speak with you?"

"He did speak with me." Her gaze was fixed on the floor. "He wanted me to dance with him."

"Damn and hell. I told Phineas to watch over you."

The look she gave him was akin to gratitude mixed with amusement. "There was little he could have done. He can hardly intervene just because a man asks me to dance."

"And did you dance with him?" Jasper felt his jaw tighten. He knew she would have had little choice but to do so, but he didn't like to think of Withernsea's hands on her.

"No. I refused him and I made an excuse so I could come home." She reached out to touch his mask. "I wanted to see you. I needed you to hold me. And kiss me."

Jasper didn't even think. He put his arms around her waist and pulled her between his legs. "So you want to use me to forget having to see him and speak to him?"

"Is that wrong?"

"Not if I don't object to being used." He bent his head and took her mouth, kissing her lightly at first and not resisting when she deepened the kiss. She needed him. Surprisingly, he needed her too. He'd been anxious and tense since leaving her after they arrived in London. As soon as she was in his arms, all of that melted away. He felt her hands reach for his mask, untying it and removing it. He let her but stiffened when she ran a hand over his scarred cheek.

"Did I hurt you?"

"No. But you needn't touch me there."

"I want to touch you everywhere."

He stilled, allowing her to caress his scar then place a soft kiss on it. He had the sense that she cherished him, every part of him, even the damaged, scarred parts he didn't want anyone to see.

She stepped back and untied her petticoats. That left her in stays and her chemise. The stays had been tied tightly, pushing her breasts up, and his mouth went slightly dry looking at the rounded flesh on display.

"Tell me what you're thinking," he said, reaching out to run the back of his hand over the soft half-moons of her breasts.

She closed her eyes and swayed. "I can't think much when you do that."

He stopped, grabbed her about the waist, and hauled her close to him. He half feared he'd scared her, but her eyes glittered with arousal. "What do you want, Olivia?"

"You."

"Be more specific. What do you want to happen tonight?"

Her cheeks turned pink, but she didn't look away from him. "I want you to take me. I want to be yours. Completely."

"You've thought this over?"

"I've thought of little else. I love you, Jasper." Her hand came up to touch his scar again, and he felt a flash of heat. He didn't know if was her touch or her admission. "I want to be with you, and I want you to make me forget everything else for a little while."

"I can make you forget without bedding you. I've done it before."

"I know you can," she said, smiling at him. "But I want more this time. I'm not scared anymore. I want to know what the act should be like. I don't want my only experience to have been with Withernsea."

How could he refuse her that? Even if he'd wanted to? "If that's what you desire, you shall have it," he said and spun her around to loosen the ties on her stays. She stood still and obedient as he wiggled the garment over her hips. Placing his hand on the bare skin near her shoulder, he murmured, "You can change your mind. Say the word, and I will stop."

"I won't change my mind."

He bent and grasped the hem of her chemise. He pulled it up slowly, revealing pale skin made golden in the light of the fire. She lifted her arms, and he tugged it over her head then let it drop on the floor. His gaze drifted lovingly over her. At her cottage he'd told himself an arse was an arse. But he'd been very, very wrong. He'd never seen an arse quite as round and lovely as hers. She started to turn around, but he put his hand lightly on her waist. "Not yet."

She stilled, glancing over her shoulder at him and smiling. His hand slid down over her hip then cupped her bottom and squeezed.

"What about your clothes?" she asked, voice low and husky.

"My clothes?" He'd never been asked to undress before. The idea that she wanted to see him, that she found his body as arousing as he found hers, made his desire flash hot. He might have ripped his clothes off if it wouldn't have meant having to make his way back through the streets of London naked.

He released her and untied his cravat, letting the snowy material tumble down his white linen shirt. Next came his coat. That took a little longer, tightly fitted as it was. By the time he tossed it aside, she'd climbed onto the bed to watch him. Her eyes were large and dark, her mouth curved in a half-smile. He unbuttoned his shirt then pulled it from his waistband and yanked it over his head. Bare-chested, he regarded her. "Do you want me to continue?"

She nodded.

He removed his shoes and stockings then reached for the buttons of his breeches. He was already hard. How couldn't he be with her lovely body on display? But the way she watched him made his cock throb.

He loosened the breeches then tugged them down over his hips. Her eyes widened slightly, and she let out a shaky breath.

"Should I put them back on?"

"No." She sat. "I suppose I'm not used to seeing a man. You're larger than I expected."

"Since I'm being compared to a five-year-old, I won't let your observations go to my head."

She smiled. "I'm sorry. It's just that I didn't see…when it happened before I didn't see him. Will this hurt?"

"No." He took her hands and lay down on the bed beside her, stretching out until their bodies touched. "You'll feel only pleasure, and if I do anything you don't like, tell me and I'll stop."

"You'll stop if I ask?"

"Always," Jasper said, his fingers caressing her cheek. "And we needn't do any more tonight." He began to pull away. She was obviously distraught after the events of the night. He didn't want her to wake up in the morning and regret anything that happened between them because she hadn't been thinking clearly.

But before he could rise, she pulled him back and kissed him. It was not the shy, tentative kiss he'd expected, but the bold kiss of a woman who knew what she wanted and had made up her mind to have it. He broke the kiss, his hands cradling her face. "I don't want you to regret this. I don't want you to remember this night as a mistake."

She shook her head. "Impossible. I could never regret even a single moment with you."

This time he was the one who kissed her, claiming first her mouth then pulling her against him and sliding over her. When the kiss broke, she looked up at him. "This feels nice. Your skin against my skin."

"I'd like to think I can do better than *nice.*" He kissed her again, then allowed his mouth to travel to her breasts where he licked and nibbled until she was panting with need. He parted her thighs with one knee and felt the heat of her. He explored her body, taking his time, watching her reactions, waiting until she was all but squirming. "Still feel nice?" he asked.

"Better than nice," she said on a gasp as he touched his tongue to her. "Oh, please. *Please*."

Rising onto his elbows, he positioned himself between her legs. His cock pulsed, eager to be sheathed in her warmth. "Do you want me inside you?"

"Yes," she said, her eyes clearing slightly. "I want…something."

He entered her slowly, making sure she could feel him, making sure she had time to stop him. Her hips arched, and he had to grit his teeth to stop from thrusting inside her. "More?" he asked.

"Is that…?"

"Yes." His gaze met hers. "More, my love, or do you want me to stop?" He kissed her lips, trying to slow the pounding of his heart.

"You can still stop?"

He laughed. "I may not want to, but I can. Your choice."

She wrapped her arms around him. "More."

He slid deeper, and she moaned. "You're right. It doesn't hurt." She looked thoughtful. "It feels rather strange actually. But in a good way."

"More?" he asked between gritted teeth.

"That's not all?"

"Not quite."

"More. All. Everything," she whispered.

He thrust inside her then, wrapping himself to the hilt. For a moment he thought he saw explosions as his pleasure heightened. She arched her hips again, and fireworks seemed to burst in his vision. He had to bring her to climax quickly now. He couldn't wait much longer. He moved inside her, thrusting slowly, his eyes locked on hers as he slid in and out. Her breathing increased until she gave short, fast gasps at his every thrust and roll. "Still nice?" he asked.

She moaned, and her fingers dug into his back. He slid his hand between their bodies and found her small nub, slick with moisture. He circled it with his thumb, in rhythm to his movements. When he felt her tighten around him, he stilled, then thrust deeply, sliding against that center of her pleasure.

She came apart, her lips pressed together to keep from making too much noise. And as she reached climax, he allowed himself to soar. He let go, burying himself deep and stifling a feral growl as he pulled out and came on the bedclothes. He tried to keep his weight off her, but his arms shook. His entire body shook from the ferocity of his climax. It had been a long time, but he didn't think that alone could account for the way he was reacting.

Every part of him felt alive, sated, replete.

And when she pulled him close to kiss him lazily, he kissed her back and realized he didn't want her to ever let go.

Nineteen

She hadn't understood before why any woman would let a man touch her. Why any woman would consent to marriage if it meant allowing a man to do what Withernsea had done to her.

She understood now. She turned to look at Jasper, who lay beside her, chest heaving and eyes closed, and she felt a rush of tenderness. He'd been so gentle, so caring, so intent upon her pleasure. Nothing had been rushed or forced or taken. They'd both given freely and taken only what was offered.

"I love you," she murmured, reaching out to touch his lips. They curved in a half smile.

"That good, was it?" he said, eyes still closed.

"No."

His eyes opened.

"I mean, yes, but that's not why I love you."

"I know. And I know you wanted to forget all about what happened tonight, but do you feel safe enough to talk about it yet?"

She buried her face in his chest, feeling his rough hair brush her cheek and inhaling his familiar scent. He hadn't told her he loved her back. Surely he did love her back. But he was correct that they had more pressing matters. "He asked me to dance," she said, looking up at Jasper. "Withernsea. My father had stepped away for a moment, and Withernsea asked me to dance. I told him no, and he became angry. He threatened to ruin my father for breaking the betrothal agreement. I don't understand, Jasper. Why doesn't he marry another woman? Why does he want me so much?"

Jasper rolled onto his back and stared at the ceiling. "I've known men like Withernsea. I've watched them, studied them. Withernsea doesn't want you. He wants what he's been told he cannot have. You defied him. You made him look like a fool, and now it's a matter of pride with him. He'll have you because he must show the world that no one is out of his reach."

"My father believes he will ruin us."

"He may sue you for breaking the betrothal contract. I can't think that would ruin you."

She shook her head and swiped at the tears pooling in her eyes. "My father says Withernsea will see us evicted from this town house. We rent it, as do most of those in our circle. Withernsea will make sure no one else will lease to us. The duke will see no one accepts our credit. He'll make certain our investments go badly. I didn't think one man could do all of that, but…"

"He's the Duke of Withernsea." Jasper's face darkened. "He has a vast fortune and incredible power. He could do it."

Olivia felt her heart plummet into her belly. She felt as though she might be sick. "My father says I must marry Withernsea."

Jasper shot up. "What?"

"He says he needs time to protect our assets, and then when we're secure, I may run away or divorce the duke or—"

Jasper took her face in his hands. "No. It's out of the question. How can your father even consider it?"

"I believe it was the plan all along."

He frowned at her and then his hazel eyes turned dark. "He used me."

She nodded.

"The bastard used me to get you back, not for your mother's sake but because Withernsea was pressuring him." He raked a hand through his hair. "The knife attack makes sense now. Once I'd found you, I was to be disposed of. I should have worked it all out."

She placed a hand on his back. "It's not your fault."

"I should have seen. And to think I made you come back."

"You didn't force me. We had no other choice. It wasn't safe at the cottage anymore." And she'd wanted to return and give Richard a family. Little chance of that. What a fool she had been.

"You will not marry Withernsea," he said, turning the full force of his penetrating gaze on her. "I'll kill him before I allow that."

"It won't come to that. I'll take Richard and run away. Perhaps if I am gone, Withernsea will leave my family alone." Somehow she doubted it. If not for Richard, she would have married the duke and sacrificed herself for the sake of her parents. As Richard's mother and protector, she had to think of him first. She could not allow Withernsea to hurt the boy or use him to bend her to his will.

"I have another idea." Jasper stood, pulled on his breeches and paced the room. Olivia found her robe and donned it as he moved rapidly back and forth before the fire. Finally, he whirled to look at her. "I'll marry you."

Her hands froze in the act of tying the sash at her waist. "You want to marry me?" This wasn't exactly the proposal she'd dreamed of.

"If I'm your husband, I can protect you and your family. I'll get a special license—"

"Are you forgetting I am already betrothed?"

He waved the impediment away. "I know a few well-placed men who owe me favors. I'll get the license. Once you and Richard are safe, we'll move to safeguard your family. The man I served under in the war, Lieutenant

Colonel Draven, has the ear of the Prince Regent. The Regent is no friend of Withernsea."

That didn't surprise her. Withernsea had deep pockets and the Regent was a notorious profligate. Withernsea had refused to loan the Regent funds and denounced his spending in the Lords, going so far as to propose legislation designed to limit the Regent's funds.

"That feud is common knowledge."

"What's not common knowledge is what Withernsea did to you. If the Regent were to be present when you accused—no, that's simply your word against his. I'd have to find a way to make the duke admit what he's done in public. Then the prince will have cause to publicly denounce Withernsea. The duke will be ruined."

Olivia considered. "It's a good plan." The problem was, of course, that Withernsea would never admit what he'd done to Olivia to Jasper. But they would face that obstacle when they came to it. There was another larger issue. "I can't ask you to marry me, though. I am grateful you wish to help me and Richard, but that's too much to ask."

Again, he waved his hand. "It's not a concern. The marriage is the easy part."

She stared at him, uncertain how to interpret his statement. She hoped it meant he cared for her as much as she did him. "What is the hard part?" she asked.

"It will take some preparation to get the special license. I'd better start immediately." He released her and bent to retrieve his shirt.

"It's the middle of the night."

"For the people I need to see, the day has just begun." He pulled the shirt over his head then yanked on his coat and shoes. "I'll have to leave Town to fetch the license."

"No!" She grasped his hand. "I don't feel safe."

He took her face in his hands. "The attacker was after me, not you. I believe your father and Withernsea will want to give you a few days to adjust to the idea of marrying the duke. Put off going out or seeing anyone until I return. I'll be back as fast as possible. Never doubt that I will come back for you."

"And Richard." She wanted to remind him she had a son, that this thing he planned would involve a child as well.

"And Richard." His tone gave no indication her son was an afterthought. "If anything should happen while I'm away, I want you to take Richard and go to my friends. They will protect you. You can find them at The Draven Club on King Street. Knock on the door and tell Porter I told you to come and you need help. You can trust the men there with your life. I have." Finally, he tied on his mask and started for the door.

"How will you get out?" she asked, realizing she had no idea how he'd managed to get in.

"The front door," he said. "How else?" He kissed her hard and then cracked her door. After looking right and left, he glanced back at her. "As soon as I'm out the door, lock it. And Olivia?"

Her gaze fastened on his, the breath catching in her throat.

He paused. "Be careful." And he was gone.

She stood rooted in place for a long moment. She'd been so certain he would tell her he loved her. But perhaps that was one more dream that would never come true.

***

Jasper wove through the alleys of Seven Dials with a practiced efficiency. He knew it well, every rat-infested hovel, every grimy corner, every dingy doorway. He rather enjoyed Seven Dials. Few people gave him a second look.

It could be dangerous to take too much notice of anyone or anything here, even a masked man ducking into a gin house at four in the morning.

Rusty bells tinkled when he opened the door, and the barkeep raised his head from a table. "Off ta yer crib!" he said, voice groggy. His eyes widened when he saw Jasper. "Oh, it's you."

"Hello, Elias."

Elias Johnson squinted bloodshot eyes at him. They'd been blue once but the blue was hardly noticeable when surrounded by puffiness and red. His hair was a brown with gray mixed in and it stood like a boar's bristles on the top of his head. His jaw was haphazardly shaven, showing patches of gray and brown there too. "Yer the only one what calls me Elias anymore," he said, kicking the other chair at the table toward Jasper. "Everyone else calls me Johnny Gin."

"I never did care for alliteration."

Elias squinted. "Wot?"

"I need a favor." Jasper sat and crossed his arms over his chest after noting the sticky surface of the table.

"I didn't think you come for the Blue Ruin, even if it is the best in London."

Jasper didn't argue, not because it was true, but because he did need a favor. Elias owed him several favors. His wife had lost a ring her mother had given to her. It was only tin and paste, but Jasper had felt sorry for the weeping woman and tracked it down in the hands of a young thief-in-training. He'd only had to hold out his hand and the little girl had dropped it into his glove without fuss. He'd tossed her a penny because even thieves had to eat. Jasper had done other jobs for Elias as well, such as warning him when the excise man might be coming his way. It was extraordinary how quickly a gin shop might be turned into coffee house.

"You had a moll working here a few years ago who claimed to know the Archbishop."

"Susie, you mean? She were a rum piece, that Susie."

She was a blowsy prostitute who could swear like a sailor, but Jasper had no reason to doubt the stories she told. And as a young girl, dear Susie had lived in Canterbury. "Where is she?"

"Caught her taking a wee nip once too often and sent her on her way. Most of my customers want to drink, not rut. They can find a girl or a boy just outside the door if that's what they're after. Besides, the whither-go-ye were always accusing me of leering at Susie, so the mort caused more harm than good."

Jasper listened to the monologue patiently, and when Elias wound down, he asked again, "Where is the mort now?"

"I don't rightly know. The missus wouldn't like it if I knew something like that. I don't need no more curtain lectures."

Jasper narrowed his eyes. "Looks to me as though Mrs. Johnson whipped off for the moment. You're free to talk."

Elias leaned close. "That's what you think, and that's what she wants you to think. But she's always here or there." He pointed to the bar and then under a table. "You ought to hire her to work for you. She knows what mischief I have planned before even I do."

Jasper sighed, heavily. "Then might we step outside for a breath of air." He'd almost said *fresh* but nothing in Seven Dials could be described as *fresh.*

"No, we mightn't not," Elias said, beginning to sound exasperated. "You think she don't have spies out there?"

"Help me here, Elias. Where wouldn't Mrs. Johnson have eyes and ears?"

"I don't think it would be wise of me to answer that. And I don't know where Susie might be." He said the last few words loudly, which Jasper assumed was for his wife's benefit.

"I know where that jilt be," came a woman's voice from the other side of the bar. Jasper wasn't easily startled, but he hadn't expected Mrs. Johnson to be awake. She rose slowly from the floor behind the bar, first an arm on the bar, then the top of her frizzy red hair, then another arm. Finally, she pulled herself up. She was thin, too thin, and her face was all green eyes and freckles surrounded by a shock of that red hair. "And I'll tell you because you found me ring for me." She touched her finger where the cheap bauble resided.

"I appreciate that, Mrs. Johnson. I have a few questions for her. I'm not after nabbing her."

"That's too bad, but don't think I don't know what sort of questions you'll be asking. You want to know about her and that black-coat. She'll tell you, but she'll want a ha'penny."

Jasper understood the system in the rookeries. One paid for information, the more valuable, the more expensive. But Susie wouldn't consider this information valuable. She risked nothing by telling him since she didn't have to snitch on someone who might later stab her in the back. "Where might I find her?"

"That queer-mort went to Mrs. Pepper's flop house. She likes it because she doesn't always have to spread her legs to earn her keep, though she never seemed to mind doing that when she were here." She gave her husband a hard look. He, in turn, seemed very interested in the wood grain on the table.

Jasper tipped his hat. "Thank you, Mrs. Johnson. Elias. You've been most helpful."

She flicked her wrist. "Good bye then, Lord Jasper. I don't expect we'll see you again."

He stood. "Why do you say that?"

She shrugged. "Elias told you I have spies. I even hear a little of what happens in Mayfair. You won't be back. Now off with ye. I want to sleep a few hours before the first customer pounds on the door."

Jasper walked out, eyes alert for danger, but part of his mind wondering if Mrs. Johnson could possibly know about Olivia.

He made his way to Mrs. Pepper's. It was a good choice for a girl like Susie, who was charming and talkative. A man might go to Mrs. Pepper's for a bed for the night, but then he'd meet a girl like Susie, who would buy him a drink and go to his room with him. When he passed out from whatever she'd put in the drink, Susie would empty his pockets and purse. And when the mark woke the next morning, Mrs. Pepper would claim she never saw or heard of any Susie, all the while counting the mark's money and paying Susie her share. It was a common enough racket.

All was quiet at Mrs. Pepper's house, a coal-blackened structure that listed to one side. He entered through the unlocked door, and the boy sleeping in front of it jolted awake. "We're full," he said. Then he got a better look at Jasper's clothing and scrambled up. "But we could make room for one more. We have a special room if you have coin." He opened the door wide to admit Jasper.

A special room where he'd be robbed blind. "I need to talk to one of your wenches."

The boy, who didn't even have whiskers yet, blinked. "No wenches work here, sir."

"Yes, they do, and I want to talk to one of them—Susie."

"I don't know a Susie."

Jasper stepped forward, towering over the lad. "Yes, you do. You can fetch her for me or I'll search the place. If you fetch her, I'll pay you a ha'penny. If I search, I'll make sure to wake half the rogues so you're sure to get an earful."

The lad stared at him, looking like he might start to cry. "I'll fetch her. You stay right here."

"I won't move." Jasper planted his feet. "But if you take more than three minutes, I'll come looking for you."

The lad blew out an angry breath and ran into the bowels of the house. Jasper crossed his arms over his chest. The house was quiet enough. Somewhere someone murmured softly and a fair number of snores floated into the vestibule. Outside a cat yowled and another cat answered. Jasper was about to start after Susie himself when the lad returned, pulling Susie behind him. She was dressed in only her shift, her large breasts swinging freely under the thin material. She was scowling, but as soon as she saw Jasper, her face brightened, and she threw back her shoulders and pushed out her chest. "I know you," she said, pointing her finger at him. "Yer the bounty hunter, you is."

"Perhaps we can find somewhere a bit more private to speak."

"If it's *privacy* you want, it will cost you. Even a whore like me 'as standards. I 'ear tell that face of yourn is 'orrible enough to make children scream."

Jasper checked his temper. Barely. "I'll pay for the information, and that's all I want. Information."

"Fine. Yer the one who loses." She gestured toward a door off to the side. "We can jabber in the parlor."

Jasper flipped the serving lad a ha'penny and followed Susie into a dark room. Susie moved to light a lamp.

"Leave it," Jasper told her. "This won't take long." He moved around the room, making sure they were alone.

"I can't see to pour."

"I'm not thirsty, and forgive me for saying so, but even if I were, I wouldn't drink anything you handed me."

He'd expected an outraged gasp or fierce denial, but she only laughed. "Yer a wily one. Out with it then. What do you want to know?"

Jasper came to stand beside her, having finished his perusal of the room. "Tell me about the Archbishop."

Susie looked at him throughout the long pause. He could barely see her face in the dim light, but he could have sworn her eyes glittered. "What makes you think I know anything about the likes of that black-coat?"

Jasper rolled his eyes. "Perhaps because every time I was in Elias's gin shop you mentioned how the Archbishop used to pinch your arse and look down your blouse when you were a serving girl in The Old Palace in Canterbury."

She tossed her hair. "Seeing as how you know everything, why come to me now?"

"I think there's more to the story, and I want details."

"Why?"

"What does it matter? I'll pay you a shilling."

"Five."

Jasper laughed. "Highway robbery. One."

"Four then."

"Two."

"Three and any less and I might forget some of the details. Like the mole on his—" She held out her hand. Jasper dropped three shillings into her palm, and he barely had time to let the last go before her hand closed and darted away.

"Listen close, Bounty Hunter. I'm only saying this once. I went to work for the Arsebishop—that's what I call him—when I was ten. I was proud to be chosen at such a young age. I shouldn't have been. He were a clinker and I was fat headed."

Twenty minutes later, Jasper left Mrs. Peppers's wanting a bath. Susie's story had been exactly what he'd expected, but the man's abuse of power disgusted him nonetheless. It would be easy to look down his nose at Susie and her ilk, but that attitude ignored the systems that led to women prostituting themselves. She'd tried honest work and been abused and prostituted by the man who should have protected her and the others in his household. She'd escaped, only to find she had few other choices. At least now she'd made her own choices.

Olivia had had the advantage of education and upper class breeding to pave her way when she ran into trouble. She'd also been lucky enough to find a remote place to hide and to spend what little money she had wisely. But one misstep and she might have found herself in Susie's position. Now Jasper would make certain that never happened.

He'd make certain Withernsea never touched her again either.

Twenty

"Mama, are you paying attention?" Richard demanded two days later as they sat in the nursery breaking their fast together, as had become their custom.

"Of course, darling."

Richard put both fists on his hips. "What did I say?"

"Er…" She sighed. She'd been thinking about Jasper again, worrying about when he'd return, if he'd return, how he would manage to acquire the license, and yes, remembering every detail of the night they'd spent together. "I'm afraid I was woolgathering. You caught me."

Richard's brow creased. "What's woolgathering?"

"It means I was allowing my thoughts to wander, not focusing on what I should. And I should have been focusing on you."

"Nanny says it's hard for little boys to focus if they cannot go outside to run until their fidgets are tired."

The nanny, who was in another corner of the room, gasped. "Master Richard! Miss Carlisle, I'm so sorry. I didn't mean—"

Olivia raised her hand. "No need to apologize, Nanny. You're quite right. Little boys do need to go outside and run and play." She looked at Richard again. "And you will be able to again. Very soon. I promise."

His expression turned mulish. "You said London had huge, huge parks. When can I go to the park?"

Olivia gathered him in her arms and set him on her lap. "I know it's been hard for you. The garden is so small."

Richard nodded.

"You will be able to go out soon."

"When?"

"Soon. I promise." When Jasper returned and she and Richard were safe from Withernsea. Until then, she couldn't risk Withernsea finding out about his son. If he did, the duke would stop at nothing to stake a claim on his child. "I have a secret for you," she said impulsively, wanting to give Richard something to smile about. The transition to life in London had been hard for Richard. He did love his grandfather, little as the man deserved it, and all the toys he'd been given and the chance to learn with books and paper and pen. His favorite part of living in Town had been the plentiful food and the variety of dishes. Her own cooking skills were basic, and there were so many dishes Richard had never tried. Despite all the advantages their new situation offered, life wasn't quite as Olivia had envisioned. Her mother was still too ill to meet Richard, and the boy must always be quiet to avoid disturbing her sleep. Richard was also inside more than she would have liked. She'd planned to take him for carriage rides, to the museums, and to play in the park.

And they would do all of that, she promised herself, when Jasper and she married. He might just be marrying her for expediency, but she knew he cared for her. Maybe he would come to love her given time? After what Withernsea had done, she'd never thought she'd want a man to touch her and kiss her and make love to her. Jasper had changed all of that. She wanted him more than anything except Richard's health and happiness.

"What's the secret?" Richard asked.

She put a finger to her lips and looked pointedly at the nanny, who was busy folding linens on the other side of the room.

"What's the secret?" Richard repeated in a stage whisper.

"I saw Lord Jasper."

Richard's little face lit like a candle. "Jasper!" Her son's excitement at the mere mention of Jasper made her smile. She was not the only one who had missed him. "Can I see him?"

"He's had to go away for a few days. When he returns, we'll both spend time with him."

Dimsdale, the butler, appeared at the door. He was breathing heavily from climbing so many stairs to reach the highest floor of the house.

"What is it, Dimsdale?" Olivia asked, giving him time to catch his breath.

"Lord Carlisle wishes to see you, Miss."

She looked down at her plate of virtually untouched toast. "I've barely had a chance to eat, and I'd planned to listen to Richard read this morning."

The butler's face showed no expression. "His Lordship said he was sorry to interrupt, but this is an urgent matter."

Olivia blew out a breath. "Fine." She tried to rise, but Richard held onto her neck.

"No, Mama. Don't go."

"I have to, darling, but I'll be right back."

Richard released her, his bright face turning dark with a scowl. "You always say that and then I don't see you until supper."

He was right. Since she'd arrived home, she'd avoided her father as much as possible. It had been easy to stay busy nursing her mother and helping the servants arrange the household matters her mother was no longer able to attend to. Her son clearly needed her more than her mother or any servants today. "Not today. I'll be back in an hour. I promise."

Richard's face looked hopeful as she followed Dimsdale out of the room. He led her to her father's library, which didn't surprise her as her father often worked here in the mornings. She was taken aback to see that his door was closed. Voices rose and fell from within. "Is my father alone, Dimsdale?"

"No, Miss Carlisle. He has a caller."

Olivia was glad she had allowed her maid to take more time with her hair and dress this morning. She wore a pale blue day dress, and a quick peek in the mirror across from the library reassured her hair remained in place. "Shall I wait?"

"No, Miss. The caller is here for you as well."

Her heart leapt then. She hadn't thought it possible Jasper could return so quickly, but she'd also learned not to underestimate him. Without waiting for the butler to introduce her, she lifted the latch and entered the library, a bright smile on her face.

The Duke of Withernsea turned to face her, and from his chair behind the large desk, her father rose and made an apologetic face. Olivia felt her face grow hot, but when she turned to leave, Dimsdale closed the door in her face.

"I hope you are in no hurry to leave, Olivia," Withernsea said. He held out a hand, but she moved out of his reach.

"I have nothing to say to you, Your Grace."

"But I have something to say to you. Do sit down."

"I prefer to stand." She was well aware this meant her father and Withernsea would have to stand as well, and that suited her mood. She tossed her father a furious glare. How dare he do this to her! But the viscount avoided her eyes.

"You were always a contrary creature," Withernsea said, sitting despite the act being considered ill-mannered. "Your father has been unable to bring you to heel, but I have faith in my own abilities."

Olivia bristled. She'd been terrified of Withernsea when she'd been a girl. She was still frightened, but she had more than herself to think of. Her fear for Richard's safety gave her the strength to stand up to the duke. "I am not a dog to be brought to heel, nor am I under your authority."

"Olivia—" Her father began.

"No." She held up a hand. "I know we have talked about this, Father, but I cannot marry him."

Withernsea sighed. "Are we to start with this again?"

Lord Carlisle cleared his throat. "Olivia, I know the duke has been less than gentlemanly in the past—"

"Oh, now, I object," Withernsea said, looking not the least offended. "Did I want to sample the goods before I bought them? I admit I did, but we were betrothed, and a little sampling before the wedding is not at all uncommon."

Cold pierced through her. "Is that what you call it? Sampling? I call it rape."

"Don't exaggerate. You wanted it as much as I did, no matter how much you do not want to admit it in front of your father."

"I did not want…what happened to happen! I told you no. I told you to stop." Tears stung her eyes, but she refused to allow them to fall.

"Yes, you did. Lord Carlisle, let the record show she certainly made a show of resisting my advances. Happy, Olivia? You acted the part of the good girl."

She was so furious she couldn't speak. Was this what the duke truly thought? That she had been merely acting? She stared at him, and the smirk on his face was all the answer she needed. Yes, it was true that women were not supposed to give in to their baser natures, but the duke had known she had not been leading him on. She'd bitten, scratched, clawed, and hit. He knew he raped her, but now he wanted to paint it as something else. "I did not want you then. You deliberately chose to misunderstand me and to violate me. I do not want you now, and I will not consent to this marriage." She turned to leave the room. Let the two of them debate how to win her over in the days to come. By the time they had a plan, Jasper would return.

She was at the door when Withernsea's hand closed on her upper arm. She tried to shake him off, but he held on with a bruising grip. He yanked her back to the chairs before her father's desk.

"Careful, Your Grace," her father admonished.

"Oh, shut up, Carlisle," Withernsea snapped. "You're too weak, and she's been allowed far too much independence. You might not want to take her over your knee and spank her, but I will enjoy doing so." He thrust her into a chair and towered over her. "I'll enjoy it very much." Leaning down, he whispered, "My bare hand on your bare arse until your skin is red and you can't sit for a week."

Olivia flinched back, not liking the flash of desire in Withernsea's eyes at the thought of hurting her.

"Your Grace," her father interjected feebly. "You promised you would treat Olivia with the utmost deference."

"Of course." Withernsea stepped back and bowed graciously. But his expression was telling. Once she was in his power, he'd do whatever he wanted to her.

"Olivia, I know you have reservations. But we've discussed this matter," her father said. "And I've had no choice but to agree to the marriage contract. You will be married tomorrow."

"What!" She rose, but at a look from Withernsea sank down again. "No!"

"Yes. The arrangements have been made."

She closed her mouth. She'd run away once, and she could do it again. She'd take Richard tonight and her father would never see her again.

"And now don't you think it's time you shared your secret with His Grace?" her father said.

She blinked at him, uncomprehending. She didn't have a secret. Except…

"No!" she screamed. "No!" She tried to run for the door, but Withernsea caught her and shoved her to the ground. Just then the door opened, and Nanny entered, Richard beside her, his small hand in hers. His eyes were huge as he took in his grandfather's stricken face, his mother lying on the floor, and the man towering above her.

Olivia saw it all clearly now. Her father had known she would run, and he wanted to prevent her from doing so. But this betrayal was too much. She would never forgive him.

Withernsea stared at the boy, his brow furrowed. Olivia pushed to her knees and held her arms open. She might have hidden the truth of who he was longer, but it would have come out at some point. Richard needed her in that moment.

"Mama!" Richard said and rushed into her embrace.

"This is your son?" Withernsea said. Then he reached out and touched the boy's hair, so like his own. "This is *our* son." He threw back his head and laughed.

Olivia held Richard tighter.

"Who is that, Mama?"

"No one. Just stay close to me, darling."

"Oh, this is too much," Withernsea chuckled. "This is too perfect. I have a son. And you, little wench, thought to keep him from me."

"Mama," Richard wailed.

"Come here, boy," Withernsea said. Richard shook his head. "Don't you know who I am?" He looked at Olivia. "Doesn't he know I'm his father?"

Richard's gaze locked with Olivia's. "Is it true?"

"No." She shook her head. "He might have been there when you were conceived, but he is not your father."

"That's not what the law says," Withernsea said.

"You cannot prove he is yours and since we are not married, you can make no claim on him," she shot back.

"That will all change tomorrow. We marry, and I'll acknowledge him. Anyone can look at him and know he's mine."

"I will not marry you!" she said, immediately regretting the words. She should have played along. She should have pretended to be agreeable.

"Oh, yes you will." Withernsea grasped Richard's arm and pulled. Olivia held on, tugging him back until Richard began to cry.

"Your Grace! Miss Carlisle! You're hurting him," the nanny cried.

Olivia immediately let go. Richard stumbled into Withernsea's clutches, and a fear unlike any Olivia had ever felt all but took the breath from her lungs.

"You will marry me tomorrow," the duke said. "Or you never see him again." And lifting the boy, he walked out of the library and then out the front door.

***

Jasper's horse had thrown a shoe in the worst possible place imaginable. Well, he amended, not the worst imaginable. He'd been in places far worse—places with soldiers holding bayonets rushing at him, places with cannon balls falling from the skies, places with snow falling so fast his feet sank in it to the ankles—and, of course, there'd been the fire.

The dark road outside Oakham was not the worst place he could remember. But with the horse limping beside him, the rain falling in a cold, wet deluge, and the night so dark he couldn't see his hand in front of his face, Jasper wasn't inclined to split hairs. He shouldn't have pushed the horse so hard. He shouldn't have pushed himself. But now that he had the special license, he wanted to be with Olivia. He didn't want to wait another day to claim her and marry her.

With the information Susie had given him about her abuse at the hands of the archbishop, it had been easy to persuade the man to overlook his reservations and issue the license. Jasper had been so elated to have it in his hands, he had ignored the rain, ignored the late hour, and set out anyway. Now, he was stuck.

Did he walk back to Oakham or did he press on?

Or did he wait out the rain and the night under a tree, with only the horse for warmth?

He walked on, pondering his options. The sound of the rain was loud, but it didn't cover the sharp *snap* of a twig breaking. Jasper froze. It might have been the horse. It might have been his imagination. But he hadn't survived as a member of Draven's suicide troop without trusting his instincts.

He was not alone.

Jasper quickly assessed the situation. He had a pistol, but it was useless to him at the moment because if he tried to prime it the powder would get wet. It might be too wet to be of any help already. He had a knife, but how was he to wield it if he couldn't see a damn thing?

On the other hand, whoever was out there faced the same obstacles. Jasper turned the horse so the beast was at his back, extracted his knife from his boot, and stood still, listening.

Nothing.

Long minutes ticked by, and finally Jasper spoke. "I know you're out there. Show yourself."

No reply. Not a sound. Not even a hint of movement—until it was too late.

The blow came from the side and knocked Jasper to the ground. The horse reared, and Jasper rolled away to avoid being trampled. The rocks in the road dug into his arms and shoulders, and he got a mouthful of muddy rain water, which he spat out. Before he could gain his feet, the attacker was on top of him. Jasper reached up blindly, searching for the man's arm. He caught it at the wrist then used his other hand to pry the man's grip off his throat. The rain made everything slick, which made it possible for Jasper to have a measure of success. He used his hold on the man to throw him off, rolling to the side and wrenching the man's body at the same time.

The man went over, his knife clattering on a nearby rock. At least Jasper assumed it was a knife. He couldn't see it, but it didn't sound heavy enough to have been a pistol. Now the rain became Jasper's enemy as he tried to restrain the man, who wriggled out of his hold like a fish. Jasper grabbed for him but caught empty air. Jasper stumbled to his feet and lunged, catching an article of clothing and yanking back. They both fell in a cold puddle, but Jasper was on top this time. He wedged his forearm across the assailant's neck and used his weight to hold him down. The man's head was in the water, only his face protruding from the puddle. Jasper released his pressure on the man's throat briefly, allowing the man to rise and gasp for air.

"Who sent you? Tell me or I shove you all the way down and let you drown."

"No one," the man gasped. "I'm a highway robber."

Jasper shoved the man down until his face was submerged and he surfaced sputtering for breath. "Liar. Two knife attacks on me in the space of a month?"

"The attack in Penbury wasn't me."

Fool, Jasper thought. He would have done better to pretend he didn't know anything of the other attack. "Then who was it? Who ordered it?"

"I can't say."

"Then there's no point keeping you alive." He pushed the man's head into the water and held it a bit longer this time.

When the man began to flail, he lessened the pressure and hauled him up by the throat. The attacker coughed and sputtered and gasped for air.

"Last chance. Next time you go down, you don't come up."

"If I tell you, you won't kill me?"

"You'll walk away from this. I give you my word."

The man hesitated. "The Duke of Withernsea hired me to follow you, and if you found anything to kill you and bring the girl to him."

The revelation wasn't a surprise, but Jasper still recoiled. He'd been right all along. Withernsea had had him followed and then tried to kill him so his own man could abduct Olivia and bring her back to him. "Miss Carlisle is in London now. Why are you still following me?"

"The duke doesn't like loose ends. He wants you dead. He'll pay twenty pounds to the man who kills you."

Twenty pounds. Was that all he was worth?

"And is twenty pounds worth your life?"

"No, sir! No!"

Jasper released him, pushing him back into the puddle and standing. When the man reemerged, Jasper hauled him to his feet. "Get out of here, and don't let me ever see you again."

The man ran away, his feet splashing in puddles as he fled.

Jasper went back to the skittish horse, calmed him, and began walking again. A few more miles and they'd reach a posting house or perhaps a farmer who could spare a horseshoe. One thing was certain, despite the dark and the rain and the cold, Jasper had to press on. If Withernsea was still sending assailants after him, he must be more determined to possess Olivia than Jasper had imagined.

She wasn't safe in London, and he now he could only pray he was not too late.

Twenty-One

People always said nothing ever changed. Although there were a great many things Olivia would have liked to see change, this afternoon she was glad nothing in her father's household appeared to have changed. The family dined at half past six and the servants took their meal an hour before. At about half past five, Olivia could count on all the servants in her father's employ to be sitting at the long table in the servants' quarters. She'd made certain her maid had no reason to check on her. As soon as Withernsea had left with Richard—*kidnapped* Richard—she'd taken to her bed and hadn't emerged again. When her maid had come into her room, Olivia pretended she was sleeping.

In reality, she'd been planning. And now she would put her plan into action. Jasper had said to go to the Draven Club if she needed help. She needed help, and St. James's was not far. The longest distance she must traverse was that from her bed chamber to the front door.

When she heard the longcase clock chime a quarter to six, Olivia rose and slipped on her half boots and a hat. She was already dressed, having donned a spencer over her day dress before pulling the covers up to her chin and pretending to sleep. She had a few coins in her valise, so she secreted them in a pocket under her skirts and tiptoed to the bed chamber door, careful to avoid any creaky floorboards. She opened the door silently, peering out to be certain the corridor was empty. She knew the servants' whereabouts. Her father was another matter. And she couldn't entirely rule out the chance that her father had posted a footman to guard the exits. He wouldn't want her to run away before he could see her married to Satan.

But then who would expect her to run when her son was in the devil's hands? No one. They thought they'd beaten her.

Withernsea didn't know her.

He thought women were weak, little more than animals to be used as men saw fit. Her father knew her a bit better—or he had. He'd known her when she'd been nothing more than a girl. She'd been obedient then and subservient. Now she was a mother, and she'd do anything to save her son. That was the only directive she felt compelled to obey.

She crept down the stairs leading to the vestibule. Halfway down, she peered over the rail. There were no footmen at the door. All appeared deserted. She started down the next step then froze when she heard her father's voice.

"Where is Dimsdale?" he asked.

"Dining in the servants' quarters, my lord," a voice replied.

Olivia let out a slow breath. She'd been right to be cautious. The footman must have been standing just out of view, near her father's library. Now she was trapped. She could exit via the servants' stairs, but if she were seen, the servants would inform her father immediately. She wouldn't get far.

"Fetch him for me, Thompkins."

"Yes, my lord."

Olivia's eyes widened as the footman's steps faded. This was her chance. She couldn't see her father's library, but she had to hope he'd retreated back inside. She took two more steps, painfully aware that the next step would render her visible to anyone in the vestibule. Trembling, she stepped down, looking over her shoulder and half expecting to see her father glaring at her.

But the vestibule was empty.

Heart thudding in her chest, she rushed to the front door, unlocked the bolt, and pulled it open. Outside, a light drizzle fell, but now that she was free of the house, she felt as though she'd stepped into sunshine after months of imprisonment. Wasting no time, she started in the direction of St. James's. She hated to spend the last of her coins, but she couldn't walk to St. James's unescorted. Custom held that ladies did not frequent St. James's after dark. It wasn't dark yet, but darkness wasn't far off. She'd be one of only a very few ladies there, and she did not relish being accosted by stupid young bucks looking for an easy target.

Walking briskly to put as much distance between her and her father's town house as possible, she finally glanced over her shoulder then lifted her hand to flag a passing hackney. It took several attempts before one stopped.

"You all by yerself?" the jarvey asked.

Olivia didn't answer the question. "Take me to The Draven Club on King Street in St. James's."

"Wot's a lady like you want with a gentleman's club?"

"That's not your concern. I have coin. I can pay. That's all you need worry about."

The jarvery shrugged. "Was just being polite, I was."

Olivia climbed into the cab and tried not to touch anything she didn't have to. The interior was filthy, the muddy, wet boots of other passengers having dirtied the straw and the seats. It smelled like wet dog, but she didn't care. She was away. She was speeding toward the people who could help her save Richard.

The journey took only a few minutes. The hackney stopped and she climbed out, tossing the driver her coins.

"Want me to wait, yer ladyship?"

"No." She had no more coin, and if she couldn't find help here, she didn't know where she would go.

The club was in a gray stone building, indistinguishable from any other on the street. It didn't sport a bow window as did White's and no men went in and out. Olivia climbed the steps and rapped on the door. It seemed an age before the door finally opened and an older gentleman with silver hair and a wooden peg for a leg stood in the doorway. He didn't seem surprised to see a woman at the door.

"May I help you?"

"I hope so. Lord Jasper sent me. He said if I needed help to come here."

"I see. Will you come in?"

She nodded, grateful to be out of the wet.

"I am Porter," the gentleman said. "Master of the House." He led her into a warm entryway, paneled in wood and lit by a large chandelier. On one wall stood a suit of armor. On the other two Scottish broadswords. Directly across from her hung a shield cut in half by a sword with a skull. Olivia shivered.

"You must be half frozen," the Master of the House said. "I'll return with hot tea."

"Really, I just need to see one of Lord Jasper's friends. He mentioned a Mr. Wraxall?"

The man's brow furrowed. "I shall see what I can do. Wait here."

Olivia would have liked to sit in one of the cushioned chairs beside the door, but she was wet and smelled of dog from her journey in the hackney. So she stood where she had been left and waited. She didn't have to wait long. Porter returned, leading a broad-shouldered man with wiry red hair behind him. Olivia didn't know who he was, but she prayed he could help her. He had the same air of authority and command about him Jasper did.

"Lieutenant Colonel Draven," Porter said with a bow. "I'll be right back with refreshment."

"That's not necessary," she told him, even as he walked away.

"You're wasting your breath," Draven said. "Porter tells me you are a friend of Lord Jasper's."

"He said to come here if I needed help."

"And here you are."

Tears began to prick her eyes, but she pressed her fingers against them, refusing to let them fall. Richard needed her. She would not give into womanly hysterics.

"Why don't we go somewhere we can sit down?" He gestured to a panel in the wall, where she could see the outline of a door. He pushed against it, and it opened into a small room with green carpeting, a couch and two chairs, and a fire. "After you, Miss."

Olivia hesitated, uncertain whether she could trust this man. But then what other choice did she have? Taking a deep breath, she entered the room, jumping when the door closed heavily behind her.

***

Jasper didn't know how long he'd been walking in the rain. The mud on the road had long since found its way into his boots and now weighed them down. His horse walked with head hung low, seemingly resigned to the rain and the dark. Why couldn't the animal have thrown the shoe closer to a posting house? Jasper hadn't even seen a farmhouse or a cottage where he might stop and ask for assistance. Nothing to do but walk on.

He concentrated on putting one foot in front of the other until one of those feet sunk deeper than the other and he found himself on the ground with a face full of mud. "What the devil?"

It didn't take long for him to realize what had happened. There's been a hole in the road and he'd been unable to see it in the dark. He'd stepped right into it and was fortunate he hadn't broken his ankle.

At least he hoped he hadn't.

He pulled himself out, testing the ankle, and relieved it only gave a mild twinge of irritation. Jasper was equally relieved the horse had not followed him into the hole and stood waiting for him on the road.

It was time Jasper faced facts. He would be no use to Olivia if he got himself killed out here in the rain and the black. As much as he felt the pressing need to return to London as quickly as possible, at this rate, he might not return at all. He would have to find shelter and wait out the storm. He could start again when it was light.

He limped off the road, leading the horse to a small group of trees. There he slid down under one and fashioned an umbrella of sorts out of his saddle bag. The horse blew out a breath, and Jasper patted his neck.

A few more hours and the sun would come up. A few more hours and he'd be back on his way to Olivia.

***

Olivia sat waiting, Lieutenant Colonel Draven's bright blue eyes trained on her face with interest. Now that she'd finished her story, his gaze shifted to the fireplace. He was a man just shy of fifty, and as she would expect of a soldier, he didn't speak much. He listened to her story without comment except to ask the occasional question. In the silence, the fire crackled and her tea cup clinked against the saucer.

"I don't know what to do," she said again, having ended her story with that phrase. "I cannot marry the Duke of Withernsea, but I would do anything for my son. I cannot lose him."

"I understand, Miss Carlisle. Lord Jasper was right to tell you to come to me. Any of my men would help you, but I am in a unique position to do so."

Olivia's spirits rose. For the first time since she'd seen Withernsea in her father's library, she felt a glimmer of hope.

"You are correct that you cannot go home. If you do, you'll be forced to marry in the morning. I need time to put Lord Jasper's plan into motion. The problem is where to put you in the meantime."

"Sir, I would rather not wait to retrieve my son. If you could go with me to Withernsea's home now—"

"As anxious as you are for your son, it would be dangerous for you to approach Withernsea right now. Surely, he will not harm his own son. He needs him to control you. Don't give up the little advantage you have now by walking straight into his net."

Olivia swiped at an errant tear. She could only imagine how terrified Richard was in a new place and without her. They'd never been apart, not even for one night, and now he'd been dragged away by strangers and unable to see his mother.

"You must be strong, Miss Carlisle. I promise it will not be long before you have your son back."

She took a deep breath and nodded.

"Would you consent to stay at my lodgings tonight? I have a spare room, though that still won't make it proper, not in the least. But I can assure you neither your father or Withernsea will ever think to look for you there."

And yet, if Lord Jasper returned to London and found out she'd run from her father's house, he would know she'd go to the Draven Club and be able to trace her to Draven's lodgings.

"I would very much appreciate that," she said.

"I'm an old bachelor, and I don't employ any maidservants, but I do have a scullery maid. I could see if she'd be willing to attend you."

Olivia waved a hand. "I promise you, sir, I can attend to myself."

"Then it's settled. With any luck, Lord Jasper will return by morning and we can have you married and safe from Withernsea. Then all we need do is retrieve your son," Draven said, pulling the cord to summon a servant. "If Lord Jasper could run into a burning building to save a man while the enemy attacked all around him, he can rescue your son from the town house of a spoiled duke."

She nodded and choked back the other tears threatening to fall.

Porter entered and Draven ordered a hackney. When Porter was gone, Olivia said, "Is that how Lord Jasper received his scar? He ran into a burning building?"

Draven gave her a long look. "He hasn't told you?"

"He's told me bits and pieces."

"Then it's not my place to say more. But I will say this—Lord Jasper is a hero. He won't admit it. In fact, he blames himself for not doing enough, but he is one of the bravest, most honorable men I know."

"Yes," she agreed. "He is that and more."

The hackney ride was not long. Olivia barely paid attention to where the driver took them, and when the conveyance stopped, she climbed out dutifully. Draven had an umbrella, and he used it to shelter her from the rain, which had turned from a drizzle into a downpour while she'd been inside the club. Now, as he ushered her to the front door of his building, Olivia noticed how dark it had become. She wondered if she had been missed yet. Surely her maid had come to dress her for dinner and reported Olivia was gone. What had her father done? Had he sent word to Withernsea? Had he gone out to search for her himself?

Draven led her into a hallway, pausing at the door to shake out the umbrella and then stowing it in a stand that held several others. "My rooms are on this floor," he said, leading her down the hallway and pausing in front of a door. Olivia could see how what had once been a grand town house had been remodeled into living quarters for several families.

He withdrew a key and unlocked his door, pushing it open and gesturing for her to enter. "After you."

She stepped into a small receiving room with doors on either side that most likely led to the more private living quarters. The room was small and sparsely furnished. There were no pictures on the wall or decorative touches. But everything looked clean and comfortable. The only thing that struck her as odd was a valise that had been left in the middle of the room. Had Draven been planning to go away?

"Ward?" Draven called, walking to the valise and tapping it with his toe. "Ward, where are you? What is this?"

The door on the right opened, but it wasn't a butler. Instead, a woman with long, dark hair down about her shoulders and large brown eyes stood in the doorway. She wore a dress in the style of the day, but something about her did not look English. Her eyes roved over Olivia and then flashed fire.

"Catarina?" Draven said, his tone incredulous. Olivia looked from the lieutenant colonel to the woman and back again. He obviously had not been expecting her. Was it her valise then? "What are you doing here?"

"Interrupting, apparently," she said, her accent definitely not British. Olivia couldn't place it, but then she'd never been out of England. "I will leave you and your whore." She marched to the valise and lifted it.

"Catarina—no. I..." He trailed off, looking completely stunned and at a loss for words.

Catarina put her hands on her hips. "I won't stay if she is here." Her gaze landed on Olivia again.

Olivia wished she could creep back out the door and away from those accusing eyes.

"Do you know how I know you are not his wife?"

Olivia shook her head.

"Because *I* am his wife!"

Olivia frowned. Hadn't Draven said he was a bachelor? "Mrs. Draven," she said, "I think you misunderstand."

"Oh, I understand!" She looked at her husband. "I understand I should never have come." She grasped her valise and stormed out, slamming the door in her wake. Draven and Olivia stood in shocked silence for a moment. Then Olivia looked at him.

"Well?" she said.

He didn't speak for several seconds. Finally, he seemed to find his voice. "I apologize. I had no idea—that is to say, I haven't seen her in years. I—"

She shook her head. She didn't want an explanation. "Aren't you going after her?"

He stared at her, clearly bewildered. Then, as though galvanized by some unseen force, he all but ran for the door and was gone. Olivia gave a long sigh, fighting exhaustion and fear. She prayed Richard was well. She prayed Jasper would come. She prayed Draven could help her.

Draven returned a short while later, alone and unwilling to speak about what had happened. He had his man show her to a guest chamber, where she sank onto the bed and fell asleep without even undressing. Sometime later—she had no idea how long she'd been sleeping—a tap on the door awakened her. Rubbing her eyes, she called out. "Who is it?"

"Draven," came the succinct answer. "Will you come to the parlor? I have something to discuss with you."

She took only a moment to straighten her hair and skirts before making her way to the parlor. The flat was not large, and she had no trouble finding the square room with walls papered in a pretty blue rose pattern. Draven stood by the fireplace, and she noted immediately he was wet and probably cold. But whatever he had to say obviously could not wait for his comfort—or for daylight, as the clock in the room gave the time as half past four in the morning.

"You've been out," she said.

"The weather is atrocious. Please sit." He indicated a blue-and-white striped chair. She took it, aware her legs wobbled with anxiety.

"I apologize for being the cause of you having to go out in such weather."

He waved a hand. "The weather was only an impediment so far as it made finding the Regent difficult. It seemed I'd reach one event and he'd have already left for the next. It took me until after midnight to catch him. But I did catch him, and I did speak with him."

"About me?"

"Yes, but more specifically about Withernsea. Once I mentioned that I had information about Withernsea, the prince gave me his full attention. I know Lord Jasper made you aware of how much the prince dislikes Withernsea. Not only has Withernsea denied the prince personal loans, he's spoken out against the Regent's largesse in the Lords. The duke has been a thorn in the Regent's side for some time. He'd like to pluck it out, and you provide the perfect implement."

"The Regent will help us then?"

Draven shrugged. "If he is able. He won't stick his neck out. He's a coward at heart. You understand that?"

She nodded. "So we need to make it easy for him."

"As Lord Jasper suggested, you must expose Withernsea for what he is. There can be no doubt. This can't be seen as political maneuvering by the prince. Withernsea has too many allies."

"The extent of the duke's abuse must be clear."

"Crystal clear. Do you think you can manage to pry a confession from him?"

Olivia considered. The duke was careful. She'd thought back a thousand times to the night he'd raped her. Withernsea had planned it perfectly so as to make certain he was not caught, and if she accused him, she would be the one held at fault. But the duke was also a proud man, and undoubtedly when he arrived at her father's house in the morning, ready to wed, only to find his bride had bolted, his pride would be nicked. Could she use that to her advantage? Did she have any choice?

"Well?" Draven asked.

"I have to do it," she said. "For Richard's sake."

"Will you be able to face the duke? To stand up to him and to the censure you will receive if he admits what he's done? It certainly isn't fair, but Society almost always blames women as much, if not more, than men. They will say you lie or seduced him or said yes and then changed your mind and cried rape."

"I know what *they* will say. All the matters to me is Richard." And Jasper. But he knew the truth, and he wanted her anyway. Jasper believed her.

Draven gave her a long look. "I see Lord Jasper chose well."

"I don't understand."

"It's obvious he cares for you, and I see why."

Her cheeks flushed warmly.

"You're braver than you look. What is that line from Shakespeare? *And though she be but little, she is fierce.*"

"I will protect my son."

"And I will help you. Now, we'll need paper and pen." He crossed to a small desk and began rummaging through a drawer. "I'm no wordsmith, but together I believe we can craft a letter that will anger Withernsea just enough to cause him to act."

"You want me to write to Withernsea?"

"We'll have to decide on the exact words, but the gist of it shall be that if he wants to marry you, he must meet you and discuss your terms." He laid a sheet of foolscap on the desk and motioned to her. "I'll have one of my servants hire a boy to deliver it. The duke won't know where you are hiding. We'll time the delivery for just after he returns home from your father's town house."

Olivia felt her belly roll. "He won't like that."

"Good. The angrier he is, the less likely he will be to think before he speaks. But where to have you meet?"

"If the prince must overhear, then we must be where he is."

"The Ashmont ball tomorrow then. The prince always attends. I'll see about securing an invitation for us. But first, the letter for Withernsea."

Olivia moved to the chair at the desk and dipped her quill in ink. "How shall I begin? *To His Grace the Duke of Withernsea*?"

"Oh, no. You will have pricked his pride by bolting from the wedding. Now we tweak his nose. *My dearest Withernsea...*"

Olivia raised a brow, but she put the pen to paper and wrote the words. She knew she played with fire, and she could only hope she would not be the one to be burned.

Twenty-Two

Jasper was in a foul mood. He'd spent the night in the rain. The skies had not cleared until dawn, and then it had taken most of the morning to walk to a posting house, have his horse reshod, and navigate the muddy roads into London. It was afternoon by the time he climbed the steps to Carlisle's town house and slammed the knocker down three times.

He had the license. Now all he needed was Olivia and Richard.

Dimsdale opened the door and then began to close it again as soon as he saw Jasper standing on the stoop. Jasper understood the compulsion. He hadn't wasted time stopping home to wash and change. When Olivia and Richard were safe, he would have time for such frivolities. Now all that mattered was making her his wife and making certain Withernsea could never touch her again.

And so when the butler tried to slam the door, Jasper stuck out a boot and wedged it open. "Not so fast, Dimsdale."

"You are not welcome here, my lord."

"Good, because I don't intend to return." He wedged his shoulder against the door and shoved until it opened and Dimsdale had no choice but to admit him. "Kindly fetch Master Richard and Miss Carlisle for me. Then you'll never have to look on me again."

"Thomas! William!" the butler called. Thundering footsteps made the house shake before two large footmen burst through the door to the servants' stairs. Dimsdale pointed at Jasper. "Help Lord Jasper find his way out."

Jasper was tired, hungry, and filthy, and that meant this was the perfect time for a fight. It had been months since he'd had a good fight. And these two liveried servants, in their brass buttons and knee breeches, were no match for the likes of the criminals Jasper dealt with daily in the London rookeries. So when the dark-haired one came for him, Jasper stepped neatly aside then turned and caught the man's flailing arm, turned it behind his back, and jerked it high until he heard the pop.

Obviously, the butler and the blond footman heard it too, though the dark-haired footman was screaming quite loudly now. That didn't stop the blond from attacking, although he was a bit more careful. He came at Jasper with his fists raised, throwing punches. Jasper wasn't as good in the ring as his friend Ewan, but he knew how to fight on the streets. Jasper allowed the blond to land a punch that glanced off his cheek, so Jasper could move in close enough to land a hard kick to the man's knee.

It was underhanded and ungentlemanly.

Jasper didn't care.

When the man faltered, Jasper grasped his throat and slammed him against a wall so hard a painting on a nearby wall collapsed to the floor.

Then he turned to the butler. The man looked as though he might run, but Jasper pointed to the floor. "If you make me chase you, you'll regret it for the rest of your life."

The butler's eyes widened with fear.

"On your knees."

He knelt without any protest. He needn't give any considering Carlisle had heard the noise and come to investigate.

"What the devil happened here? What do you think you are about?"

Jasper stalked toward Olivia's father. Something in his eyes must have alerted the viscount that Jasper meant to hurt him because he stumbled to reverse his path. Jasper reached out and grasped his shoulder, pushing the man down to his knees beside the butler.

"Where is she?"

The viscount's gaze was defiant, but the butler began to weep and cried out, "I don't know, my lord. Please don't kill me."

"Do you mean to tell me Miss Carlisle is not here?" Jasper's chest tightened.

The butler shook his head. "She ran away last night. We don't know where she is."

Jasper turned his attention to the viscount. Olivia would never leave Richard. If she'd run, something must have happened to the boy. Jasper leaned down to stare into her father's eyes. "What did you do?"

"It's not your business."

Jasper grabbed the man by the throat and hauled him up. "I'm making it my business. What did you do?"

"Kill me if you like," the viscount gasped out. "I won't help you."

"I will," said a female voice from the stairs leading to the upper floors. Jasper glanced up and saw a woman in a long white night rail and a flowing white robe. Her gray hair was down about her shoulders, and she was so thin and frail she looked as though a summer breeze would topple her. But the resemblance between Lady Carlisle and her daughter was unmistakable.

"Caroline!" the viscount rasped. "Go back to bed! You don't have the strength—"

"Someone must, and it's clearly not you. You think I don't know what goes on in this house? You think you can dose me with laudanum and keep me oblivious?"

Jasper lowered the viscount to the floor, loosening his grip on the man's neck but keeping him within reach.

"I was only following the doctor's orders," Carlisle said.

"I know the doctor's orders. Keep me comfortable. Did you think I didn't know I was dying?" She swayed, but reached for the banister, catching it to stabilize herself. "You can keep me comfortable tomorrow. Today I will help my daughter. I should have done it a long time ago." She looked at Lord Jasper.

"Where is she?" he asked.

"I don't know," she said softly, seeming to crumple. "Lord Carlisle does not know either. She's run away. Again." She gave her husband a chastising look. "Just when we had her back with us."

The fear slicing through Jasper lessened slightly at her words. Withernsea didn't have her. He knew where she'd go if she ran. To the Draven Club. At least, he hoped to God she'd listened when he told her to go there if she needed help while he was away.

"Why did she run?" he asked. "She must have had a reason to take her son and flee."

Carlisle put a hand on his neck, as though worried Jasper would grab him again.

"You'll have to ask him." Lady Carlisle pointed to her husband. "I assume it has something to do with Withernsea's visit yesterday."

Jasper took a step toward Carlisle. "What did you do?" He'd never wanted to hurt a man so much. He shook with the effort of holding his anger in check. This was Olivia's father and Richard's grandfather. He was an old man. Hurting him was unforgivable.

"I didn't have any choice," Carlisle said, retreating until his back thumped against the wall. "He would have ruined us if I didn't agree."

"Agree to what? Marriage? To that monster?"

The viscount winced. "And it was only for a little while, to give me time to find a way around him…"

"Richard, no." The viscountess covered her face.

He stared up at her. "I was doing it for you. To keep you from being thrust out on the street!"

"I'd rather that than lose my child. I thought I'd never see her again, and now…now…"

Jasper raised a hand. "I know where she is. She should be safe enough. Calm yourself, Lady Carlisle." He looked at the viscount. "You should have come to me for help. If you think I'll allow Withernsea to destroy her or you, think again. Although, maybe you're not worth saving."

He turned to go. He couldn't reach the Draven Club quickly enough.

"Withernsea has Master Richard." Carlisle's words were like ice on bare skin. Jasper froze.

"What did you say?" Jasper turned slowly. He advanced on the viscount until the man lifted his hands before him in a protective gesture.

"The duke took the child. What could I do?"

"And you call yourself a father, a grandfather." Jasper started for the door. It seemed the Draven Club would be his second stop.

"And what do you propose to do about it?" the viscount called after him. "If you marry her, Withernsea will ruin me and you."

"Withernsea can't ruin me," Jasper called over his shoulder before opening the door. "I'm already ruined."

And Jasper would ruin the duke first.

***

Slipping inside the duke's large house in Grosvernor Square was a simple matter. Jasper had slinked behind the heavily guarded and fortified lines of the French dozens of times, but it was the deadly alleys and sewers of the

London rookeries where he'd honed his skills. If he could bypass the cutthroats and thieves of London's underground, he could avoid detection by a handful of footmen and maids.

He entered through the servants' kitchen door on the ground floor while the servants were having supper. He caught snatches of their conversation and quickly learned the duke was dining at his club and would then attend a ball. Consequently, some of the staff had been given the night off. That made Jasper's task even easier.

He made his way to the family quarters on the second floor without seeing another servant. He had no illusions wherever Richard was being kept would be unguarded. But that worked in his favor as well. He wouldn't have to search every bed chamber. Richard would be held in the one with a footman outside.

When Jasper emerged onto the floor from the servants' stairs, he peered down the corridor, immediately spotting a man sitting outside a door. The man was bent over a plate, shoveling potatoes into his mouth. He grumbled to himself, and Jasper imagined he groused about having to sit up here while his friends dined together below.

If Jasper moved down the corridor, he'd be spotted immediately. A man in a mask was always suspicious, especially here, where he did not belong. Jasper reached into his pocket and found a pair of dice. He usually had a pair. They were good for passing the time or running his fingers over when he was thinking. He withdrew them silently, mentally measuring the distance between himself and the other end of the corridor. If he could slide the die silently along the carpet until it pinged against the wall on the far side, the footman might rise to investigate it. That would be enough of a distraction for Jasper to incapacitate him. But he had to throw the die without the footman seeing it roll past and with enough strength so it made it all the way to the other end of the corridor, no small distance.

Jasper knew how to toss the dice, but he'd never faced this much pressure. One yell, one holler, and Jasper would be discovered. That didn't mean he'd leave without Richard, but he'd have to hurt a lot of people to do so.

Crouching low, Jasper hefted a die in his hand. He'd have to send it rolling under the footman's chair and far enough past him to encourage him to rise and turn his back to Jasper to investigate. Jasper rubbed his hands over the die quickly, then balanced it on one finger and flicked it hard with his thumb.

The roll was perfect. The die sailed low over the carpet, rolling under the footman's chair and coming to rest a few feet past the servant. On the carpet. Silently.

Jasper swore under his breath. Not only had the die not rolled far enough, he knew he couldn't roll it further, not with any accuracy. He'd have to throw the other so that it curved at the end and clattered against the wall. It was not so different from billiards. And Jasper excelled at billiards. He rubbed the die again, positioned it on his thumb, and with a small prayer, flicked it. This time it hit the carpet before the chair, but it rolled underneath and then clinked against the wall on the other side. The footman was immediately alert. He rose and peered down the corridor, facing away from Jasper.

"What was that?" he muttered.

In a moment, Jasper was behind him. A well-placed thud on the back of the head and the man went down. Jasper searched his pockets, found the key, and opened the bed chamber door. The room was dark but warm from the fire in the hearth. As soon as he stepped inside, Jasper heard whimpering. "Richard," he said quietly. "It's Jasper."

"Jasper?"

Suddenly a form raced out of the darkness and slammed into Jasper, almost knocking him over. He lifted the boy and held him tightly, ignoring the sting of tears that pricked behind his eyes. The room was dusty. That had to be it.

"You're safe. I'm taking you out of here." He ran his hands all along the boy, checking for bumps or breaks. "Are you hurt? Did he hurt you?"

"No. He didn't hurt me. Where's Mama?"

"She's safe. You'll see her soon. We're leaving, but you must be very quiet. Can you do that?"

"Yes," he whispered.

Carrying the boy the entire time, Jasper took him out the same way he'd come in. The servants still sat at their table, no one aware that upstairs one of their own lay unconscious.

Once outside, Jasper didn't hesitate. He knew where to take the boy. Neil Wraxall had been his commander in Draven's troop, and he'd married a woman who ran an orphanage for boys. They were building a new orphanage, but in the meantime, the boys as well as Neil and his wife lived in the Earl St. Maur's town house. That wasn't far from here.

Jasper might have put the boy down as he made his way there, but he didn't mind holding him. In fact, he rather liked the feel of the boy's arms about his neck and his head resting on his shoulder. Jasper swore that if he had anything to say about it, Richard would never spend another night frightened again.

They arrived at the Earl St. Maur's town house a quarter hour later just as the family had sat down to supper. The family, by the sound of it, was a hundred boys and a crying baby. The butler hadn't said a word upon seeing

Jasper and Richard. He'd merely held up a finger, indicating he would return in a moment. If he'd spoken, Jasper wouldn't have heard him at any rate.

"What is this place?" Richard had whispered.

"My friend and his wife live here with about a dozen orphans. I thought you might stay here until I can bring your mother."

"But I want to see her now."

"I know." Jasper squeezed the boy. "I'll bring her as soon as I can. In the meantime, there will be other children to play with."

Richard looked somewhat interested at that prospect.

Neil stepped into the vestibule, his hair rumpled and aggravation on his features. But his expression changed to bemusement when he saw Jasper. "This is a picture I never thought I'd see."

Jasper didn't set Richard down. "It's a long story, but I need you to keep him safe for me for a few hours."

"We always have room for one more. Is he yours?"

Jasper looked at Richard, and the boy looked back at him.

"He will be," Jasper said. The look in Richard's eyes was like the warmth of the sun on his face. Jasper had never felt such love.

"I'll keep him safe," Neil said, "but I'll want the story."

"Later," Jasper said. "Over a brandy. Or three."

Neil nodded. Finally, Jasper set Richard down. Neil went on one knee and held out his hand. "Major Wraxall. Who are you?"

Richard looked at Jasper, who nodded. "Richard," the boy said quietly.

"Richard, do you want to have supper with my wife and the other boys? Afterward you can play. We have dozens of toys."

Richard looked at the floor then reached out for Jasper's leg and pulled himself behind it.

"Richard, you'll be safe here," Jasper told him, trying without success to dislodge the boy. "I'll bring your Mama as soon as I can. Go."

Neil held up a hand to still Jasper. "Have you ever petted a rat, Richard?"

Richard stopped trying to curl up behind Jasper. "Rats bite," he said.

"Not these. These love to be petted and will eat right from your fingers."

"Can I see?"

"Of course. We have three. You can pet them and tell me which is the softest—Matthew, Mark, or Luke."

"No John?" Jasper asked.

"We don't talk about John," Neil said. Then he looked back at Richard and held out a hand. "What do you say? We feed them after supper."

Richard looked from Jasper to Neil then back again. "You will bring Mama?"

"As soon as I can."

The little boy nodded and put his hand in Neil's. Neil rose and led him back toward the dining room.

"Thank you." His throat tightened as he watched Richard led away. "Neil," he said, voice husky. "One more thing."

Neil raised a brow in question.

"Do you have something I might borrow to wear to a ball?"

***

The dress was too long and large, and the pins holding the bodice in place pricked her skin. But Olivia held her head high. It was a small inconvenience. The fact that Draven had found her a dress, ensuring she looked presentable for a ball, was no small miracle. If she made it through the evening, it would be a huge miracle. There had been times tonight when she thought she might collapse into tears.

She did not want to face Withernsea.

But she'd do it. Richard needed her. Thoughts of Richard made her brave. Thoughts of Jasper too. Draven told her now that the rain had passed Jasper would return any hour. She just needed to get through this confrontation. She had to show the world what Withernsea was. If all she succeeded in doing was making a scandal of herself, she didn't care. Jasper would come for her. He would help her get Richard back.

She and Draven had arrived at the ball on time, a thing that was not done. Most people preferred to make an entrance. But since so few guests had arrived, it gave Olivia and Draven time to plan where she would confront Withernsea. It must be near enough to the dance floor so that Prinny could overhear but secluded enough that they would not be interrupted. They'd walked the ballroom several times before they found a suitable location. In each corner of the ballroom, small rounded alcoves held Greek- or Roman-inspired statues. The areas seemed to replicate small ancient temples. But one alcove was missing its statue. Perhaps it had been taken for repair or moved to another area of the house. Instead a set of chairs had been placed inside, and currently two older ladies sat sipping tea and chatting quietly.

"That's it," Draven said.

Olivia nodded. "I believe I can tug at the blue material draping the alcove so it partially shields us."

"It's most likely held by a cord. When those ladies leave, make your way there and investigate."

But the ladies sat in the alcove for the next several hours. Olivia exchanged more than one look with Draven, fearful she would have to find a new location. And when Withernsea arrived at the ball, just after eleven, her anxiety increased. She tried to make conversation with the few acquaintances who still spoke to her, but she had difficulty keeping her mind on any one topic.

And then at quarter to twelve, two things happened. The prince regent arrived with much fanfare and Draven interrupted her, pretending to claim a dance. As he spun her around the dance floor, he nodded to the now-empty alcove. “This is your chance.”

Her entire body felt cold. “Where’s Withernsea?” she asked. Her teeth threatened to chatter from fear, and her lips felt numb.

”Just over there. You know what to do, Miss Carlisle, and you can do this. You’ve been waiting five years to tell him how you feel. Now is your chance.”

She pressed her lips together. “I don’t think I can do it. I won’t be able to speak. I’ll break into tears—”

Draven gave her a hard look, the kind she imagined he’d given to countless soldiers under his command. “Carlisle, failure is not an option. You won’t accept it, and neither will I.”

He was right. She couldn’t fail. Richard needed her.

“Do you know what my men used to say before they went into battle?”

She shook her head. She hadn’t thought of this like a battle, but in many ways, it was. It had been her private battle for a long time. She was making it public.

“They would say, *I have on my dancing shoes.*”

“Why?”

“Because they knew that every mission might be their last. They fully expected to find themselves dancing with the devil in hell before the day was out. Miss Carlisle, you have your dancing shoes on. I know because I bought them."

She gave him a wan smile.

"You can do this."

"Yes, I can." She took Draven's proffered arm, and he led her off the dance floor. Then he escorted her close to Withernsea before pausing to engage a man he knew in conversation. Olivia listened politely, or at least pretended to, for several moments, all the while her gaze on Withernsea. The duke watched her too, the anger in his expression not difficult to read. So he hadn't liked being left at the proverbial altar a second time. She'd use his anger against him.

Olivia excused herself from Draven and made her way to Withernsea. His eyes widened slightly at her approach, but he also stepped away from those with whom he conversed.

"Might we speak in private?" she asked.

"I'll call for my carriage."

"No." Panic rose in her at the thought of being alone in a carriage with him. She spotted Draven speaking to the prince, and she knew the lieutenant colonel would lead the prince toward the alcove as soon as she was inside with Withernsea. "Let's speak here." She pointed to the alcove, which was still, mercifully, empty.

"You seem to forget, Miss Carlisle," Withernsea said, leaning down so that his broad lips were close to her face, "I hold all the cards."

"There you are wrong. You cannot force me to marry you. If you want me to agree, then humor me for a few moments." She gestured to the alcove and started toward it. She wasn't certain whether Withernsea would follow or not, but she didn't look back. And when she stepped inside, he was right behind her. Her skin crawled and her belly roiled. She wanted to vomit, but she refused to give into her fear and dread.

Hands shaking, she tugged the blue drapery closed. It did not cover the entire entry, but it was enough to shield them from onlookers—and anyone standing on the other side from Withernsea.

"Well," Withernsea crossed his arms over his chest. "This is cozy."

"I wanted to have an intimate conversation about what happened before."

Withernsea sighed. "Are you still on about that? I did not rape you. Everyone knows you cannot conceive a child from rape. And there's no question that boy is mine."

"Actually, there is a question," she said. "You see, after I ran away from London, I found myself alone and destitute. I'm afraid I had to rely on the generosity of quite a few men. Richard might be the child of any one of those." This was a lie, but Draven had been right to suggest it. Withernsea's face went from pink to red with anger.

"You little slut. And to think how you carried on when I took your virginity. I knew you wanted me."

"I carried on because I did not want you," she said loudly, hoping Draven was on the other side of the drapery. "I told you no. I fought you."

"Oh, but that only makes it more fun. I like it when they scream and cry. I like a challenge."

Anger coursed through her, and her hands shook not with fear but rage. "So you admit you raped me?"

"I don't need to admit anything. You and I know the truth. You wanted what I gave you."

"I didn't want you then, and I don't want you now."

His lip curled in a snarl. “But I will have you. You won’t see your bastard again if you don’t marry me. You won’t run away without him. I knew I’d see you again.”

“And what happens when we marry?”

He chuckled long and low, and she actually felt the bile rise in her throat.

“You will call what happened all those years ago a blessing. You’ll come to believe rape was the least of your worries.”

She should have been terrified, but her heart pounded because she knew she had him. She’d seen movement on the other side of the curtain. Now she needed Withernsea to admit what he’d done.

“I’ll agree to marry you, but you have to admit the truth to me.”

“What truth?”

“You raped me five years ago. I was a virgin. I told you no. You forced yourself on me.”

“Fine.” He reached for her, but she snatched her wrist away.

“Say it. Tell the truth here and now.”

He gave her an impatient growl. “Very well, yes, I raped you. Yes, you said *no, no, no! Stop! Please!”* He mocked her cries in a high tone. “I forced you, and I liked it. You liked it too.”

“No.” She grasped the drapery and pulled it back, praying someone would be on the other side. “I did not.”

Withernsea turned toward the drapery and balked as the forms of the prince, Draven, and a dozen others stood on the other side. At some point the orchestra had ceased playing, and their voices had carried enough to attract a crowd.

At the sight of the regent, Olivia curtsied. “Your Highness.”

The prince barely acknowledged her. "Your Grace," he said as the duke made a perfunctory bow. "I'm afraid what I heard just now is quite distressing. It's always been rumored you were a rapist and a sadist. But to hear it from your own lips." He shook his head with disgust. "I want this man removed from my presence."

"Your Highness," Withernsea said quickly, "she lies. She trapped me. I didn't touch her."

"I heard the words from your own lips. You admitted you raped a lady, a gentlewoman."

"Gentlewoman." Withernsea scoffed. "She's a whore. She's had a dozen lovers. Everyone knows women lie."

"I am not lying," Olivia said, her gaze on the faces in the crowd. Plenty looked down their nose at her, but there were a few with sympathy written on their faces. "He hurt me. I said no, and he forced himself on me."

"She was alone with me. She let me kiss her," Withernsea argued. "She led me on. It's her own fault. She should have stayed with her chaperone."

There were a few murmurs of assent, and Olivia's face felt warm. So this was the way it would be. She would be vilified and her rapist exonerated.

"That makes no difference," Draven said. "Rape is rape."

The prince hesitated, sending the crowd was not on his side.

"He did it to me too," a voice called from the crowd.

Olivia's eyes widened. Was another woman coming to her aid?

"Who said that?" the prince demanded. At first no one moved, then the crowd parted and a woman with pale blond hair and a yellow dress made her way through. Olivia didn't know her, but she heard whispers of "The Countess of Rockwell."

"I said it, and it's true." The countess raised her chin. "Withernsea tried to rape me. I managed to scratch him and get away, but if I hadn't, my fate would have been the same as Miss Carlisle's."

"That's simply not true," Withernsea argued. "I never touched you."

"Will you argue you never touched me?" another woman demanded, stepping forward. She wore jewels and a dress that must have come from Paris. "I was not as fortunate as Lady Rockwell. Withernsea violated me, even after I said no and fought him off."

"Ha!" Withernsea said, scoffing. "Everyone knows she's a whore. The baron has been cuckolded a hundred times over. You can't rape a whore."

But apparently the regent had heard enough. "And you, sir, are no gentleman. I want you out of my sight. Out of my presence."

"I quite agree, Your Highness," Lord Ashmont, the ball's host, said, appearing by the prince's side. He motioned to two footmen. "Escort this man out, and make sure he is not admitted again."

"You are throwing me out?" Withernsea screeched. "Throw her out!" He pointed to Olivia. "She's the trash. She has a bastard. She doesn't even know who the father is."

"Furthermore," the regent went on, ignoring the duke, "I want it known that I will not be in the same room, nay the same building, as that man. He shall attend no events I attend, and consider your membership to White's revoked, Withernsea."

"You can't do that!"

The footmen grabbed Withernsea's arms and began to drag him away. "Get your hands off me. You'll pay for this, Olivia. You will never see your son again!"

Olivia felt the lump in her throat rise. This was what she'd feared he would say. Draven had assured her he would find a way to get the boy back, but what if Withernsea went home and took his anger out on Richard? What if he hurt her son or killed him?

"I think you're the one who will never see the boy again," came a familiar voice.

Olivia spun around and watched as Jasper stepped out of the crowd. She had no idea how long he'd been there, but she wanted to weep with joy at seeing him.

Jasper's gaze met Olivia's. "I have your son. He's safe, and Withernsea will never touch him again."

Her knees buckled, and Jasper moved quickly to catch her. Above the ringing in her ears, she heard the shouts of Withernsea as he was tossed into the street. Jasper grasped her arms and pulled her against his chest, and she rested her head against him, grateful he'd come for her. She needed his strength now. She needed his love.

"Richard is safe?" she whispered.

"Safe and well. He's unhurt and when I left him, he was laughing and playing. I imagine he's sleeping peacefully now."

She looked up at him and his smile was beautiful and reassuring. There was something different about him tonight. He seemed more confident, more himself.

"I have the license," he said.

"Then we can marry?"

"As soon as we like. Tonight even."

"I'd like to wait until—"

"We talk to Richard about it?" He laughed. "Of course. Then if you won't become my wife tonight, will you at least do me the honor of dancing a waltz?"

The music had started again, and the crowd around them had thinned. But there were still plenty of curious onlookers. People who stared at her and Jasper with blatant curiosity. She took Jasper's hand, and he led her to the center of the dance floor. Taking her into his arms, he led her around the floor with a skill that left her breathless. It was only then she realized what was different about him.

He did not wear his mask.

"You aren't wearing your mask!" she cried.

"It doesn't match this coat," he said casually.

"But you never go out without it." She looked about her. It was clear to see everyone at the ball was watching them and almost certainly whispering about Jasper, whose face had not been seen by any but his close family since he'd left for the war. "Aren't you afraid people are looking at you? Talking about you?"

He raised her hand to his lips and kissed it. "I'm done hiding. Are you?"

She scanned the room, noting the men and women who sneered at her, those who smiled, and the place where Withernsea had been dragged away. She might never be accepted into Society again. This might very well be her last ball. But Jasper was correct. She was through hiding.

"Yes," she said. "I am. Thank you."

His brows rose. "For what?"

"For loving me." She gave him an expectant look. "You *do* love me, don't you?" Her heart caught in her throat.

"I love you, Olivia."

Her heart warmed in her chest and thudded hard.

"You made it impossible not to." He smiled.

"I didn't want to love you either."

"But my good looks won you over."

She laughed.

"My charm then."

"Your kindness. Your gentleness. Your patience."

"Are you trying to ruin my reputation?"

"Mine is already ruined."

"Then we have nothing to lose." And he kissed her in the middle of the ballroom before sweeping her into his arms and carrying her away.

Twenty-Three

The wedding was small. Jasper had asked Neil and Ewan to attend as well as his father and brothers. Neil and Ewan had come. His family had not. Draven had also come, standing in the back and looking rather uncomfortable. He hadn't stayed for the breakfast, claiming he had matters to attend to.

Richard had made fast friends with one of Neil's orphans, a lad named Charlie, and they'd invited the boy to attend so Richard might have a friend. Jasper had also persuaded Olivia to invite her mother. She had, but Lady Carlisle had been too ill. Her father had not attended either, not that he'd been invited. Withernsea was ruined now and her family safe from his vengeance. Jasper knew that as angry as Olivia was with her father, she was relieved that he would not suffer at Withernsea's hands. He did not know if she would ever be able to forgive the viscount. In Jasper's opinion, the man's actions had been unforgiveable.

And so Jasper married Olivia very much as he'd found her—alone except for her son, who would be his son as soon as all the documents were signed by the appropriate people. But she wouldn't be alone for long. He would be her family, and perhaps they would have a family together, brothers and sisters for Richard to play with.

After the wedding breakfast, which had been held at the Earl St. Maur's residence, he took Olivia and Richard home. It wasn't much of a home as he didn't spend much time at his rooms near Lincolns Inn Fields, but he'd told Olivia they could look for somewhere together. He'd always kept his residence a secret to protect himself from his enemies. But now he'd retire from hunting those who did not want to be found. Perhaps he could help Neil with the orphanage—or perhaps not. Perhaps he could help Ewan in the boxing studio. That was a more likely scenario. And his father and brothers could always use assistance managing the Strathern estates. It was time he did his part there as well. They might not approve of his bride, but they would accept his help.

By the time Richard was tucked into his new bed in his new bedroom for the night and Olivia came to him, Jasper was having difficulty keeping his eyes open. He hadn't slept the last several days, and the prospect of sleep was appealing—just not as appealing as Olivia in a revealing night rail.

She entered the bedroom, and Jasper sat up from where he'd been reclining on the bed. "Where did you find that?"

"A little something Lady Julia gave me. She said all brides need something pretty for their trousseau."

She sat in the edge of the bed and he reached out to finger the lace and ribbons at her breasts. He could see the outline of them through the fine material. "I have a newfound respect for Lady Julia," he said, tugging at a ribbon.

Olivia kissed him, and he pulled her down beside him, kissing her back and forcing himself to move slowly. He did not want to rush this. He did not want to rush her.

He kissed her until she was breathless and pressing seductively against him, then he began loosening the ribbons holding the bodice of the night rail in place. With his teeth.

As more flesh was revealed to him, Jasper used lips, teeth, and tongue to taste, tempt, and tease. When he had her almost naked, he reached for his own shirt, pulling it over his head.

And then he paused, just looking down at her.

This was his wife. In the home where he'd never brought a guest. In his bed, a bed no other woman had ever shared. She'd given him her trust and her life. She'd even given him her son. He wanted to give her something.

She reached up and stroked his cheek, just below his scar. He caught her hand, but instead of moving it away, he pressed it against the ruined flesh. Her eyes widened. "I didn't think you liked to be touched there."

"I like it when you touch me. Anywhere you touch me."

Her fingers moved over the scar tenderly, then she raised her head and kissed him there. Her mouth slid back to his, but he pulled back slightly.

"I said I wasn't hiding anymore. That wasn't quite true."

"What do you mean?"

He looked at her. She was so beautiful—her dark hair about her white shoulders, her cheeks flushed pink, her rounded breasts rosy-tipped and waiting for his lips.

"I've never told you how I got this scar."

"You said it was a fire."

"It was. We'd been ambushed." He wanted to lay back and close his eyes, but he forced himself to look at her as he spoke. "Ewan, Peter, and I had gone into a warehouse looking for arms. Rafe had good intelligence that the French stored guns and ammunition there. Turns out the French knew we were coming. When we arrived, they tried to kill us. When that didn't work and we took refuge in the building, they locked the doors and set it on fire."

"Jasper, you don't have to tell me this."

"Yes, I do. I have to tell someone. I've never spoken of it before, and it's time I took it out of the darkness."

"Go on then." She took his hand and twined her fingers with his.

"We were trapped, and Ewan, being the biggest of the three of us, argued he should be the one to break down the door. We knew there would be men outside waiting to kill us, but we'd rather die from a ball than burn to death. It took precious minutes for Ewan to break down the back door, the one we thought fewer soldiers would cover. Peter and I waited out of the way as Ewan rushed outside and into the line of fire. I went next and joined Ewan in combat. The smoke had obscured the soldiers' line of sight, and they'd fired and missed. Now they had to fight Ewan hand to hand."

"Not a winning prospect," she observed.

"No. I fought with him, and then several others from our troop arrived and lent their support. It wasn't until most of the French were dead or wounded that I noticed Peter wasn't with us." Jasper did close his eyes now. This was the part he dreaded. "No one had seen him, and I ran back inside the building. Everyone told me no, but I went anyway. He was there. He'd been trapped by a beam that had fallen as soon as I went through the door. He was alive and burning, screaming for help. I tried to lift that beam. I used every ounce of strength I possessed, but I couldn't make it move. And all I could hear was Peter's screams as he burned alive."

He swallowed hard, taking comfort from the way Olivia squeezed his hand. "Then something hit me. A board, a piece of debris. I don't know what it was. I just remember the pain was like nothing else I'd ever felt. I must have been rendered unconscious. They told me later Ewan carried me out. He couldn't get Peter out. He was…"

She put a finger over his lips. "It's over now."

He nodded. It was over now. He'd told her and the last of the shame he'd felt faded with the confession. He'd worn the mask to hide his face because of the ugly scar but also because of the shame he felt at having survived when Peter had not. But he couldn't let the past determine his future, any more than Olivia would let her past determine hers. They would begin again. Together.

"It is over now," he said. "And this"—he kissed her gently—"is just beginning."

"And what is *this*? Our marriage?" she teased.

"That, and also this night. I intend to make the best of the night." He kissed her neck.

"You do know Richard will wake us at dawn."

"Then I'd better not waste any time." He kissed her again and pulled her close. She wrapped her arms around his neck.

"I love you."

"And I you." And he went about showing her just how very much he did indeed love her.

Acknowledgements

Thank you to all of my readers who asked for Jasper's story. I loved him the first time he stepped on the page in *Third Son's a Charm*, and I'm so glad some of you did too. Special thanks go Michelle Arnold for suggesting the title of the book and also to Abby Saul for her help with editing and production. Of course, any and all mistakes are my own.

More from Shana Galen

If you enjoyed this book, try Shana's Scarlet Chronicles series, set during the tumultuous years of the French Revolution. The first in the series, *To Ruin a Gentleman*, is available for pre-order now.

The true story of the Scarlet Pimpernel…

Angelette, the recently widowed Comtesse d'Avignon, only invited Viscount Daventry to her country house party as a favor to her sister. When the handsome British lord arrives—two days late—he's full of unnerving tales of unrest and violence in Paris. Angelette assumes it's all exaggeration…until her chateau is attacked and her life threatened. Daventry rescues her, and the two are forced to run for their lives. But when danger closes in, will the viscount stand at her side or save himself?

Is not the one you've been told.

Hugh Daventry visits France frequently to import wine for the family business. On his way out of the country, he stops at the comtesse's house party out of obligation. But after meeting the raven-haired beauty, he tries to persuade her to leave France with him. When the peasants attack, he realizes he's already too late, and now he must protect Angelette, whose sharp tongue is far from angelic. Too soon the couple is caught up in the rising revolution, dodging bloodthirsty mobs, hiding from soldiers, and embroiled in the attack of the Bastille. Hugh wants nothing but to leave tumultuous France for the calm of England. He knows Angelette is intelligent and resourceful—a survivor. But can Hugh survive without her?

One

Hampshire 1812

The Right Honorable Thomas Daventry, only son of the Viscount Daventry, hadn't been home in ages. It wasn't that he didn't get on with his parents. He did. It was more that he didn't get on with Hampshire. The rolling fields dotted with puffy white sheep were certainly bucolic, but they were also tedious as hell. At nineteen, what did Thomas want with sheep and fields and an old drafty pile? London with its artists and theaters and clubs was far more exciting than Daventry Hall.

Or was it?

After last night, Thomas wondered if perhaps the old pile and his staid father and mother had unplumbed depths. And if his father was keeping secrets, Thomas wanted to know.

Which was precisely why he'd ridden hell-for-leather the last few hours to reach home.

Just after noon the sun peeked out from behind low-hanging clouds that had threatened rain, and Thomas crested the rise overlooking the stately house. It had been built in the last century by some famous architect or another. Thomas considered the man an architect with little imagination. How difficult was it to design a gray stone rectangular building? Daventry Hall was all symmetry and proportion, right angles and clean lines. Not a column, not a tower, not a turret (whatever that was) to be seen. It was stable and predictable, like his parents.

Seeing the house again, Thomas almost turned right back around. It was foolishness coming here and confronting his parent about the information he'd received last night.

On the other hand, as long as he was here, he might as well have a meal.

Half an hour later, Thomas joined his father in the library. This dark-paneled room with plush couches and heavy draperies had always been his favorite room in the house, and he'd read most of the books it contained. Thomas had done his share of writing as well. He fancied himself a bit of a poet, though he'd yet to sell any of his verse.

Like the library, the viscount looked much as he always had, though his dark hair was mostly gray now, and he wore his spectacles more often than in the past. The viscount removed them now and gave Thomas a long look from behind the polished desk.

"What have you done now?"

Thomas scowled. "What's that supposed to mean? Can't I come for a visit?" He sat in one of the chairs across from the desk and admired the shelves of books.

The viscount tapped his fingers on the desk, while the low fire in the hearth crackled. "Have you gambled away your allowance?"

"No. Of course not."

"Fallen in love with an actress?"

"You'll need to increase my allowance if I'm to catch the eye of any actresses."

"Noted. What is it then? Been challenged to a duel? Lost your credit—"

"None of those. I haven't done anything except attend a dinner party."

The viscount steepled his hands. "Go on."

"I met an interesting gentleman there. A Sir Andrew Ffoulkes. He claims to know you."

Thomas had been watching his father's face, else he would not have noticed how all expression was wiped away. The viscount looked perfectly blank.

"Do you know him?" Thomas asked.

"No." His father's voice was level and without tone.

"That's funny. He…well, it's ludicrous really. I shouldn't have bothered you with it." He stood.

"What did this Ffoulkes say?"

Thomas shrugged. "He said to tell you hello and for me to ask you about the real Scarlet Pimpernel."

The viscount's fingers, steepled a moment before, now locked together. "The Scarlet Pimpernel."

"You know, the old story about the Englishman who rescued Frenchies during their revolution. Everyone says Sir Percy Blakeney was the pimpernel, but this Ffoulkes said to ask you about the real pimpernel."

The viscount rose and crossed to a small table with a crystal decanter. It wasn't dusty—nothing in the house was dusty—but Thomas had never seen his father drink from its contents before. Now, he poured himself two fingers of the amber liquid and drank it down before pouring another two.

"Are quite you well?" Thomas asked, concern, and not a little excitement, beginning to grow. "Did you know the Scarlet Pimpernel? Was it Sir Percy?"

His father looked at him. "I suppose there's no point in keeping it hidden any longer."

Thomas sank back into his chair, his gaze fixed on his father. This was what he had come for, and yet, he couldn't quite believe his father had a story to tell. Viscount Daventry—Dull Daventry, as everyone called him in Town.

"I did know Ffoulkes," the viscount said. "It's habit to deny it, but the truth is I knew him well. I knew Blakeney too. I knew them all—Dewhurst, Hastings, the whole league." He sipped his drink. "And I suppose you are correct that Sir Percy was part of the League of the Scarlet Pimpernel."

"He wasn't the Scarlet Pimpernel?"

"He was *a* pimpernel, not *the* pimpernel."

"I'm not sure I follow. If he was not *the* pimpernel, who was?"

His father set his drink on the desk and gave Thomas a hard look.

"Are you saying?" Thomas shook his head. It was not possible. His father could not be the Scarlet Pimpernel. "I-I cannot believe it."

***

Hugh could hardly fault his son for the look of pure incredulity that crossed his face. It wasn't every day a child's parent admitted to being England's most celebrated hero. Hugh had never wanted acclaim or recognition. That's why he'd given it to Blakeney, but he couldn't start there. If he was to tell his son the tale, he should start at the beginning. But what exactly was the beginning?

Even as he thought it, the remembered scent of fresh apples and cut hay and sweet clover seemed to infuse the room. Because, of course, it all began in Versailles, and it all began with her.

Pre-order *To Ruin a Gentleman* now!

About Shana Galen

Shana Galen is three-time Rita award nominee and the bestselling author of passionate Regency romps. "The road to happily-ever-after is intense, conflicted, suspenseful and fun," and *RT Bookreviews* calls her books "lighthearted yet poignant, humorous yet touching." She taught English at the middle and high school level off and on for eleven years. Most of those years were spent working in Houston's inner city. Now she writes full time, surrounded by three cats and one spoiled dog. She's happily married and has a daughter who is most definitely a romance heroine in the making.

Would you like exclusive content, book news, and a chance to win early copies of Shana's books? Sign up for monthly emails for exclusive news and giveaways on Shana's website, www.shanagalen.com.

Made in the USA
San Bernardino, CA
11 November 2018